THE LAST DEBUTANTE

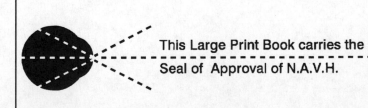

THE LAST DEBUTANTE

JULIA LONDON

THORNDIKE PRESS
A part of Gale, Cengage Learning

GALE
CENGAGE Learning·

Detroit • New York • San Francisco • New Haven, Conn • Waterville, Maine • London

GALE
CENGAGE Learning®

LIBRARY OF CONGRESS CATALOGING-IN-PUBLICATION DATA

London, Julia.
    The last debutante / by Julia London. — Large Print edition.
        pages cm. — (Thorndike Press Large Print Romance)
    ISBN 978-1-4104-5936-7 (hardcover) — ISBN 1-4104-5936-5 (hardcover)
    1. Regency—Fiction. 2. Scotland—Fiction. 3. Large type books. I. Title.
PS3562.O78745L37 2013
813'.54—dc23   2013007604

Published in 2013 by arrangement with Pocket Books, a division of Simon & Schuster, Inc.

Printed In the United States of America
1 2 3 4 5 6 7 17 16 15 14 13

THE LAST DEBUTANTE

ONE

Dundavie, the Scottish Highlands, 1811

Jamie Campbell wasn't alarmed when the old woman pointed her gun at his head — he was galled. He'd ridden up to her fence and had just come off his saddle when the cottage door opened and she appeared with her blunderbuss.

He'd suffered more than his fair share of vexations these last few weeks. Things had gone to hell when his brother, Geordie, had called out Cormag Brodie and very nearly killed him. Not unreasonably, that had prompted Cormag's sister Isabella, who was Jamie's fiancée, to cry off their engagement. That was almost enough to drive a man to the nearest bottle of barley-bree, but to finish off that spectacularly bad event, Jamie then discovered that his uncle Hamish, who was losing a wee bit of his mind every day, had given away the money Jamie had managed to save in the family coffers. That money was all Jamie had to help support his clan, who had seen their livelihoods erode with the encroachment of Lord Murchison's sheep onto their small parcels of land, and many had left for better occupations in Glasgow and beyond.

For the nine years Jamie had sat as laird of the Dundavie Campbells, he'd tried to lead them into the winds of change while holding on to as much of their way of life as possible. The Brodies were key to his plan, so it was all bloody well vexing — as was this woman and her gun. Jamie was descended from a long line of scrappy, argumentative Highland Campbells, men whose mettle had been tested at war, during famines, and in the throes of great change. They were not the sort of men to be put off by duels or broken engagements, or an old woman and her blunderbuss — which was shaking a little as she struggled to hold the thing up.

"There's no call for that now, aye?" he said, pausing outside the gate. He held up both hands to show he was unarmed.

"As you are standing on my property, I'll be the one to judge," the woman retorted in a crisp English accent.

Sassenach. Mary, Queen of Scots, another one. Jamie's hackles rose.

"What business have you here, sir?"

What business had *he* here? He was born and reared here, in these very hills. He knew them all, every path, every stream, every tree. What the devil was *she* doing here? *Ach,* he shouldn't have come. He didn't generally act in haste; at the very least, he should have brought Duff, his cousin and right hand, along.

But Old Willie had told him that the woman who lived in this cottage on Brodie lands was the one who had used Hamish so ill, and it had made Jamie feel a wee bit murderous. What sort of person took advantage of an old man who possessed only half his mind? Jamie was so intent on discovering the answer that he'd immediately ridden in the direction of the Brodie lands.

He sighed and looked at the neat little thatched-roof cottage. It was set back against towering firs on the edge of a small field where chickens wandered about, pecking at the ground. The cottage had been whitewashed and the fence recently mended, judging by the fresh yellow lumber. A wiggen tree, which superstitious Highlanders often planted near their cottages to ward off witches, shaded the front garden, and in one open window loaves of freshly baked brown bread were cooling.

9

It was idyllic, the sort of tidy vista that had lately brought Englishmen flocking to the Highlands.

The woman, however, was not what Jamie had expected. Old Willie had said she was English, but he'd not mentioned her gray hair or her rounded middle. Jamie had expected a vixen with a sultry gaze and curving figure, a woman who was a master at depriving men of their money.

This woman looked as if she ought to be waulking wool.

Jamie lowered his hands. "I am Jamie Campbell, Laird of Dundavie." He waited for her inevitable gasp of alarm when she realized she had done the unthinkable by threatening a man of power and means.

She did not gasp. She hoisted her gun up a wee bit more. "That means naught to me. There are more Campbells roaming these hills than there are trees. Go on, then — off with you. I think it best you not be seen on this side of the hills," she said. "The Brodies have no love for the Campbells."

"The feeling," he said, a little miffed that she would so eagerly embrace the Brodies' side, "is entirely mutual. Nevertheless, I have come in search of a woman who has become financially involved with my uncle Hamish." He cocked a brow at her, silently daring her to deny it.

"If you mean to imply that *I* am involved with him, I am most assuredly *not.*"

She was quick to deny it, wasn't she? And a wee bit nervous, as well, which Jamie read as guilt. "Might I at least know to whom I am speaking?" He took a step closer, putting his hand on the swing gate.

"*Stop!* You are trespassing on my land!"

He snorted. "This land belongs to Gordon Brodie."

"That," she sniffed, "is but a small detail. He has let me this land, and therefore it is mine. Now please take your leave before I am pressed to defend myself in a most violent manner."

If she thought she could shoo him away like a fly, she was mistaken. Jamie pushed the gate open. "*Diah,* for someone who claims no' to be acquainted with Hamish, you are eager to see me gone, are you no', then? Have you attended the pony races near Nairn?"

"I *will* shoot you if you come one step closer, and the Brodie boys who come round every Monday will cart your carcass off and toss it into the sea."

"I've yet to meet a Brodie who was willing to expend that much effort. Much less one capable of carting me anywhere," he said

11

brusquely. "Madam, I shall speak even more plainly. I am in search of the Englishwoman who lives in the cottage by the old Norse cairn." He pointed grandly up the path he'd traveled from Dundavie to a crumbling old cairn plainly visible at the top of the hill.

He continued, "There are some who believe she has divested my uncle of one thousand pounds, a mighty sum. And while I would be the first to say a man is free to give his money to any lass he wants, I take issue when the man is no' in his right mind. This is a man who forgets to belt his plaid and believes that he is the friend of an English lord who lives alone in the hills here. He canna remember the names of his children, yet he knows the names of the angels who visit him at night. Anyone who might take money from my uncle takes cruel advantage."

Her cheeks reddened like a pair of apples; she cocked the trigger. "Leave me now, or die in the garden."

Jamie frowned. He did not relish the thought of corralling an old woman and taking her gun. The best course of action was to return with Duff and a few of his men. "Very well," he said with a shrug. "Perhaps you might be persuaded to recall your acquaintance when I bring a witness or two

12

round to remind you, aye? Good day, madam." He touched his hat and turned away toward his horse.

He heard the blunderbuss fire a split second before he felt the burn of lead enter his body. He fell, landing with a great *thud,* his head striking a rock — and then everything went black.

Funny how small, chance moments could alter one's world so completely. Daria Babcock had never really thought of it until now. She wasn't generally one to contemplate fate or the meaning of life; she'd never engaged in such lengthy introspection. But then again, she'd never found herself on the side of a road in the Scottish wilds, utterly alone, until today.

Well. Not *utterly,* as there was a dog, but she hardly counted him. After her initial fear of being mauled when he'd wandered out of the forest, she'd quickly discovered him to be completely useless. He was black, with spots of white on his paws and his chest, and presently had folded his legs to lie beside her trunk, his head propped against it, his eyes closed, as if he had no more pressing issues to attend to than his nap.

Mr. Mungo Brodie hadn't seemed particularly concerned when he'd deposited her here — he'd mentioned only that her destination was "just a wee bit up the road, then."

That "road" was little more than a rabbit trail. Into dark woods. With not a soul in sight.

Daria glanced up to the treetops and the robin's-egg-blue sky. She guessed it was the middle of the afternoon, which meant she still had a bit of time before it turned dark.

Which in turn gave her more time to study the ridiculous twists of fate that had brought her here. For her current predicament — side of road, all alone — clearly deserved some study. "I wish I knew the moment that everything changed," she said aloud.

The dog's ear twitched.

Perhaps it had begun a month or so ago, when she was feeling rather cross. It had seemed to her that a veritable explosion of births had occurred in and around Hadley Green, and that scores of pink-cheeked cherubs in carriages were being pushed about by their nurses as their gurgling laughter drifted in through open windows.

On one particularly sobering afternoon, she'd attended tea at the Ashwood estate, where she'd been gobsmacked at Lady Ashwood's coy announcement to the assembled group of Hadley Green ladies that she was expecting her second child.

"A *child*!" Lady Horncastle, the grand dame of Hadley Green, had swiveled her silver head around to squint at the fair-haired Lady Ashwood through her lorgnette, clearly as stunned as Daria. "But you were only *just* delivered of your son, my dear," she said, as if Lady Ashwood might rethink her pregnancy with the startling news that she already *had* a child.

Lady Ashwood had blushed and laughingly said, "I remarked the same to my husband, but I think he will not be happy until every room at Ashwood is occupied by a child."

"That is *quite* a lot of children," Lady Horncastle had sniffed. "Your husband is surely aware that if one desires a herd, one may invest in cattle. It is really much simpler."

The announcement had made Daria quite cross, too. She desperately wanted a baby of her own, even a herd of them. Every time Daria held a baby she felt an uncomfortably deep tug in her chest. She would like to be married, to be a mother, a wife, to have some purpose other than to attend teas. Yet in spite of having spent the last three years endeavoring to put herself in every conceivable avenue of society, she had

15

not even a whiff of a proper marriage prospect. That wound was being liberally salted by the fact that all of her close acquaintances were now married and bearing children, and on that particular day, it had sent Daria drifting onto a sea of melancholy.

She was the last debutante of Hadley Green. The last one of her social circle, the last one without an offer.

Daria had drifted home on that sea, but it was no better there, for she had the misfortune of living with two constant reminders of what was missing from her life. Her parents were like two cooing doves, forever in each other's company, content with their own society. Daria often felt as if even she were intruding on their secret little world. At times she was touched by their devotion to one another, but at other times, she was annoyed by it.

When Daria had arrived home from the tea, she'd found her parents huddled together before the hearth in the salon against the chill of an early spring day, their heads bent together over a letter. Daria had thought nothing of it.

"I will admit," she said, holding up one gloved finger to the dog, "that there are times I am entirely distracted by my own pathetic state of being."

He gave her a single thump of his tail.

It wasn't until supper that Daria had even noticed the subtle change in her parents. The evening lacked their typical effusive commentary on their blissful day.

So Daria had filled the air with a recitation of events from that afternoon, eager to relieve herself of her vexations. However, she was not rewarded with an appropriately commiserating response to her complaints of having no prospects or hope for a future. She'd sighed loudly to demonstrate her exasperation as Griswold, their butler-groundskeeper-footman-valet, lumbered about the table, removing their soup bowls.

"Is anyone listening?" Daria demanded.

"Of course!" her mother said. "You were saying, dearest?"

"That my life is not to be borne, that's what," Daria said a bit missishly. "And that you and Pappa might take me to London for the Season," she added hopefully.

"Oh, I think not," her father had said, his attention on the plate Griswold placed before him.

"Why not?" Daria had asked, stung by the swiftness of his dismissal. "It's not as if I have any prospects here."

"We are not suited to London," her

mother said. "And you do have prospects, darling. Lord Horncastle is very attentive to you —"

"I should rather perish than marry Lord Horncastle! I am aware that Horncastle is the only gentleman in Hadley Green with a fortune, but it does not make up for his odious tendencies to drink and pout!"

Yet her mother had smiled thinly and said with great condescension, "You will find a nice young man when the time is right, dearest."

"The time is far past *right,* Mamma. I am one and *twenty*! Am I to waste away in this tiny little village without an occupation? I feel restless and useless." She could almost hear her good friend Charity Scott whispering in her ear: *"The point is that here in Hadley Green, you are without true society. There might be members of the Quality milling about from time to time, but the* real *society is in London. You* must *go to London."*

"You are very useful to us," her father had objected.

Daria had groaned. She loved her parents, of course she did. She was their only child, and they'd doted on her all her life. If they had one failing, it was that they did not concern themselves with the proper way things were done. They were quite content with their private life and seemed to think Daria should be just as content. "Really, Pappa, what woman is not married at my age?"

Her father had shrugged thoughtfully. "Charity Scott is not."

Yes, well, Charity was not married because she'd borne a child out of wedlock years ago and refused to name the father. "Charity said her brother, Lord Eberlin, would give me a proper letter of introduction, and that one could put oneself at the top of society with such a letter. Charity said that all one must do is wedge her foot firmly in the door, and the rest is up to her."

"It would seem Miss Scott is a font of knowledge about town," her mother had mused.

Daria had looked at her mother, and then her father, who was gazing at his wife with such concern that Daria felt herself on the verge of shrieking to the heavens for someone, anyone, to *listen* to her. It was just as she'd said to Charity that very day: no one understood how bleak her situation was.

She'd looked at her parents, thoroughly exasperated. "All right," she'd said firmly. "You must tell me what is the matter. Why are you both acting so strangely? And what is the letter you are holding in your lap,

Mamma?"

"Your mother has received a bit of unwelcome news," Daria's father had said.

"Richard!"

"She's not a child, Beth. You can't hide it from her."

"What has happened?" Fear began to bloom. "Is it Mamie? Has something happened to Mamie?" she demanded, referring to her grandmother.

"Yes," her father said.

"No!" her mother cried at the same time. "No, she is very well, Daria."

"But the letter is from her," Daria had pressed. "And she has told you something that has distressed you."

"I don't want to trouble you with it —"

"For God's sake, Beth," Daria's father had said. Then to Daria, "Mamie is in a bit of financial difficulty. But it's nothing that a few pounds won't remedy straightaway."

Daria might have believed that was true had her mother not bitten her lip to keep from speaking. "I don't understand. She's needed money before and it hasn't distressed you like this."

"This time it is quite a large sum," her mother had explained. "Your father must travel to Scotland. We cannot possibly entrust that sum to anyone else."

"Honestly, I don't see why she doesn't come home," Daria had complained. "She went to care for her sister, and her sister has been gone for two years. There is nothing to keep her there."

"She is not ready to return to England," her mother said quickly. "Really, love, this is nothing over which you should concern yourself. Your father will go to her and that is that."

"It's decided, then, is it? I'm to have no say in it?" her father had responded. "Beth, darling . . . I can't imagine making the journey without you. What if —"

"Someone should be here with Daria," her mother had firmly interrupted.

"Oh please, no, Mamma. The summer will be tedious enough without having to graft orchids for the two of you. *I'll* go," she had said suddenly.

It had seemed such a brilliant idea, the perfect solution to her doldrums — a summer in Scotland, away from Hadley Green and all her happy friends with their beautiful babies.

But her mother said instantly, "That's absurd."

Those two words had sealed Daria's determination. What was absurd was to continue on as she had been. "Why?" she'd

21

demanded. "I am perfectly capable of carrying a bit of money, and I've missed Mamie terribly. She's not been home in ages."

"To begin, you cannot travel all that way without your parents or a chaperone. What would people think?"

Better they think she'd at least found some adventure than that she was well on her way to being the Hadley Green Spinster. "I can find a proper companion."

Her father had chuckled. "Forgive me, Daria, but your mother is quite right in this. You will stay here at Hadley Green and amuse your mother with your company while I go."

Even now, seated on her trunk in the middle of a Scottish forest, Daria shook her head. Her parents had never understood how determined she could be. That evening she had told Griswold to bring the carriage around, and off she'd gone to Tiber Park. She'd banged the brass knocker three times, marched into midst of the Scott family, and with frustration still heating her blood, she'd said, "Charity, will you accompany me to Scotland?"

Much to Daria's great surprise, Charity had looked at her brother and shrugged. "Why not? Scotland is the thing now, is it

22

not? I've been at Tiber Park too long, and I think it might be nice to see a change of scenery."

Daria's parents had refused this idea, of course, but Charity was persuasive with them. It was agreed that her daughter, Catherine, would stay behind, as the eleven-year-old girl was far more enamored of Lady Eberlin's new baby than the prospect of Scotland. Further, Lord Eberlin's closest friend, Captain Robert Mackenzie, would bring them to Scotland aboard his merchant ship.

Charity and Daria had set sail for Nairn a fortnight later, at which point Daria unfortunately discovered she easily became seasick. Despite how much ginger beer she was made to drink to quell her nausea, she'd spent the two-day voyage in her bunk, groaning through wave after wave of illness. She scarcely remembered any of it at all, other than Charity slipping in and out of the room, the scent of her perfume making Daria even sicker.

Even when the ship stopped rocking.

Charity had said, "We are moored, and still you do not rally. I think Mackenzie is right. I think we must send for a physician."

"We are moored?" Daria had asked, and had pushed herself up, blinking against the bright sunlight streaming in through the porthole.

Charity had given her a rare smile. "I've already taken the liberty of going ashore while you recuperated. It's rather a rustic village, but not without its charm. Oh, and I arranged transportation to your grandmother's house. It is very near here, as luck would have it. You will have a seat on a private tour of the Highlands that will deposit you in Glenferness. That is where you will find your grandmother." She had turned to the small mirror bolted to the wall, looking one way, then the other as she checked her hair.

"What of a seat for you?"

"I've arranged one for me, as well. But on a different coach, for I am to Edinburgh."

"What?" Daria exclaimed. "We meant to see Edinburgh together, on the way home from seeing Mamie. That was our plan, Charity."

"We *will* see it together, of course we shall! You will come to me in Edinburgh when you've seen your grandmother. You don't need me for that."

It had been too much for Daria to absorb, since even thinking gave her a headache. She'd forced herself up. "How will you get there? What coach will take you there?"

Charity's smile had deepened a little more. "Captain Mackenzie has kindly arranged it."

Daria knew in that moment that even Charity would desert her. She truly *was* the last debutante of Hadley Green.

"Don't look so distressed!" Charity had said. "You are off to a grand adventure! Isn't that what you hoped for? You will accompany a delightful set of sisters. Mrs. Gant and Mrs. Bretton are both widows and they've planned their holiday for quite some time. They are eager to see the Highlands and just as eager to offer you a seat in their coach. They seem quite lively."

Daria had found the ladies to be lively, all right, but not in the way Charity had meant.

A brilliantly blue spring sky greeted Daria that morning when she'd boarded the coach. She was cross with Charity for having abandoned her, and she was sure that ten miles would seem like ten days in the company of Mrs. Gant and Mrs. Bretton.

The two sisters, both plump and gray and fond of matching hats, had hired Mr. Mungo Brodie to drive them. After demanding he speak his native language, they realized there was no way to understand what he was saying, so they expressed their desire that he be "as native as he might."

25

"Their language is too harsh on our ears," Mrs. Bretton had confided to Daria, who agreed. The language was too harsh, and the roads too pitted.

Their slow progress along the narrow road into the hills allowed the sisters the opportunity to pepper Daria and Mr. Brodie with several questions. That was when they were not demanding that Mr. Brodie come to a halt so they might pile out of the coach, dragging Daria along with them. They shared a pair of opera glasses to have a look about, and liberally pressed them into Daria's use so that she might view the birch and oak that grew so thickly beside the road, or try to see the crossbill birds seated high in the trees, or catch a glimpse of the ospreys flying overhead. They would then climb back into the coach, and off they would go, inching along for another few yards.

As the day crept by, Daria began to fret. She didn't want to spend an entire evening with these women, but they had yet to see any signs of civilization, and they hadn't met a soul on that road. Daria was peering out the window with the hope of seeing a village ahead when the coach suddenly came to a halt, sagging to one side as Mr. Brodie came down. A moment later, he opened the door. "Glenferness."

The sisters looked at Daria.

But they were in the middle of nowhere, with nothing around them but forest.

Daria's heart climbed right into her throat. "Pardon?" she croaked.

"Glenferness." He walked away, and Daria could hear him unlashing her trunk.

Now Daria's pulse began to pound. "Oh no — there must be some mistake." She hastily climbed over the sisters' legs and leapt out of the coach. "Mr. Brodie!"

He appeared from the back of the coach with her trunk on his shoulder, then dropped it like a bundle of hay at the side of the road. "Aye?"

"There is no house here," Daria said, gesturing to the forest alongside the road.

"Aye, there is. Just a wee walk."

Daria looked at the thick wall of trees. "A wee walk to *where*? I see nothing but forest."

"There," he said, and pointed.

Daria saw it then — a path no wider than a rabbit trail.

"You can't possibly mean there is a house on *that* path."

"Ach, lass, walk up the road, then. Ye'll find it well enough." He reached for her smaller portmanteau and placed it on top of her trunk.

"But what of my things?" Daria asked, panicking now. "Is there no footman? No conveyance? Am I expected to walk through those woods in these shoes and carry my own things?"

"Brodie lads will come round and bring the trunk, miss. No time to dawdle, now — I'm to have the ladies to Piperhill Inn by nightfall, and we're a wee bit behind schedule." He walked to the head of the coach.

"Good day, Miss Babcock!" Mrs. Gant called, sticking her silver head out the coach door. "Our regards to your grandmother!"

"But . . ."

Mrs. Bretton gave her a cheery wave as they rolled away.

That was how Daria had come to be utterly alone on the side of the road, thinking unkind thoughts about Mr. Brodie and Scotland.

"Quite a deep pit of muck you've walked into, Daria," she sniffed. She glanced at the rabbit trail that passed for a road here. She'd never believed herself one to wilt at the first sign of trouble, but she felt on the verge of doing just that. She reminded herself that if Mamie — elegant, sophisticated Mamie — had come to Scotland and managed, then so could she. She had only to decide whether she would remain seated on the road waiting for marauders and murderers to come along or do as Mr. Brodie suggested and walk up that tiny, overgrown trail.

She stood up and looked at the dog. "Do you intend to accompany me? Or will you sleep the day away?"

The dog sat up, his tail wagging.

"Very well. But you must be responsible for yourself. I am not a nursemaid," she warned him, and picked up her portmanteau. She took a deep breath, muttered a small prayer, and stepped onto the rabbit trail, almost toppling over when the dog rushed past her in order to be first on the path.

Two

A reddish mist clouded Jamie's vision. Pain burned in full conflagration at his ribs, then down his left side to his toes. He was lying on his back, and when he tried to lift his head, searing pain blinded him. Feeling the back of his head for the source of the pain, he found a thick bandage. Along with the scent of witch hazel, commonly used to dress wounds, there was a sweet, cloying smell that he didn't recognize.

He struggled to remember what had happened, where he was.

"You're awake!"

The moment he heard the Sassenach's voice, everything came flooding back. The old woman. The blunderbuss. Uncle Hamish. He tried to focus on her, but the haze in his vision was too dense.

"For heaven's sake. She told me the valerian would keep you sleeping for hours!" She made a clucking, impatient sound.

"One should not call oneself a healer if one cannot concoct a proper sedative. You mustn't worry, Mr. Campbell. I shall give you more."

The woman suddenly loomed over him, giving his heart a start. She was smiling like a kindly grandmamma, with her hair knotted atop her head and her apple cheeks. "Feeling improved?" she asked hopefully. "I've some laudanum if the pain is too deep."

Valerian and laudanum. Was she trying to kill him?

"Stay right where you are. I have a broth." She disappeared from his sight as suddenly as she'd appeared.

She was barmy, this Sassenach. Jamie had to think his way out of this, but the fog in his brain and the pain in his side were making that impossible.

The woman appeared again. She was humming a jaunty little tune as she sat on the bed beside him, holding a wooden bowl, the contents of which smelled quite foul. She smiled as she leaned over once more, and a spoon began to dance before Jamie's face.

Jamie pressed away from her, biting back the pain that ripped through him as he turned his head.

31

"Oh dear, you shouldn't resist me, Mr. Campbell. How shall you ever regain your strength?" She grabbed his chin with her hand. Jamie tried to push her off, but the pain was so intense he began to see spots before his eyes. He must have opened his mouth to gasp as well, for the next moment the bitter broth was sliding down his throat.

"A few spoons more and you will rest peacefully."

Peacefully in his grave. How was it that an old Englishwoman was holding him, the Laird of Dundavie, prisoner? What feat of magic was this?

The woman smiled and held up another spoonful. Jamie jerked his head away and felt a wave of nausea at the pain. *"Tha thu as do chiall,"* he gasped, telling her she was mad.

"I think you should try not to speak, Mr. Campbell," she said brightly. "Firstly, I don't speak your language. Secondly, you should allow your body to rest and heal." She bounced the spoon against his gritted teeth. Jamie sealed his lips against the assault of her spoon. When he refused to open, she sighed and pinched his nose shut. "I've reared children, Mr. Campbell. You cannot win in this."

She was right. When at last he was forced

to take a breath, she tossed more of the foul liquid down his throat.

"You'll feel much recovered in no time, mark me," she said soothingly, her words drifting somewhere high above him. He could feel himself sliding down the slope into oblivion, and his last conscious thought was that not only was he going to die in the hands of this madwoman, but he was going to die on Brodie land.

Daria hadn't taken more than a few steps when a stone pierced the sole of her shoe. She uttered a mild curse beneath her breath and carried on, choosing her steps carefully. The shadows were much deeper in the forest, making it difficult to see. More than once, the dog had darted ahead and then suddenly reappeared before her, startling her. "Walk on, you ridiculous mongrel," she chastised him.

Her arms began to burn with the weight of her portmanteau. She swore to herself that if vultures did not carry her off, she would never travel with so many items again. "*One* gown," she said aloud, seeking company in the sound of her own voice. "One gown for evening, one for morning, and one for day. But no more than *three* gowns." She shifted her portmanteau into the other hand. "And certainly no more than two pairs of shoes —"

The familiar smell of woodsmoke wafted to her now, bringing her to a halt. Where there was smoke, there was life, and hopefully that life was her grandmother. If not, well . . . Daria would face that conundrum if and when she met it. At that moment, she believed she could face any danger if it meant she could put down her portmanteau and take off her shoes.

She quickened her step, climbing up the path to the crest. There, on the edge of a green field where some cows were grazing and chickens were waddling about, was a cottage. And what a charming little cottage it was, with a thatched roof and blue flowers in the window boxes — the sort of cottage Mrs. Gant and Mrs. Bretton were determined to see on their tour.

"The peasants of Scotland take great pride in their cottages," Mrs. Gant had told her with the authority of someone who had studied her guidebook carefully.

"Please, dear Lord, let it be Mamie taking pride in this one." Daria sighed, adjusted her portmanteau, and began picking her way along the path as the dog raced after something that had caught his attention.

Daria arrived at the fence that surrounded

34

the garden. The swing gate was unlatched, and inside the fence was a large patch of glorious color — yellow, blue, and pink flowers springing up, looking slightly untended. In the other half of the small garden were green plants that Daria assumed were root vegetables. *This* was where her grandmother lived? In a crofter's cottage? Her elegant grandmother was a *crofter*? Daria pushed through the little gate and shooed a rogue chicken out of her path with her foot. "Mamie?" she called.

No answer.

Daria walked up to the rough-hewn door and hammered it with the flat of her hand. "Surprise, Mamie! It's me, Daria!" She waited a moment, then added unnecessarily, "Your granddaughter!" She stepped back and stood with the portmanteau clasped in both hands, her smile deepening as she imagined Mamie's great surprise and pleasure at finding her only granddaughter on her doorstep.

But Mamie didn't open the door. No one opened the door. Was she mistaken? Was this not Mamie's cottage after all? But Mr. Brodie had assured her that he knew precisely where it was. And he had seemed quite certain of himself when he'd deposited her on the side of the road.

35

Daria leaned forward and pressed her ear to the door, but she couldn't hear anything. She debated for one long moment, then very gingerly and reluctantly put her hand on the latch. "Mamie?" she said again, and quietly, slowly, opened the door a tiny bit.

Through the crack she could see a wooden table with four wooden chairs around it. In the center was a porcelain bowl. On one end of the table was a black iron pot, covered with a lid. On the wall behind the table was a shelf with some books and a basket that held some balls of yarn and knitting needles, and dangling from a hook just below that was an apron. A stack of china plates and four crystal wineglasses looked vaguely familiar to her.

Daria pushed the door open a little wider and stuck her head in. Behind the door she could see that the kitchen was only one end of a much larger room. On the other end were a settee and two overstuffed chairs. A woolen rug covered the floor just before a stone hearth, in which a fire was cheerfully blazing. It looked as if someone had just stoked it. A pair of books was stacked neatly atop an end table, and next to that was Mamie's favorite clock, the one Charity's father had carved from cherrywood many years ago. On the mantel above the hearth were two silver candlesticks that Daria recognized as a gift her mother had given Mamie one year.

A rush of relief washed over her. This *was* Mamie's cottage! She beamed now, proud of herself for having found it, for having braved her first solo journey. Eager to see her grandmother, she stepped inside, dropping her portmanteau on the floor. She removed her bonnet and tossed it on top of the portmanteau, then smoothed her hair as she walked into the room to look around.

"Mamie?" she called softly. Surely she was close by; the scent of freshly baked bread lingered in the air.

There was a corridor before Daria with two doors on one side and another at the end. She unfastened her cloak and draped it over the back of a chair. Perhaps Mamie was sleeping. She moved quietly, pausing to look inside the first room. There was a feather bed with a satin coverlet, a pair of slippers beside the bed. This would be Mamie's room, but Mamie was not within.

Daria walked into the room and glanced around. There was no water in the porcelain basin and the hearth was cold. The wildflowers in the crystal vase on the mantel had wilted and hung like ruined ribbons over the lip of the vase. There was no evidence of servants. Goodness, how did one live without at least one servant to help with things?

Daria moved on, past another sparsely furnished but tidy little bedroom. When she reached the closed door at the end of the hall, she knocked. Hearing nothing, she cautiously opened the door.

It was dark within, and the smell fetid. She pushed the door open wider and stepped just over the threshold, giving her sight time to adjust to the dim light. It was quite warm, and she glanced in the direction of another hearth, the fourth in the house, where embers still glowed. In a chair beside it was a heavy quilt of the plaid she'd seen a few men wearing in Nairn. Daria moved deeper into the room — and was brought to an abrupt halt by the sound of someone's breath. The hair on the back of her neck rose; she whirled about, expecting to find something horrible behind her. What she saw caused her to clamp a hand over her mouth, capturing the shriek just before it left her.

A man was lying on a bed against the wall. A completely *naked* man. Bandages were wrapped around his torso and around one thigh, and another one around his head. But he was completely free of any covering. He lay motionless, his eyes closed, his chest slowly rising, then slowly falling.

Daria's breath deserted her. She stood rooted to the floor, her gaze locked on him, a tremor of fear building in the pit of her belly. He was . . . a very big man. *All* of him was big. Daria had seen a little boy without his breeches, but she had never seen a fully grown man in all his splendor. She'd had no idea that boys turned into *this.*

Dark hair spilled onto the pillow around his head. His jaw was square, his chest corded with muscle, his shoulders broad, and his arms finely shaped by his strength. He was trim at the waist, and he looked quite . . . *firm.*

And then there was the rest of him.

The rest of him was, in a word, astonishing. Daria madly wished Charity were here to see this with her, to gaze in astonishment with her. To feel the heat of curiosity swirling in her cheeks, too, to feel her pulse begin to quicken —

"Cé tú féin?"

Daria gasped. She had been so intent on his body she hadn't realized he'd awakened; he was staring at her with dark, glassy eyes.

He spoke again in the foreign language, his voice hoarse as if unused for a time. He pushed himself up on one elbow, grimacing with pain.

Awareness of him flooded Daria's cheeks and neck with uncomfortable warmth. She tried to think of what to say, of how to extract herself, but before she could do it, the man glanced down at his body, then at her again. With his gaze locked on hers, he grabbed the end of a linen and slowly pulled it over his body, covering his groin. *Only* his groin. And then he spoke again, repeating the same strange words.

It flustered Daria even more. *Was* she in the wrong cottage? "I beg your pardon," she said. "I don't speak your language." What a ridiculous thing to say, standing in this man's bedchamber, having a good long look at him while he slept. "I did not mean to . . . to see." She gestured vaguely at him. "It was an accident. I must have come to the wrong cottage."

His gaze remained locked on hers, his expression inscrutable.

"I came in quite by mistake. Mr. Brodie said her cottage was here, but she's not about. I . . . I entered without permission, but I had walked quite a long way, and the portmanteau was so heavy." She was babbling now. He probably didn't even understand her, but it didn't stop her from trying to make a right from a very horrible wrong.

40

"Yes, I must have the wrong cottage," she said apologetically, as if it were perfectly natural to walk into someone's home and into their bedchamber. She took a step back.

The man leaned forward a little. She thought he was going to speak. But instead, he fell forward with a grunt, his forehead striking the wooden frame of the bed. Daria cried out in alarm and stood paralyzed, waiting for him to move.

He did not move.

She leaned forward, her heart pounding. Had he *died*? A bubble of hysteria rose up; she could feel the scream about to leave her throat when he rolled onto his back with a grunt, his eyes closed, the grimace deeply etched into the skin around his eyes.

The bed linen, she could scarcely keep from noticing, had slipped from his body again.

"I'll show myself out," she whispered, feeling hot with embarrassment.

"Halt!"

The word was spoken soft and low, but Daria would have known Mamie's voice anywhere. She whirled about — to look straight into the barrel of the large gun her grandmother held.

THREE

"Mamie!" Daria cried.

"*Daria?*" Mamie lowered the gun, but before Daria could ask when Mamie had taken to carrying firearms, much less housing naked men, Mamie grabbed her arm and yanked her out of the room, then quickly pulled the door to as Daria's mind raced through all the possible reasons why her grandmother might have a bandaged, naked man in her house.

"Who —"

"Come," Mamie said softly, and with her gun in one hand and Daria's elbow firmly in the other, she steered her down the hall to the main living area. She let go of Daria's elbow and put her large gun on the table, whirled around, and stretched her arms wide. "Darling!" she said, her face suddenly a wreath of smiles. "What a beautiful surprise!" She grabbed Daria up and held her tightly to her chest, cooing that it was so good to see her. Daria was surrounded by the familiar scent of lavender, and she pressed her cheek against her grandmother's soft shoulder.

"My goodness, how did you come to be here? Are Richard and Beth with you?" Mamie leaned back, holding Daria at arm's length, smiling as she examined her. "My, but haven't you become a beautiful young woman! You surely have squads of suitors!"

"Mamie, why is there —"

"So you and your parents have come to see me? Oh, how that warms my poor old heart! Sit, sit," she said, nudging Daria toward the table. "I shall pour you tea. Are my daughter and Richard in Nairn? I should think Richard wouldn't like the travel up into the hills." She turned to the shelves, reaching for a small basket.

Daria remained standing, studying her grandmother. She looked a little rounder than when Daria had last seen her. And a little plain — her clothing was not the fine silks and brocades she'd always preferred. But never mind that. "Mamie," Daria exclaimed breathlessly, "there is a naked man in that room!"

With her back to Daria, Mamie nodded. "Yes, I know. That must have come as quite a shock, but you mustn't fret about him.

43

He'll be fine. Oh, how you startled me, Daria!" She laughed suddenly as she put a basket of tea tins on the table. "I thought someone had come to rob me! Is Beth coming?"

"No, it's only me — Mamma and Pappa are in Hadley Green." Daria pressed her fingers to her forehead. "Please, Mamie — *why* is there a naked man in that room?"

"Hmm?" her grandmother asked, bustling around the hearth as if nothing were wrong. "Oh! I shall tell you, my love, I will. But first I insist on hearing all about *you*. You cannot imagine how I have missed you! And now to find you in Scotland? It's as if I were dreaming!" She suddenly paused and pinned Daria with a look. "Your parents are *aware* you are here, are they not?"

"Of course! They wanted to come themselves when they received your letter, but I —"

"You read the letter?" Mamie interrupted quickly.

"No," Daria said, eyeing Mamie curiously. "Mamma told me you needed help, and I wanted to come —"

"I should hope my daughter has not lost her senses and sent you across the country all alone!"

Daria's head was beginning to spin. "No,

44

Mamie. I came with Charity."

"Who?"

Daria shook her head. "Mamie, who *is* that man?"

"I will explain it, of course I will, darling. But you've come a long way and you should have your tea. I have some freshly baked biscuits —"

"I don't want biscuits. You are right that I have come a very long way. I made that journey in the anticipation of a lovely reunion with my grandmother and I imagined something vastly different — a house, a small village. A servant! But I find you in a crofter's cottage without any help at all, with a wounded, *naked* man."

Mamie clucked her tongue at Daria. "You make it sound nefarious."

"Yes," Daria said, nodding furiously, "it rather seems nefarious to me."

Mamie sighed. "All right, then. I will tell you. But I assure you that you and your imagination will be quite disappointed. Sit down, my love."

Daria didn't move.

Mamie grabbed her hand and dragged her to the kitchen table. *"Sit,"* she said again. She reached around to a smaller table to fetch a plate of biscuits and placed them before Daria.

"Well?" Daria asked, folding her arms over her middle and ignoring the biscuits.

Mamie took the apron from its hook and draped it around her belly. "I found him."

Daria snorted.

"Well, I did. In the woods." Mamie turned away, tied the apron at her back, and leaned over the hearth to check the kettle. "He'd been shot."

"Shot." Daria frowned. "By whom? Why?"

"I haven't the slightest idea! Robbers, perhaps? But I couldn't very well leave him there to die, could I? So I brought him here."

Mamie's explanation didn't ring true, perhaps because she offered it with her back turned. Or because now, as she turned, her smile seemed a little too wide, a little too . . . fixed.

"*You* brought him here," Daria repeated, her gaze narrowing.

"I did."

"By yourself?"

"No! No, no, of course not. Ah . . . one of the Brodie men helped me. The Brodies are thick as midges in summer; one can scarcely walk without tripping over them." She busied herself with the tea tins, examining them all as if she'd never seen them until now.

"And then . . ."

"And then?" Mamie asked absently.

"And then you sent for a doctor to tend to him," Daria suggested, trying to move the story along.

"A doctor? No."

"No?"

"Daria, this is not England. It would take far too long for a doctor to arrive and the poor man might have died. I sought the counsel of a healer and mended him myself."

Daria stared hard at her grandmother. How could Mamie possibly know how to mend a man who had been shot?

Mamie turned away, back to the hearth. "Splendid — the water was still warm and boiled quickly." She removed it from the fire.

"I am fairly certain," Daria said evenly, "that when a man has been shot with lead, it is prudent to have the lead removed."

"Yes, that is true. So I did," Mamie said, as if it were a matter of course to remove lead from a human body. "Don't look so alarmed, sweetling. One learns quite a lot when living in Scotland. Handy things they don't teach you in England." She chuckled as she made tea.

Daria's stomach began to roil with nerves

and not a little bit of horror. "I am aghast, Mamie. You *seem* to be the same person who was my grandmother. But my grandmother, who left England seven years ago, was a lady. She had never, to my knowledge, carried a gun or dug lead out of human flesh, much less the flesh of a strange man."

Mamie shrugged. "I suppose people change."

Daria leaned forward, peering into her grandmother's face. "Mamie? Are you all right?"

Mamie laughed. "I am perfectly fine! There is nothing to warrant such a look of concern, my love. When the gentleman is better — and he will be, as soon as the fever breaks — we might ask him a bit more about himself and send for his family." She waved her hand. "Let him sleep. I want to know about *you.*"

Daria could scarcely think how to proceed when a low, rumbling groan from the back room caused both women to still. Daria looked over her shoulder, then at her grandmother.

Mamie smiled thinly. "Poor thing is in need of some medicine. I'll be but a moment." She stood up and hurried to the shelf on the wall. She reached high on her tiptoes and stretched her arm up, feeling about the shelf and then pulling down a brown vial. She glanced at Daria from the corner of her eye. "It's just a bit of laudanum. Do stay seated," she said, and disappeared down the hallway. Her hair, Daria noticed, was coming undone from her uncharacteristically haphazard bun.

She heard Mamie open the door, heard her say, "There now, just a bit of this will aid you."

"No," the man said in English, his voice deep and as rough as tree bark.

"I am only trying to help you."

Daria stood up. She moved hesitantly down the hall, but as she reached the door, Mamie appeared. "Daria, I asked you to stay seated," she said coolly as she pulled the door shut behind her. "You must leave him be. He will not heal if he does not rest." She moved past Daria.

Daria stared at the closed door for a long moment, debating. She would get to the truth of what had happened here. She only had to determine how to do it.

She turned around and walked back into the main living area. Mamie was up on her toes, putting the brown vial away.

"Do you not think that man requires medical attention?"

Mamie whirled around to face Daria, her

mouth in a grim line. "Daria, my love, as I said, when he is recovered, we might learn more from him. In the meantime, I need to make a poultice to draw the infection out of his wounds, and I will need you to help me gather some devil's bit." She picked up a basket and thrust it at Daria.

Daria stared at the basket. "I don't know what that is!"

"You will learn," Mamie said firmly. She marched to the door and flung it open, almost tripping over the dog that had followed Daria here. "You wretched dog!" she said sternly. "Off with you! Come along, Daria! Don't mind the dog — he roams the hills rather freely. Now, tell me all your news," she said, reaching for Daria's hand. "I want to hear everything. About my daughter, about Hadley Green, and of course I want to know which handsome young gentlemen have caught your eye."

She would speak of suitors *now*? Before Mamie could shut the door, Daria glanced back at the end of the corridor. Foreboding sank into her bones.

FOUR

In what was optimistically called the throne room at Dundavie, there was a chair in which the Campbell lairds had sat for hundreds of years to receive members of the clan. The seat's leather was cracked now, and the paint peeling from the arms. Duff had long wanted to replace the leather and paint the wood, but Jamie wouldn't allow it. That chair was as familiar to him as the back of his hand. He knew every sag, every lump, every crack.

He was tracing a tear in the leather next to his knee with his thumb while Gwain Campbell expounded vociferously upon his latest complaint. Gwain had thatches of unruly red hair on his chin, which were almost indistinguishable from his ruddy cheeks. He was a man who was rarely satisfied, and when he was, it was not without qualification. He'd had a prosperous year, for example, but not without working himself to the bloody bone. His infant son, born one month before he should have been, had survived and was now thriving with a great personal sacrifice of sleep on Gwain's part.

His complaint this day was something about sheep, but his gravelly voice was only a distant noise to Jamie, whose attention had wandered to the tapestry behind Gwain's head. It had hung there forever, but until now he hadn't really noticed the pale white unicorn with the flowing mane. Or that it romped in a field of yellow spring flowers. Today, the flowers were moving. They were swaying left and right on a slight breeze that he could feel slip down his body. He could hear the trees rustling overhead, could smell the sweet scent of the flowers.

Something about those flowers stirred Jamie deep within — they were too close, the color of their petals too deep. He turned his head from the tapestry and a sharp pain shot through him. The crack in the leather seemed to have deepened, growing rough as stone on one side. His head was foggy and it seemed as if everything around him was just beneath the surface of water, shadowy figures. He saw something move above him. *A unicorn.* No, not a unicorn. *A woman.* A woman with a long tail of hair that brushed against his cheek. Isabella? *Ah, Issy . . .* He lifted his hand to her nape, stroked her ear-lobe with his thumb. She smelled sweet, so sweet. *"Leannan,"* he whispered.

Isabella whispered to him, but Jamie couldn't make out her words. His hand was drifting down, brushing against the swell of her bosom, and he was pleasantly, warmly, reminded of how it was to hold her, to kiss her, to feel her. An overpowering need to fill her now began to pulse in him, and Jamie pulled her down to him, whispering, *"Leannan,"* before he kissed her.

The kiss sent a shiver through him. It was so delicate, so reverent. He shaped his lips around hers, and warmth filled him, sliding out to his limbs, swirling around his wounds. The sensation was so light that it seemed almost a dream, as if he were drift-ing on a cloud. Maybe this was an angel's kiss for a dying man.

He felt pressure against his shoulder. She was pushing against him. He felt her knee move against his hand and knock into his side, causing fire to streak down his leg. Jamie groaned and opened his eyes; his gaze was blurred, but he was aware that weak light was filtering in from someplace above him. It slowly began to dawn on him: he was not at Dundavie.

He was in the Sassenach's cottage.

A small hatch of a window above his head was open to allow a soft breeze and what seemed like morning light. His finger was between the bed and a rough stone wall. Jamie slowly turned his head, saw the vase of wildflowers beside him. He blinked, his vision coming into focus. He moved his head again. The pain was bearable; he glanced down the length of his body and his gaze fell on a young woman.

She was sitting in a chair near the foot of the bed, a plaid around her shoulders. Her knees were tucked up under her chin, her arms wrapped around her shins. And her hair, tied into one long tail, hung over her shoulder. *Honey,* he thought. The color of her hair made him think of warm honey.

He remembered her — he'd seen her before.

She blinked. "Sir?"

Sir? No one called him sir. They called him laird.

"Are you awake?"

English. It was coming back to him. He vaguely recalled her standing rigidly, gaping at him. Aye, now he remembered — she'd been staring at his cock. Who was this English female, and why did it suddenly seem as if the Highlands were teeming with them? Was this the woman he'd kissed, or

54

had he dreamed it?

"You've been asleep for two days, I think," she said. "Or rather, two days that I know of."

Two days?

She inched to the edge of her chair. "Do you speak English?" She stood up, warily coming closer, as if she expected him to suddenly snatch her like a corpse rising from his grave. She glanced nervously at the door and shifted even closer, hesitantly reaching out her hand. Long, elegant fingers. Jamie realized she meant to touch him and reacted unthinkingly, jerking his head away. He instantly felt the throb of pain in the back of his head and was momentarily stunned by it, at which point she pressed the flat of her palm lightly against his forehead.

Jamie grabbed her wrist and pulled her down so that he might see her in the fog that surrounded his brain and his vision. Her face was close to his, a young, beautiful face. His gaze roamed over her features, trying to understand. Deep golden-brown eyes, dark brows, a slender nose, and full lips. "Who are you, kitten?" he asked in Gaelic. "The devil in disguise?" His mouth was dry; he licked his cracked lips. Her gaze fell to his mouth. Jamie tightened his grip, felt the small, slender bones of her wrist, the way she strained against him.

"I think your fever has broken," she murmured, and tugged at her arm. Jamie let it go, and she slipped away from him like a whisper of silk. "Thank the Lord for it; I've feared for your health." She knelt down beside the bed, just beyond his reach. Her eyes, Jamie noticed, were only slightly darker than her hair. "Why are you here?" she asked softly. "What happened to you? Who shot you?"

How could she not know who had shot him? Was he not lying in the bed of his enemy? Surely she'd seen his horse — where *was* his horse? If the witch had done something to Niall, he would hang her from the highest wiggen tree —

"I want to help you," she said earnestly. "But I cannot help you if I don't know who you are and why someone would shoot you."

She wasn't making sense. Where was the old woman? The thought of that old witch made him eager to move. He tested the leg that didn't burn, moving it under the coverlet. He had one good leg, then. With effort, he pushed himself up onto his elbows, testing his arms.

"No, no, you mustn't!" the woman said frantically. "My grandmother will be quite upset, for you are too badly wounded —"

The sound of a door closing somewhere in the house made her gasp; she scrambled to her feet as determined footsteps moved down the hall toward them. She cast about the room as if she were seeking a place to hide and looked frantically at him just as the door swung open and the Witch of Clan Brodie entered the room.

"Daria! What in heaven's name are you doing in here?" she whispered loudly, and then looked at the bed. She was clearly quite surprised to see Jamie propped up on his elbows. "Oh!"

Jamie steadily returned her gaze.

The old woman's breath hitched. She nervously smoothed the lap of her apron and tried to force a smile. "Has the pain awakened you, sir? I shall fetch some medicine —"

"No," he said quickly, his voice scratchy and low. He knew her medicine and suspected she'd been trying to kill him with it.

"His fever has broken, Mamie," the young woman said, her voice hopeful.

"Has it?" The old woman did not sound terribly excited by the news. "Then . . . I should have a look at his wounds."

"No," Jamie growled. He'd fight her if necessary — he wasn't yet dead.

"I really think I ought," she said. "We cannot risk them turning septic, can we?"

"No," he said again.

"Mamie, he does not want it," the young woman said pleadingly.

Mary, Queen of Scots, what in blazes was going on here? Jamie looked at the two women. He could see a resemblance: full bottom lips, light brown eyes, and even in the old woman strands of golden hair peeked out from amid the gray.

"I was hoping he would help us determine what has happened to him, but I think he does not have a basic command of the English language," the young woman said.

Diah. He had been educated at Oxford. "I understand," he said gruffly. "I understand everything you've said."

The moment he spoke, Mamie — as the younger woman had referred to the older — seemed on the verge of bursting with trepidation. He could see it in her eyes, in the set of her mouth and the nervous fluttering of her fingers on one hand.

But the younger one was clearly relieved. "You speak English! Can you help us, then, sir? Can you say who might have shot you?"

"Daria!" Mamie said quickly. "The poor man has only just awakened! He needs a pillow. Let me put a pillow —"

Jamie threw up his hand, stopping her as she took a step toward him. Grimacing, he eased himself up, propping himself against the wall behind his head.

"Oh! Splendid!" the younger one said, clasping her hands together in such an enthusiastic manner that Jamie thought she was restraining herself from applauding outright. "He's much improved, Mamie!"

"For heaven's sake, Daria, let the poor soul rest —"

"But if he knows who might have done this, we can help him!"

They were speaking to each other as if he were dumb and could not hear them. Jamie looked at the younger one. *Daria.* He liked that. It sounded lyrical. Independent. She seemed hopeful and earnest, and, he thought in that foggy moment as he took in the thick tail of hair, she truly did not seem to know that this old woman was determined to kill him.

"Do you know who has harmed you?" she asked, stepping closer. Her gaze was on his mouth, as if she expected to see the words as they emerged from his lips. Behind her, the one called Mamie looked as if she might faint.

Jamie could not begin to guess what was happening with these two Englishwomen

59

on Brodie lands. Were they in bed with the Brodies? But as he could scarcely move, he decided in that moment to play dumb until he could at least stand. "I donna recall," he said simply.

Daria's shoulders sagged; she looked entirely deflated. But behind her, Mamie puffed up with relief that her secret was intact. "There, you see?" she said brightly. "We should allow him to rest now —"

"Do you know your name?" Daria asked, ignoring the old woman. She was a determined young thing, which Jamie found a wee bit incongruent with her age and the fact that she was English. He'd always found Englishwomen a bit spineless. They were not the hardy women of the Highlands, to be sure.

At the moment, however, her determined questions were complicating things. He couldn't think clearly and was fearful of revealing too much before he knew how he might need to defend himself. "No," he said simply.

Mamie's breath caught; she quickly turned away, no doubt to hide her great surprise.

"No?" Daria repeated disappointedly. "Not even your given name?"

He merely looked at her.

Daria frowned uncertainly. "You should

rest. In the meantime, we will summon the authorities."

"What?" Mamie very nearly shouted. "No!"

Daria looked back at the older woman. "Whyever not?" she asked. "Surely someone around here knows him and can vouch for his identity."

"No!" Mamie said. "Oh no, I cannot think that is a good idea at all!"

"No," Jamie hoarsely agreed. The last thing he needed was Brodie men finding him incapacitated before his own men did. They'd make quick work of him after what his brother had done to Cormag.

Daria looked between the two of them. "Why *not*?"

"Suppose he is wanted," Mamie said. She was rubbing her forehead with her fingers, as if she were trying to tease out her thoughts. "What if he has done something quite wrong?"

"Diabhal," Jamie muttered under his breath — *devil.* Aye, she was the devil, this one. Now she would paint the picture as if *he* had done something wrong?

"Him?" Daria asked. "But he's the one who's been shot —"

"Yes, but someone obviously had cause to shoot him, don't you see?"

61

Daria seemed to consider that.

"I didna deserve to be shot," Jamie said, his gaze fixed on the old woman.

That drew a curious look from Daria, but Mamie said impatiently, "Daria, you do not understand how things are done here. Scotland is not the least bit like England. People here tend to take matters into their own hands. They don't live by the strict rule of law as we do."

What were the Scots, then? A lot of savages gallivanting across the Highlands?

"But if he is a criminal, then should we not bring the authorities to our aid?" Daria asked.

That gave the old woman pause. She swallowed and glanced nervously at Jamie. "Let's discuss this in another room so the poor man might rest. Come along, Daria," she said primly, and ushered the younger woman out before her.

Daria reluctantly allowed it, but she was staring at Jamie over her shoulder as she went, her expression skeptical.

Mamie, on the other hand, could scarcely bring herself to look at him at all.

When they'd gone, Jamie moved gingerly, painfully, onto his side. The scent of wildflowers washed over him again; he sighed and closed his eyes. *Duff, for God's sake,*

62

where are you?

Bloody hell, he'd have to break free of this cottage by himself, then. Just wait until the other Campbells heard that he'd been held captive by a grandmother. There'd be no end to it.

With a groan, Jamie forced himself to move his good leg, testing its strength.

FIVE

Had she truly left England for this? Daria was accustomed to dining on fine china, at a set hour, in an actual dining room. She was accustomed to spending her days calling on friends and receiving callers, to servants and carriages and footmen and fine linens.

She was most certainly not accustomed to preparing food and sweeping floors and hunting in the woods for "healing plants." She'd ruined her best shoes and the hems of her gowns, and worse, and no one had brought her trunk up from the road. It had probably been eaten by bears. Or worse.

Neither was she accustomed to being so tenderly kissed by wild, muscular men. The memory of it made her shiver. It had happened so quickly! She couldn't stop him from pulling her down . . . Well, perhaps she might have stopped him if she'd tried. But his touch was so moving, and his mouth so warm, so soft. She'd felt a thousand tiny sparks of light flare in her the moment his mouth had met hers.

It was almost as surprising as finding Mamie in the state she had. *What in blazes had happened to her grandmother?* Daria could see no reason for her to remain in Scotland. The standard of living here was agrarian, beneath what Mamie had known all her life. There was no society, nothing to keep her — it made no sense. Daria recalled a sophisticated woman who smelled of lavender and slipped her sweetmeats and told her fantastic stories of princesses and princes. After her husband had died, the widowers in and around Hadley Green had courted Mamie, and she'd seemed happy to entertain their attentions. She'd gone on picnics, she'd dined at important tables, she'd hosted society teas. She had been, to Daria's young eyes, quite lovely.

That woman was not in this cottage.

The woman in the kitchen moved as if she weren't certain what she was to do next. She pulled bowls from the shelf and set them on the table, then picked them up and replaced them, only to find another size.

"What is the matter?" Daria asked.

"What is the matter?" Mamie repeated sharply, and slapped the bowl on the table before whirling about to face a surprised Daria. "I told you to leave the poor gentleman alone, that's what! I specifically asked you not to enter that room, and look what you've done!"

Girlish panic raced through Daria. Did Mamie know he'd kissed her? Could she see that the kiss was still singing through her? Daria was prepared to confess he was delirious, calling her by another name.

"I didn't do anything!" Daria protested. At least she didn't think she had. There had been a bit of a contretemps between her and her grandmother this morning, as Daria had refused to accompany her into the forest again, on the grounds that she did *not* gather berries like a farmer, and certainly not in forests full of wild animals and men who shot other men and left them to die. Mamie had seemed confused by her refusal, desperate to go out, and just as desperate not to leave Daria alone with the stranger. She had indeed forbidden Daria from entering his room while she went out to gather whatever in heaven's name it was she gathered in the woods.

"Well, now he's awake and I've nothing to ease his pain!" Mamie added, and pivoted around to the shelf. "You have vexed him with your meddling."

"*My* meddling?" Daria exclaimed. "He awakened all on his own —" Another pointless argument. She had begged, argued, and cajoled her grandmother to summon help, but Mamie was steadfast in her refusal to seek it, and seemed quite perturbed with Daria for even asking.

But now, she was suddenly smiling as if she'd not been the least bit cross only moments before. "Be a sweetling and go out to fetch the bandages I've hung out to dry. We must change them." She winked at Daria, then rose up on her tiptoes to the shelf to reach the brown vial.

"He doesn't want a tincture," Daria said reprovingly.

Mamie's face darkened again. "Darling, please don't argue — I really must change his bandages."

The bandage argument was one Daria could not win. She sighed and picked up a roughly woven basket from the floor, stalked to the door and yanked it open, and nearly stumbled over the dog. He was lying across the stones, a large bone between his paws. He sprang to his feet and stuck his snout in the space between the door and the frame, his tail wagging madly.

Daria stepped over him and pulled the door shut. She frowned down at him and his bone. It was a *ham* bone, and given its size and the distance she guessed he could have carried it, she presumed that he'd procured it from someone nearby. Unless Mamie had slaughtered a pig, which, after two days in this cottage with this madwoman, would not surprise Daria in the least.

The dog bounded into the garden before her, leaping over weedy plants. Daria grimaced as her shoe sank into the dark soil. By the time she reached the line where the linens were lifting lazily on the morning breeze, the dog had disappeared onto the path she had walked from the main road, leaving his bone behind.

She dropped the basket, put her hands on her hips, and surveyed the linens Mamie had washed. Her grandmother was, if nothing else, rather industrious. Daria pulled a sheet down, folded it carelessly, and tossed it in the basket. She happened to glance up and saw Mamie in the window of the man's room. Mamie was looking at Daria, watching her, too. Mamie smiled thinly and cranked the window shut.

Daria sighed irritably. She tried to picture *this* Mamie in Hadley Green. She tried to picture her in their family home.

Daria's family home wasn't the largest

68

house by any means, but it was very lovely. It had two stories and an attic, where Mr. Griswold had a pair of rooms on one end and old Mrs. Bromley, who did the cooking and housekeeping, had a pair on the other.

The house had six bedrooms, as well as a drawing room, dining and sitting rooms, and a small library where her parents kept their notes and books. They fancied themselves botanists, and in recent years they had taken on the complex task of grafting a new strain of orchid. Daria didn't know all the details, and it wouldn't matter if she did — she was not invited to their private orchid party.

They spent their time in the hothouse, their forms barely distinguishable from one another. Daria spent her time in the main house, with its ivy-covered walls that had ten large-paned windows facing the lane. Daria couldn't picture her grandmother in that house any longer — at least not like this.

She pulled the bandages from the drying line and tossed them in the basket. Removing the largest of the bed linens next, she tucked it under her chin and was attempting to fold it when she heard a horse coming down the path.

Daria looked up to see a horse and rider

ambling down from the hills to the west. Not just any rider, mind you, but a bear of a man who seemed almost as tall as his horse. His feet scarcely cleared the ground. His hair was pulled back in an old-fashioned queue. He was wearing a dark coat and buckskins.

The dog suddenly appeared, barking furiously at the intrusion, racing through the woods to the path. He stopped in the middle of the path, and with his legs braced wide apart, he barked.

"Uist!" the man shouted. *"Suidh!"* The dog instantly sat, his tail brushing the ground behind him in a happy wag. A moment later, he suddenly hopped up and trotted forward to sniff the horse.

The man's gaze had locked on Daria, his expression cold and stern. A flutter of fear swept up her spine. She glanced nervously at the cottage, debating whether she should call Mamie. In the moment that took, he'd reined up beside the fence. And the dog, the worthless dog, had trotted back into the field.

"Madainn mhath." The man's voice was low and soft, belying the dark look in his black eyes. He didn't move, but he seemed coiled, ready to strike.

Daria blinked. "Ah . . . English, please?"

One wildly thick, dark brow arched high above the other. "Good morning, then," he said in heavily accented English. She slowly lowered the linen sheet she was holding and glanced at the cottage again, assessing how quickly she could run inside and bar the door. Where were Mamie and that enormous gun? Daria would very much like to see her with it at present. She thought of screaming, but then worried that Mamie might do something rash and put herself in harm's way. So Daria stood rooted to the ground, the linen clutched tightly in her hand.

"Perhaps you might help me, aye? I'm in search of a man who's gone missing nigh on two days."

Daria's heart suddenly leapt. What if this was the man who had shot the stranger inside? "I cannot help you," she said quickly. "I am here alone with my grandmother." She realized the moment she said it that it was not a wise thing to say. If he was a robber, she'd just opened up to him the possibility of robbing this cottage.

In fact, his gaze narrowed, as if he were assessing the feasibility of it. He shifted slightly in his saddle, the leather creaking and moaning under his weight, and glanced back at the cottage.

"We cannot help you."

He took her in once more, from her braided hair to her soiled hem. "He's a tall man, the one I want. Long in the hair," he said, gesturing to his shoulder. "Broad in the chest. Eyes the color of acorns."

"No." Daria shook her head. "No one like that." She could feel the beat of her heart ratcheting up, making her breathless. She was teetering between confessing he was inside and praying for mercy, and running for her life and praying for deliverance.

He studied her closely.

Daria's heart was nearly pounding out of her chest. This bear of a man could crush her with one of his giant paws, if he were of a mind. "No one but us and the Brodie lads," she blurted, summoning up the mysterious young men Mamie had referenced. "*Three* of them." She smiled. Nervously, uncertainly, but she smiled.

The man's jaw clenched. He looked her up and down once more, muttering something in his language. "Aye, then." He made a clicking sound, and the horse ambled on.

Paralyzed with fear, Daria stood watching until he'd turned down the path that led to the main road, not daring to run and give herself away until he was gone. Until she realized he would find her trunk on the road. Lord knew what he would believe then. She balled the linen into the basket, picked it up, and fled inside the cottage.

Mamie was there, waiting. She latched the door behind Daria and gave her a grim look as she wrapped her arms tightly around her. "Are you all right?"

"Yes, yes, I'm all right," Daria said, in spite of her racing heart. "I've never seen a man as big as that. Who was he?"

"I don't know," Mamie said, and dropped her arms from around Daria. "Oh, my darling, that must have been such a fright! One must have a care in these Highlands. There are scofflaws and bandits roaming about."

Daria's panic ratcheted up even more.

"What did he want?"

"Him!" Daria cried, pointing to the hall. "He was looking for *him,* Mamie. I told him that we'd seen no one but the Brodie lads."

"Which way did he go?" she asked anxiously.

"Down the path to the main road," Daria said, gesturing wildly. "Where, I might add, my trunk still sits. I *hope* it sits there. He will see it, and he will know it belongs to us. He will know something is not right, for who leaves a trunk on the road? And if there are Brodie lads, as you say, why have they not carried it up? What if he comes back,

Mamie? What if he is the one who shot him? What if he comes back for him and shoots *us*?"

Before they could answer, they were both startled by a shout of the unintelligible language from the back room.

Mamie quickly dug the bandages out of the basket, pressed them into Daria's hands, then hurried into the kitchen and picked up a bowl from the table. The bowl contained a dark liquid that smelled like burnt wood. "You'll have to do it, Daria," she said gravely.

"What? What am I to do?"

"Dress his wounds."

Daria gasped. She shoved the bandages back at her grandmother. "Mamie, *no!* I *cannot* —"

"You can, and must! His bandages must be changed and I . . . I agree, I must seek help."

"You agree *now*? You agree to go for help and leave me to change his bandages while a man the size of a beast roams about outside? No, Mamie, I will not!"

But Mamie wasn't listening. She had already removed her apron and was reaching for her cloak. "You have argued that I should go to the authorities, and now I am going to go. It is imperative! But we cannot in good conscience leave his wounds to fester —"

"Don't leave me alone, Mamie. Please," Daria pleaded.

It was too late. Mamie was already at the door. "You'll do very well, my love. Spread the salve on his wounds and wrap clean bandages about them. Lock the door behind me, Daria, and open it *only* to me."

More shouting from the back made Daria jump what felt like a foot off the ground. *"Mamie!"*

Mamie suddenly grabbed Daria's hands and squeezed them tightly. "Please, for God's sake, do as I ask! I will be back before nightfall, I swear to you. But we cannot let his wounds fester — he could lose a limb!" She let go of Daria's hands, picked up the big blunderbuss that was leaning up against the door, and slid the bolt open. "Lock the door," she warned Daria, and slipped out.

Daria gaped at the closed door. Her grandmother had just left her alone to clean the wounds of a strange man while another one roamed about outside.

"The bolt!" she heard her grandmother call.

Daria scurried forward to slide the bolt and lock the door, then dashed to one of the small windows to look out. Her grandmother was marching toward the path that led to the road, the gun on her shoulder, the dog trotting behind her. *"Mad,"* Daria muttered. "She's gone quite mad."

The man shouted again, causing Daria to jump again. She tried to breathe deeply to calm her racing heart, but it was no use.

"Bloody hell, where have you gone?" the man bellowed in English.

Daria whirled around and looked at the closed bedroom door. All right, then. There was no use crying over it. She squared her shoulders, then picked up the bandages and the bowl.

How was she to do it? How could she remove the bandages from his naked body, touch his flesh, and then wrap the bandages around him again? It was beyond anything she knew. She was quite happy to be courted and wooed by men, but she realized that she didn't really *know* men. Lord Horncastle had kissed her once and left her feeling cold. Mr. Reston, who had come down last summer, had courted her intently and had kissed her more than once, his hands wandering her body in a rather pleasant interlude. But Daria had felt nothing but his arms and shoulders beneath his proper shirt and coat. She had never, in all her life, touched a strange man's skin. The memory of that stranger's kiss, that mad, drugged kiss, slipped down her like warm milk.

Another string of the Scottish language shook her; Daria paused to grab a cleaving knife from the shelf and tucked it up under her arm. Her hands were shaking, she noticed with chagrin. So she drew another breath to steady herself and marched down the hall.

SIX

Jamie had rallied enough that he could feel his fury beginning to strengthen him. He shouted once more in Gaelic, since ladies shouldn't hear what invective he said, even if they were evil.

At last he heard footsteps coming down the hall, and he could tell from the delicate tread that it was the younger one. *Daria.* Seated upright with his back to the stone wall, he watched the door slowly open, creaking loudly on its hinges.

A head of honey-gold appeared. Her gaze met his, and her eyes widened slightly.

Jamie did not speak; he could not trust himself to speak civilly.

"Ahem." She stepped into the room. Her eyes skated over his bare chest and arms and his hair, which had felt matted and rough when he'd touched his head earlier. She was holding a bowl and some rags, both of which shook. And tucked up under one

78

arm was a rather large knife.

He smirked at that, which seemed to un-nerve her; she suddenly moved and put everything down on a small table, then grasped the knife, holding it down by her side, her fingers curling around the hilt. "I have come to change your bandages," she announced grandly.

Jamie couldn't help a small smile or the cock of his brow.

She lifted her chin. "And I will not toler-ate any foolishness."

An interesting thing to say, given that he was the one who had suffered all the foolish-ness in this house.

She stood as if she were expecting him to agree to her terms, and when he did not, her grip on the knife tightened. "Why do you not speak?"

Jamie could see every frayed nerve in her, every quiver, every shortened breath. He looked pointedly at her knife, then lifted his gaze to hers again. "Do you fear me, then, lass?" he asked quietly.

Color began to seep from her cheeks. "It's rather a big knife," she said, as if he hadn't noticed. "Should you not fear me?"

Foolish chit. If Jamie ever had a daughter — and God help him if he did, for he found females to be the most exasperating and confusing creatures on earth — he would explain in no uncertain terms that if a man wishes to subdue a woman, he will. There is nothing — no knife, no club — that will stop him. Not even a one-legged man with a hole in his side and a wee bit of renewed strength could be stopped from subduing her if necessary.

"I mean only to change your bandages," she added, as if he might believe she was accosting him. "The wounds must be kept clean."

Jamie shrugged. "Then change them."

The chit pressed her lips together and frowned at his bandages. The witch had wrapped them around his torso and his thigh, knotting the ends together. This one would have to crawl onto the bed to change them, since he was sitting up. He could see that she'd worked that out for herself, and he almost chuckled at her expression. An English rose, as fresh as the morning dew, unhinged by the sight of a man. "I'll no' bite, if that's what gives you pause."

Her gaze flew up to his; her cheeks were stained an appealing shade of pink.

"Come, then. Have done before I expire."

She drew a breath so great that her shoulders lifted with it. She moved hesitantly to the edge of the bed and stood, clearly

80

expecting him to move, to put his legs over the side and give her room to work. But Jamie was in no mood to help her. To her credit, she did not demand it. She put the knife on a pillow — just beyond his reach but well within hers — then hiked up the hem of her gown to give her a bit of leg room and put one knee on the bed. Then the other. She still wasn't close enough — she tried to lean over and untie the ends of the cloth, but she couldn't leverage her body at that distance. She sat back on her heels, her hands on her knees, examining the situation.

Jamie smiled.

"Don't you dare smile at me as if this is some sort of game," she said, her voice low and full of warning. She shifted closer, studiously avoiding his gaze as she gingerly worked the ends of the bandage free.

Jamie couldn't take his eyes from her. Her skin was remarkably smooth, unmarked by the effects of childhood illness or even a single freckle. Her wine-colored lips looked especially full against her pale skin, and Jamie felt a faint stirring deep in his groin. He thought of Isabella, and wondered if he'd ever seen her as clearly as he was seeing this English rose.

His gaze fixed on her lips. He remembered

that hazy kiss, the plump, firm flesh of her lips, the moist warmth against his mouth. She was now biting one of those lips in concentration. He scarcely noticed what she was doing to his body; he only knew that the moment she lifted her gaze to his, triumph shone in her eyes at having untied the bandages. Eyes that, under the right circumstance, could be a man's undoing.

The right circumstance. That was laughable, for he wasn't entirely certain that she wouldn't try to kill him, too.

When she saw him looking at her as he was — a man taken with feminine beauty — she froze. Their faces were only inches apart, and her golden-brown eyes — flecked with a silvery blue, he noted — locked on his. "What are you doing here, so far from home?" he murmured, and casually lifted his hand to touch her cheek.

Her eyes widened. But she didn't pull away; she held his gaze. "How do you know that I am far from home?"

"You speak like a Sassenach."

Her lashes fluttered uncertainly.

He brushed her cheek with his knuckles. *Smooth.* Silk and cream. "And you're no' sturdy enough to survive life in the Highlands . . . your knife notwithstanding."

Her brows dipped. "I'm sturdy —"

"No," Jamie said, shaking his head. "You wish you were in England, with your tea and your feathers —"

"Feathers?"

He gestured to her head. "For the hats." He'd never seen such ridiculous millinery as he had in London.

The color in her cheeks deepened. "I am sturdy enough, I assure you, if one considers that I came to see my grandmother and discovered that not only has she lost her mind, but there is a strange and completely incapacitated man in her house. And now, I am tending to his wounds. Wounds which he has no memory of receiving," she added suspiciously. "I rather think no one can fault me for being a bit hesitant, but I assure you, I am *sturdy.*"

He gave her a lopsided smile. "Aye, no one can fault an English rose for changing a poor man's bandages." He let his hand drop, brazenly brushing her décolletage as he did.

Her blush deepened and she leaned back on her heels. "Please sit up a bit so that I might . . ." She made a circling gesture with her hand. "Unwrap them."

"Why is it you, then, and no' the old woman to tend me?"

She did not answer. Jamie did not take his

eyes from her as he put his hand on her shoulder. He felt her flinch, heard her sharp intake of breath, and gave her a slight smile as he used her as an anchor to pull up and away from the wall, clenching his jaw against the pain this caused him.

She had to reach around him to unwind the bandage on his torso, giving him a lovely view of a flawless décolletage and the creamy mounds of flesh that rose out of her bodice. At any other time, in any other place, he would have persuaded her to allow him to touch her breasts, to bury his face in them. Jamie was not unsuccessful in wooing women to do as he pleased. But at that moment, he was far more concerned with personal survival and escaping this bloody cottage, and he contented himself with merely looking. Openly and admiringly.

"I believe your wounds have impaired your sense of propriety, sir," she said with a pointed look.

Jamie smiled. "Perhaps a wee bit," he conceded. "I heard a man outside, aye?"

She did not respond except to frown, then leaned into him once more to unwrap the bandage.

"Who was it, then?"

"No one."

"No one," he repeated.

"A passerby," she said, leaning in to reach around him once more.

"Aye, and what did the passerby want?" he asked as he breathed in the scent of rose-water.

She hesitated in her work, then said softly, "You."

Duff. Duff had found him, he was certain of it. And if he had, he'd be back, for Duff was the canniest, most perceptive man Jamie had ever known.

"Are you surprised?" she asked, peeking up at him. "Does it not give you cause for concern?"

"What concern should I have, lass?"

"What if he is the man who shot you? What if he would like to finish what he failed to do the first time?"

Jamie smiled a little. "I suppose, then, that you'd have to protect me from him, aye?"

"Why would I do that?"

"Why are you trying to save me now? Why have you no' summoned someone to come for me?"

She dropped her gaze again. "I don't rightly know, to be quite honest." She pulled the bandage completely free of his body, then her face fell. "Dear God."

Jamie bent his head to see the wound the

old woman had inflicted upon him. He probed it gingerly, wincing in pain.

She gasped. "Don't touch it!"

"It's no' as bad as I feared," he said with some relief. "The lead went through."

It hurt like hell, but at least it didn't burn like fire any longer.

"Leave it be, please," she begged, and scooted off the bed, fetching the bowl and the clean bandages. "I am to apply this liberally to your wound," she said apologetically.

"What is it?"

She looked down at the bowl. "I am not certain, in truth. I only know that she scoured the woods looking for the right plants to make the salve."

"The right plants," he scoffed. "There are plants that grow in these hills that are poisonous."

"She's been working very hard to save your life since she found you in the woods."

Surely the chit did not believe the old woman had found him in the woods! "I wonder," he said casually, "how she managed to bring me here."

"The Brodie lads helped her," the English rose said as she dabbed a cloth into the bowl.

"Ah, of course. One wonders why the

Brodie lads have no' come round to find out why I've been shot, aye?" Or to complete the killing the old woman had botched. He could well imagine there would be any number of Brodies queuing to have a go at that.

Her gaze met his for a moment before she turned her attention to the wound, applying a salve that smelled foul and stung like nettles.

"Were I your . . . Mamie," Jamie continued, "I'd seek help. For all she knows, I am the one who shot first, aye?"

That brought her head up. "*Did* you?"

"I donna know," he said, steadily returning her gaze.

She flushed, dipped the cloth into the bowl, then dabbed it on the wound. Jamie tensed, his jaw clenched against the burn.

She put the bowl aside and picked up the new bandage. "It would be helpful if you could remember what happened."

"Did you say, then, where the wi— your grandmamma has gone?"

"I didn't," she said distrustfully. "As it happens, she has at last gone for help."

Ho now, here was an interesting turn. The old bat must believe that since he claimed not to remember, she might actually convince the authorities of her innocence.

The English rose made quick work of the bandage and tied it off neatly, then stepped down off the bed to admire her handiwork.

"Well done," he said, a little breathlessly; his side throbbed painfully. "Are you a nurse, then?"

"A nurse?" She smiled as if that amused her. "No."

"Then who are you, *leannan*? What is your name?"

"You'd like a proper introduction?" She folded her arms across her middle. "Miss Daria Babcock of Hadley Green. It's a village in West Sussex. Who are you?"

He smiled. "I hope we will learn that together. Now then, what of the hole in my leg? Do you intend to change that bandage as well?"

Daria Babcock of Hadley Green glanced at his leg. He was reminded of that hazy image of her standing in the middle of the room, gaping at his naked body when he'd been half-mad with the concoction the old woman had given him. He slowly, deliberately, pushed the bed linen from his wounded leg, revealing his bare thigh and leaving just enough to cover his groin.

The English rose paled. Her gaze flicked to the bulge between his legs, still covered by the bedsheet, then back to the bandage.

"Ah . . ."

He bent his knee, bringing his thigh off the bed so that she could reach around it. "You look like a ghost, Miss Babcock." He couldn't help grinning.

Her expression darkened. "You must think me very naïve, Mr. No Name." She moved to the bed and began to tug at the knot in the bandage around his thigh. She made quick work of unwrapping it, grimacing when she saw the wound. This shot had not been so clean, and was made even uglier from the removal of the lead. It looked as if someone had dug with a shovel in his thigh. Miss Babcock was looking a little gray at the sight of it, and honestly, Jamie felt a little gray himself.

He took the cloth from her hand, jabbed it into the bowl she held, and ignored her gasp as he dabbed the ghastly stuff onto the wound. He hissed at the burn, then did it again, putting a generous dollop into the cavity of the wound. He'd either die of gangrene or he'd heal, but in either case, he would move things along.

The English rose was still gaping at his wound, so he grabbed up the fresh bandage and wrapped it around his leg himself, then tied it off. "There's a good lass — fetch my plaid."

"What?"

He nodded to the plaid, folded neatly and draped on the back of the chair.

She did as he asked, fetching it from the chair and unfolding it, approaching him as if she meant to drape it over him like a blanket.

"Lay it flat on the bed beside me," he said, patting the bed. "Aye, that's it. Now, please turn your back."

"Why?"

"I intend to dress," he said, and began to move the sheet from his body. "And I fear your tender nature will cause you to faint."

She whirled about so quickly that her braid swung out wide. "You mean to *dress*?"

"To don clothing. But as the buckskins I was wearing seem to have disappeared, I shall dress in the traditional garb of the Highlanders. Is it no' what the English tourists prefer from a Scot now? To see us clothed in the *breacan feile*?"

"I don't prefer anything from a Scot," she said. "I am quite content with England, thank you."

Bloody good for her.

"But you can't dress. You can scarcely sit up in your bed."

"You don't know the will of a Highlander," he said, and clenched his jaw against the pain as he eased himself onto the plaid and wrapped it around his waist, rolling a bit to get it around him.

"Perhaps not. But I am well acquainted with the stubborn nature of men in general," she said pertly.

Behind her, Jamie rolled his eyes. He grabbed up the soiled bandage she'd unwrapped from his leg and used that to belt the plaid to him. "All right then, give us a hand."

She glanced over her shoulder; Jamie was slowly inching his way to the edge of the bed. He beckoned her near, but the lass seemed dumbstruck. With a grunt, Jamie tried to stand. His injured leg buckled beneath him and a wave of dizziness came over him. She rushed to him then, and he quickly pulled her against his side with an arm draped heavily around her shoulders. Leaning against her, he tested his weight as she braced her hands on his back and abdomen, struggling to hold him upright.

"Augh," he uttered as he shifted forward, moving his injured leg.

"I beg you not to do this! Please go back to your bed before you hurt yourself. It's too soon!"

"Never known a man to heal by lying about in his bed," he muttered. Something wasn't right. The far edges of his vision were beginning to swim. *The salve.* Jamie cursed in his native tongue. That witch — if she couldn't force it down his throat, she would put it in his wound.

"Oh dear, you don't look well at all," he heard the lass say, but her voice seemed disembodied. He looked down at her and watched her features melt just before he felt his legs give way beneath him.

SEVEN

When the man fell, he took Daria with him. She landed half on top of him, half off, and had to work her arm out from beneath his shoulder. She put her hand beneath his nose. She felt the warmth of his breath and a rush of relief went through her.

She lay there for a moment or two, that sliver of a thought skipping through her mind of how — no, *why* — she was here. She'd scarcely gained her feet when she heard pounding on the cottage door. "Off with you, you mangy dog!" Mamie shouted. That was followed by the sound of more banging.

"Now you've done it," Daria whispered to the man lying on the floor.

She hurried to the door and slid the bolt open. Mamie swept in, slamming the door shut on the dog. "Did you bandage him?"

"I did —" Daria started, but Mamie was already striding to the back room. Daria ran to catch up.

Mamie cried out when she saw the man on the floor. "What in heaven's name has happened?" she demanded as Daria entered the room behind her.

"He wanted to test the strength of his leg," Daria said. "One moment he seemed fine, and the next, he . . . he just fell."

"Well, of course he did. The salve had something in it to help him sleep," Mamie said, and knelt to press the back of her hand against the stubble on his cheek. "He's not feverish."

Daria stared at Mamie. "You put something in the salve? That's a rather dark shade of deceit, is it not?"

Mamie clucked and gave Daria a dismissive wave of her hand.

"Honestly, Mamie, if I didn't know you better, I'd think you put something in the salve because you know he doesn't want it, and then gave it to me to administer so he'd not suspect it," Daria said accusingly.

"What an imagination you have!" Mamie said, but the color in her cheeks was rising. "Help me, darling. We must return him to his bed."

The man sprawled on the floor weighed fifteen stone if he weighed one. "We can't possibly lift him. We'll have to leave him on

94

the floor until he comes to."

"We can't very well leave him on the floor!"

Daria stood up and stalked to the bed, grabbing up a pair of pillows. "Then perhaps the Brodie lads might finally appear to help you."

Mamie gave her a dark look but did not give her the satisfaction of a reply.

Daria knelt down, lifted the man's head, and slid the pillow underneath him. His head lolled to one side.

"He'll catch his death here," Mamie said.

The fleeting thought that if he were to die, then Mamie would have succeeded swept through Daria's mind. She quickly forced it out. "Pray that he'll not sleep as long as that," she said crisply, and stood again to retrieve a blanket from the bed, which she draped over his body.

She paused, staring down at him. For a potential criminal, he looked handsome in his sleep, really. There was the dark growth of beard on his face, and his hair was matted from lying in bed, but there was a softness in his features that she did not see when he was awake. He didn't look as hard or as angry.

"Come, Daria," Mamie said, and Daria reached down to help her as she clumsily gained her feet. Her grandmother paused, her hands to her back, bending backward, then walked out of the room.

Daria followed her. "Did you find help?" she asked when they were in the kitchen.

"Hmm?" Mamie said, as if she'd momentarily forgotten what she'd gone out to do. "Unfortunately, not as yet. The Brodie lads were not to be found."

The mysterious Brodie lads were never quite where anyone needed them, were they? But why in God's name would Mamie lie about this? What possible reason could she have to keep this man sedated in her house?

The question of what to do plagued Daria well into the night. She tossed and turned in the freezing third bedroom, wrapped in a wool shawl and huddled beneath the coverlet. There was no hearth in this room, and it was cold as ice. She burrowed down and closed her eyes, but could see only a pair of hazel eyes, a square chin covered with dark stubble, a jagged wound in a man's thigh.

She'd never been so challenged. A life of tea and dancing and gossip had left her woefully ill-prepared for these obstacles. But if Mamie would not seek help, Daria would have to. The only thing she knew to do was to walk the ten miles or so to Nairn.

All right then, she would have to plan for it. First, there was the issue of shoes. Perhaps Mamie had some boots she might borrow. She would need to pack a bit of food, wouldn't she? And then . . . then she would follow the road. It couldn't be that difficult, could it? Follow the road to Nairn, where she would send a letter to Charity and ask her to come straightaway. And then she would prevail on any authority there to help her. All very easy!

She had to believe it was easy because she had no other hope. If she was successful, Daria couldn't even guess what it might mean for Mamie. She feared for her grandmother. But she feared more for the stranger's life.

Morning came quite early after such a sleepless night. Daria pulled on a woolen robe Mamie had given her and combed her hair, letting it fall loose down her back. She padded down the little hallway to the main living area. She could smell ham, and found the one Mamie had buried beneath the hot coals at the hearth last night. She dug it out and removed it from the covered cast iron skillet, placed it on a platter, and put that in the middle of the table. Funny, she thought sleepily, that after only a matter of days, she was quite comfortable pulling hams from glowing embers. As she stirred the embers she heard a door open. She expected to hear footsteps, but the heavy, lurching step and dragging foot were decidedly *not* Mamie's.

Daria quickly stood and wrapped the robe tightly around her. The stranger came into view, dragging his injured leg. He was wrapped in his plaid, belted precariously with a soiled bandage. His matted hair stood on end, his beard had thickened, and dear God, how his eyes were blazing. Not with fever. With anger. He glared at Daria as he wordlessly passed her and roughly pulled a wooden chair from the table, landing on it with a grunt and then laboriously arranging his leg beneath the table. He saw the ham and instantly leaned forward, his hand reaching —

"I'll carve some for you," she said quickly, and picked up the knife that she'd used to protect herself from him the day before.

He responded with a menacing look, but he shifted back, his hand sliding down the table and into his lap.

She sliced off a thick slab of ham, put it on a plate along with some of Mamie's bread, and slid it across the table to him.

He ate as if he were starved. "More?" she asked when he'd devoured the food. He nodded curtly. Daria sliced off more of the ham and bread. He'd eaten almost all of it when Mamie scurried into their midst, coming to an abrupt halt when she saw him sitting there, eating ravenously. She was still clothed in the gown she'd worn yesterday, her graying hair half up on her head and half down. She looked exhausted and half-crazed. "Oh dear," she said anxiously. "No, Daria, you shouldn't give him so much food. I've made a broth —"

"Enough of your broth," he said through a mouthful of ham.

Mamie pushed her hair back and looked wildly at Daria, then at him. "Please come back to your bed, sir. Allow yourself to heal properly — it's been only three days."

"I'll no' return to that bloody bed," he said firmly, and dragged the back of his hand across his mouth.

"I only want to help you —"

"You've a peculiar way of helping."

"Mamie," Daria said, coming around to put her hand on her grandmother's arm. "Sit, please. Clearly he prefers to recuperate on his own terms. And it would be in your best interests to find another occupation than nursemaid to a stranger, don't you agree?"

"Aye, she's right."

Mamie cast him a glare that would have

frozen the North Sea, which was met with an equally chilling look from him. The tension between them was palpable. Lord, there was so much unspoken in this room! Daria felt as if she were in the parlor at Rochfeld, the Horncastle estate, trying to sort out one of the infernal riddles Lord Horncastle was so fond of forcing onto everyone.

"I've come to the end of my patience with the two of you," she snapped. "It is quite obvious to me that we'd all benefit if one of you would kindly own to what has happened here!"

"I don't see how he can own to anything," Mamie said pertly. "He can't recall how he came to be here." She stood abruptly before anyone might posit a different theory and went to the hearth to toss another log on the fire.

"*You,* sir, know more about what happened to you than you have admitted," Daria said, pointing at him. "And *you,* Mamie, can't seem to find anyone in all of Scotland to help you! Yet you have a ham and chopped wood — *someone* has helped you."

"All from Nairn," Mamie said with a flick of her wrist.

"I find that impossible to believe. So

please stop being untruthful about what happened here!"

The stranger snorted as if that amused him.

Daria's anger soared just as high as if he had laughed outright at her. "And *you,* sir," she said, turning on him. "You claim not to recall what happened to you, and yet you can recall what you were wearing at the time you were filled with lead. Furthermore, you were not the least bit surprised that someone was looking for you, which suggests to me that you know *why* you were shot. And I think you know your name!"

His smile faded and he looked at Mamie. "Aye," he said with a shrug.

"Aye?" Daria echoed, surprised by his agreement.

"Aye," he repeated and turned his hazel eyes to Daria. "But I've no' even a wee idea why I was shot." He arched a dark brow in Mamie's direction.

Mamie clamped her mouth shut. She hung the kettle over the fire with such force that it swung and hit the stone wall at the back of the hearth.

Daria didn't relish the idea of walking to Nairn, but she was determined to find the answers to what had happened here if it killed her. "Very well," she said, irritably. "I should like to borrow some boots, Mamie. I am to Nairn."

The stranger's brow arched high, and one corner of his mouth lifted as he took her in. "I canna have you walk to Nairn, lass. It's too far for an English rose, aye? So I shall tell you the truth as I know it."

Mamie turned so quickly that she almost collided with Daria. "Don't listen to anything he says. He knows nothing. How could he? He has been wounded in the head — he will remember nothing useful, I assure you."

Daria ignored her grandmother. She braced her hands against the table and leaned across, glaring at him. "*Tell* me."

A slight shadow of a smile lit his eyes as he shifted forward with some effort. "I am Jamie Campbell, Laird of Dundavie."

"As if that has any bearing on anything," Mamie muttered.

"What does 'laird' mean?" Daria asked, sinking into a chair beside him.

"It is something akin to a lord," Mamie sniffed. "But *not* a lord. A decided step down from that."

Daria waved her grandmother off. "Go on," she urged him.

"The truth, lass, is that your Mamie is the one who shot me."

Daria reared back and slapped a hand on the table. As opposed to his face, as was her instinct. "Do you take me for a fool?"

A slow smile appeared on his lips, and he shook his head. "No' even a wee bit, *leannan.*"

The way he said that word, whatever it meant, sent a shiver down Daria's spine. What wretched game was he playing with her? She looked to Mamie for help, but Mamie had sunk down onto a chair, looking suddenly much older than her sixty-some-odd years. And something in her expression made Daria's belly knot.

"That's ridiculous," Daria said angrily, appealing to her grandmother to correct the record, to offer a reasonable explanation, *any* explanation.

But Mamie seemed only to sink lower into her chair, her lips pressed together into an intractable line.

Daria's belly began to churn and she pressed the flat of her hand to her abdomen. "Mamie, please, I am begging you — the *truth.*"

Mamie sighed. She pushed her hair back from her forehead and lifted her gaze to Daria. "Is a woman not permitted to defend herself?"

Daria's heart sank as Jamie Campbell

erupted.

"*Defend* yourself! Madam, I was unarmed!"

"I didn't *mean* to shoot you," Mamie said to him, and to Daria, "I had the gun for protection, naturally. I am here alone, and a strange man had come to my door. It . . . it went off —"

"When my back was turned," Mr. Campbell said. "*Ach,* woman, you dissemble yet!"

"Did you announce yourself?" Daria demanded of him. "You must admit that you are intimidating in your appearance, especially to a woman who resides alone."

He looked very surprised by that. "Intimidating? In what way?"

"Well, your size, for one." And his hair, hanging to his shoulders. Broad, barely clothed shoulders. "And your . . . dress," she added carefully.

His brows dipped into a dark frown. "My *dress*? Buckskins? A linen shirt? A coat and a plaid for warmth? These are intimidating? What, must a man wear lace to quell the fears of an English rose?"

"I am *not* an English rose! I mean that you might appear, at first glance, perhaps a bit . . ." She shifted in her seat. "Savage."

"*Savage!*" he bellowed. "I will have you know that I've been welcomed into ballrooms across London and was no' thought a *savage*!"

"I don't mean that you *are* a savage, but only that to a woman's eye, there might be a moment of consternation if one is not acquainted. That's all."

He was not appeased. He shifted forward again, propping his good arm against the table so that he could pierce her with his dangerously dark eyes. "Allow me to tell you why your grandmamma shot an unarmed man," he said, his voice dangerously low. "I didna intimidate her. I scarcely had opportunity, aye? She met me at the door with a gun. I *announced* myself. I told her I had come to inquire why she unlawfully divested my addlepated uncle of one thousand pounds. Her response was to shoot me. Now — have you any whisky? I find all this more than a wee bit trying."

Daria was appalled. "Now you accuse Mamie of not only shooting you with your back turned, but *stealing* as well? I think you are as mad as she!"

"I beg your pardon, I am not *mad*." Mamie stood, reached up to the top shelf, and brought down a green bottle. She took down three small glasses as well, and put them all down with a loud *clap* before Jamie Campbell.

Daria did not generally imbibe. But in this extraordinary circumstance, she eyed that bottle of whisky. So did Jamie Campbell. He reached for it, filling the three glasses, then making quick work of one. As he poured another tot of whisky for himself, Daria moaned, laid her arms on the table, and rested her forehead against them, her eyes closed, trying to absorb another impossible turn of events.

"Oh, Daria, dearest," Mamie said sweetly, and Daria felt her grandmother's hand on the back of her head, stroking her. "I am so very sorry for the trouble I've caused you."

Daria was beyond apologies. She was wildly alarmed. She had no idea what she was to do, and Daria always, *always* knew what to do. When Mr. Anders, a bachelor with thinning hair and bony fingers, had pursued her quite ardently last year, she'd known precisely what to do. When Mrs. Morton had confided in her that Daria's good friend Lady Ashwood was rumored to have contributed in a nefarious way to the death of her first husband, Lord Carey, Daria had known precisely how to scotch the rumors. But God help her if she knew what to do in this little cottage with these two.

"Go on, then. Tell her," Jamie Campbell

rumbled. "Tell your granddaughter why you robbed my uncle of one thousand pounds, aye?"

"I didn't rob him of a thousand pounds!" Mamie said angrily, causing Daria to lift her head. "Do I look as if I have even five pounds to my name? If you must know, Daria has come to Scotland to deliver a banknote —" She stopped herself and closed her eyes a moment, her fingers wrapping around one of the glasses of whisky. "Never mind that. The point, Mr. Campbell, is that I shot you quite by accident and I have endeavored to repair the harm and save your life in the process."

"Diah," he muttered, throwing up a hand in frustration.

Mamie pushed a tot of whisky across the table to Daria. "Drink it. For your nerves. It's Irish, superior to anything you will find here."

Jamie Campbell slammed his fist on the table at that remark.

Daria ignored the whisky. "I don't quite understand, Mamie. Were you defending yourself, or was it an accident? And how does one shoot a man by accident? That is to say, why were you pointing a gun at him? If he announced who he was, if he stated his business, would you not have lowered your gun?"

Mamie tossed back the whisky as if she were quite practiced at it.

"I think your grandmamma does no' care to be questioned," Campbell scoffed.

"My *name*, Mr. Campbell, is Mrs. Frances Moss," Mamie said sternly.

"Will you still deny, Mrs. Moss, that you have made Hamish Campbell's acquaintance, then?"

"She has admitted shooting you by mistake — must you badger her about this ridiculous accusation of stealing?" Daria asked angrily.

But Jamie Campbell ignored her, keeping his gaze steady on Mamie.

"Well . . ." Mamie's voice trailed off as if she had more to say.

Daria's heart began to pound. She couldn't have possibly taken one thousand pounds. "Well? Well *what*?"

"It is possible that I have made his acquaintance," Mamie said uncertainly.

"Aha!" Mr. Campbell said triumphantly, jabbing his arm in the air and instantly grimacing in pain, doubling over his injured side.

"You *know* him?" Daria cried.

"I wouldn't say that I *know* him, no," Mamie said. "But I might have met him. At the pony races, perhaps. But more to the point, I most certainly did *not* swindle one thousand pounds from him." She snorted as if that were preposterous, apparently missing the irony that since she had been untruthful about everything else, it was impossible to believe her now.

Daria dared not look at Campbell as she rose up from her chair. She drew Mamie up from hers, held her by the arms, and looked into her blue eyes. "Have you received any money from him, Mamie?"

Mamie gave Campbell a sidelong glance, but Daria gave her a gentle shake. "Mamie? Have you accepted any money from Mr. Hamish?"

"Mr. Campbell. Hamish Campbell," Jamie Campbell said behind her.

Mamie's lashes fluttered and she looked down. "He might have given me a gift —"

"Bloody *hell*!" Jamie Campbell exploded, and brought his fist down on the table again, rattling the bottle and the whisky glasses. "Woman, I am of a mind to drag you to Edinburra on a charge of thievery!"

Daria's hands fell from her grandmother's arms. She couldn't think, her mind suddenly a blank slate. She couldn't *breathe.* She put her hand to her throat; fear was welling up in her, choking her. Something was horribly wrong with her grandmother. Mamie had heretofore been scrupulously honest. How could it have come to this? And what of her parents? How would she ever explain this to them?

Daria instinctively stepped back, away from the woman she had loved with all her heart, her mind racing. She looked at Jamie Campbell, who, to his credit, looked at her with a bit of sympathy. Her only hope for Mamie was to appeal to him for forgiveness, for help. But if Mamie had stolen *one thousand pounds* . . . the amount stunned her. What hope did she have that she would not be caught and prosecuted for thievery, just as Jamie Campbell had said?

Daria desperately tried to think.

"Where is my horse?" Jamie Campbell asked quietly.

"Quite safe," Mamie said. "I've a paddock nearby, and he's been properly fed."

"My dog as well?"

Mamie frowned. "He has a ham bone as large as he is. I think he has fared well enough."

That was *his* dog? Daria suddenly marched to the door and threw it open. The dog was sitting patiently beside the door. "Come," she said, gesturing inside. The dog cocked his head to one side.

"Trobhad!" Campbell called, and the dog rushed inside, his tail wagging furiously, his nose sniffing his master and his wounds.

Jamie Campbell put his hand on the dog, stroking his head, and turned a cold gaze to Mamie. "I will no' allow you to walk free from this, Mrs. Moss."

"Whatever she has taken, we will repay," Daria said quickly. Campbell looked as if he were prepared to argue. "Mamie," Daria said quickly, and put her hands on Mamie's shoulders. "Will you please go and dress?"

Mamie's eyes widened with surprise. "But I —"

"Please, darling," Daria pleaded with her. "You're wearing yesterday's gown."

Mamie glanced down. She pressed a hand to her hair and frowned at the feel of it. "Yes, all right; perhaps I ought." She walked out of the little kitchen, looking defeated.

Daria waited until she heard the door of Mamie's room open and close, then whirled toward Jamie Campbell.

"Donna even try," he said. "I do no' give quarter to thieves and liars."

This was clearly going to be a tussle.

EIGHT

On an early-summer day the previous year,
much like this one, Jamie had sat in the
laird's chair at Dundavie, his finger tracing
over the crack in the leather, and received
the Murchisons, a well-to-do English family
who had purchased the land next to the
Campbell clan lands and infested it with
sheep. Mr. Murchison had made an enticing offer to some Campbells to buy their
parcels of land, which they had accepted.
Many in Jamie's clan didn't fully grasp that
the ability of each of them to prosper was
based on their ability to prosper as a whole.
Each clan member owned his or her parcels
of land, but the yields from those lands went
into clan coffers and benefited the entire
clan. So when parcels were sold, it reduced
the land available for the clan to profit from.

Change was coming swiftly to Dundavie,
and Jamie was trying his best to steer a rocking ship to the new reality. However, he was

naturally predisposed to dislike the Murchisons, who had come that summer day with an offer to buy more acreage.

But what Jamie recalled about that day was how Murchison's daughter had interrupted her father twice to make a point of her own that she seemed to think critical to the conversation. He'd been surprised by it, for women generally were not present when matters of business were discussed, and if they were, they certainly didn't speak. Particularly Englishwomen. He'd never known a young, unmarried Englishwoman to be any more engaged than a piece of furniture in matters of business.

Miss Daria Babcock, he was learning, was in some regard much like that young Englishwoman. Give her a podium and a proper cause, and he'd wager she could beat men into submission with her tongue. She was certainly trying to subdue *his* rage, talking quite a lot as she paced before the table, her robe trailing behind her, her knotted hair swinging loosely above her waist, her arms wrapped tightly around her.

He liked the way her hips swung as she paced, the way she knit her brows as she concentrated on her argument. He liked the curve of her neck, the swell of her bosom above her folded arms. If the circumstances

113

were different, he would like her quite a lot.

Miss Babcock suddenly halted and stared at him, clearly waiting for a response. When he did not offer one, she demanded, "Have you heard a word I've said?"

Jamie shifted uncomfortably. He'd heard some of her words, although which ones he could not say. It hardly mattered — nothing she could say to him would change his mind. He was of the firm opinion that Mrs. Moss should be cast into gaol and left to rot. But as he had no gaol to cast her into, he'd not decided what he would do with the old woman quite yet.

Miss Babcock suddenly leaned across the table so that she was at eye level with him. "She's ill, Mr. Campbell, quite ill, deserving of your compassion. You have my word that I shall see your uncle's money repaid if you will allow me to escort her home to Hadley Green, where my mother might care for her as she needs."

Jamie cocked his head to one side. "Do you suggest that I allow you and the old woman to leave Scotland, then wait patiently for one thousand pounds to magically appear?"

"I gave you my word."

Jamie smiled. He slid his hand across the table and wrapped his fingers around her wrist before she knew what he was about. She tried to yank free, but he pulled her closer until she was forced to brace herself on her elbows, bent halfway over the table, her face only inches from his, her light brown eyes sparkling with ire. "Your *word* will no' be sufficient. That old woman deserves to be put away, if not hanged, aye?" His gaze slipped to her mouth. "Consider yourself fortunate that she's no' been dealt a Scot's justice quite yet. Or you, for that matter."

"*Me?* What have I done?"

"In the Highlands, a family stands on the actions of one."

Miss Babcock yanked her hand free and stood back, glaring down at him. "You will not frighten me with threats, sir. I think it is clear that my grandmother is *not herself.* I've known her for one and twenty years and I've never known her to do the slightest bit of wrong." Her expression softened, and the young woman suddenly looked very weary. She sighed and slipped into the chair directly across from Jamie. "She is the kindest, most generous woman," she said sadly. "I have always adored her."

"Touching," Jamie said. "But no' enough to sway me."

"*Oh!*" she snapped, and shifted around in

her chair so she was facing to the side, her arms folded tightly across her chest once more.

"I beg your pardon if you are offended. I donna know how the English treat those who will, unprovoked, shoot a man in the back, but in Scotland, generally speaking, they are no' allowed to roam freely."

Miss Babcock glanced heavenward and closed her eyes. "Then would you at least consider helping *me*?"

He snorted. "You?"

She cast a cow-eyed look at him. "Surely you can appreciate how difficult this is for me."

He could not begin to guess why he should care, given the injustice that had been done to him. He suspected the Brodies were behind it all somehow, seeking vengeance for the trouble with Geordie. If that were true, it only made Jamie want to put the old woman away that much more. But he could not look into the lovely eyes in the lovely face across from him now and say so, though he would like to. He gave her an indifferent shrug.

She twisted in her chair once more to face him. "The irony, Mr. Campbell, is that you are the only one who can help me now. Isn't that absurd? But it's true! Who else but *you* can help me discover what has happened to my grandmother?"

"No."

"I am new to Scotland," she doggedly pressed on. "I can't even tell you where in Scotland we are at present. How could I possibly go about the business of discovering what has happened to my beloved grandmother? But you . . . you seem to know some things, and you are clearly in a position to learn more. There is no one else I can turn to for help."

"Very touching," he said, and looked away from those pleading eyes. "But no." His leg was beginning to ache fiercely. He picked up the tot she'd left untouched and downed it.

"How can you refuse me?" she pressed. "Will you not put yourself in my shoes for a moment?"

He pushed himself up, determined to walk on his injured leg.

The moment he did, Miss Babcock was up, too, darting around the table and tucking herself up under his arm, draping it over her shoulders to help him walk. Jamie debated not using her as a crutch, but the sooner he could move, the sooner he could leave this wretched little cottage.

He began to move, leaning heavily on her.

"I don't understand your reluctance," she said as she slipped her arm around his waist to bear his weight.

Jamie grimaced with the pain that sliced through him at each step, shooting up his side and back, into his shoulder.

"Are you all right? Perhaps you should sit."

"I'm fine." He gritted his teeth against the searing pain as they moved into the small parlor. An ornate clock ticked the seconds by with each excruciating step. He didn't need to be reminded how slow and infirm he was, and turned away toward the windows. Surprise and relief filled him when he saw Duff and two of his men making their way down the path.

Jamie turned Miss Babcock about so that she would not see them.

She was oblivious to the change in direction, so intent was she on convincing Jamie to let them go unscathed. "I refuse to believe a man of your obvious stature would truly desire to see an old woman pay unfairly for her madness."

"Then you would be disappointed," he said gruffly. His dog Aedus pricked his ears up and looked to the door.

"Perhaps I could give you the banknote I brought Mamie? It's not enough to cover your entire loss, but you might hold it as collateral until my father can send what is owed. That's all I have to offer at present," she said impatiently. "I didn't come prepared to bargain on her behalf. How could I have — What is that noise?" she said, pausing, trying to turn her head to the window.

Jamie prevented her from turning completely, but he couldn't prevent Aedus from rushing to the door, his tail wagging furiously, dancing to be let out.

"Is someone here?" Miss Babcock tried to move away from Jamie, but he sank against her at the same moment someone knocked on the door. "Mr. Campbell, if you please," she said, pushing against him and exhaling with her effort when he would not release her.

"Who is it?" Mrs. Moss cried, emerging from her exile. She looked frantic, her cheeks tear-stained and the skin beneath her eyes dark. She had changed her gown and tucked up her hair, but there was a wildness yet in her eyes.

"Go on, then," Jamie said to her. "Open the door."

"Let *go,*" Miss Babcock said.

Jamie did not let her go. "Open it," he said again to Mrs. Moss.

The old woman paled even more. But she

walked to the door, pushed the dog aside, and opened it. She instantly stood back, lifting her chin high, defiant.

Duff's large frame filled the doorway. His gaze swept over Mrs. Moss, the room, and then fixed on Jamie. *" 'S fhada bho nach fhaca mi thu."*

I've not seen you in a while.

And Jamie had never been quite as pleased to see Duff as he was now. "Aye. Ran into a spot of trouble. What took you?"

Duff glanced at the two women. He put his hand on the dog's head, scratched him behind the ears, and responded in Gaelic, "I went back to fetch some men. I wasn't certain what I might find. What in hell has happened to you, then?"

"She shot me," Jamie responded in their tongue.

Duff looked at Miss Babcock.

"No' her," Jamie added in English. "The other one."

Mrs. Moss gasped and took a step backward as Duff turned his large head in her direction. *"Carson a?"*

"Why? I have my theories. But the lady will tell you it was quite by accident."

Duff's face darkened as he stared at Mrs. Moss.

Mrs. Moss, however, had made a slight

recovery. "And who are *you,* sir?" she asked imperiously.

"One of my men." Jamie coaxed Miss Babcock forward. "Duff Campbell is his name." The pain in his leg was excruciating now. But Miss Babcock's loyalties lay elsewhere, and she tried to wrest herself free of him. Jamie clamped his arm around her, pulling her back against his chest, her bum against his groin. He clenched his teeth against the pain — or something else, he wasn't certain. "My horse is somewhere nearby."

"Aye, we found him. Robbie's gone to fetch him," Duff said. "He's well, he is."

Relief swelled in Jamie; at least the old woman hadn't harmed his horse or his dog. "Good. We'll have one more with us."

Miss Babcock cried out in alarm and struggled again, causing him such discomfort that he let go of her. She leapt to stand before her grandmother, her arms outstretched, and declared dramatically, "You'll have to shoot me. I will not allow you to harm her!"

"*Ach,* lass, there's been enough shooting," Jamie said.

"And just where do you propose to take me?" Mrs. Moss demanded. "This is Brodie land! They'll not abide your savagery!"

Jamie groaned at that word. "I am well aware it is Brodie land, but that has little bearing on the wrong done to me. Rest easy, old woman — I donna mean to take you. I mean to take her," he said, nodding to Miss Babcock.

Both women cried out in unison. "Me!" Miss Babcock exclaimed. "What have *I* done? You can't take me against my will!"

"You have made your argument for it yourself, lass. Your desire is that I do no harm to your grandmamma. My desire is that we handle this matter by applying the rules of Highland justice. Plainly put, if your grandmamma wants to see you returned to England, she will repay the money she took from Uncle Hamish."

"What?" Mrs. Moss cried. "Are you implying that you intend to hold her for *ransom*?"

"No' implying it at all. I am stating it quite plainly." Jamie reached for a chair to hold himself up at the same moment Duff moved, with startling quickness, to apprehend Miss Babcock before anyone could pick up another blunderbuss. The lass was no match for Duff. She struggled, but Duff clamped her to his chest with one arm so that she could not move.

Mrs. Moss began to panic, gasping for breath. Duff stoically placed his free hand on her head and pushed it down, forcing it between her knees. "Breathe, then," he ordered.

"You *cannot* take me as your hostage!" Miss Babcock shouted, struggling futilely.

In no mood to argue, Jamie began his arduous journey to the door, thankful to see his cousin Robbie and MacKellan there, wearing twin expressions of surprise.

"This is unlawful!" Miss Babcock shouted. "If you so much as try to remove me from this property, I shall see that you are brought to the courts to answer for your actions!"

"I donna see how you will do that." Jamie nodded at the men who were gaping at him, looking rather startled to see how oddly bent over he was, wearing nothing but a plaid. Even his boots were missing.

"I will send for the authorities at once," Mrs. Moss said. "I shall have the Brodies down around your ears before you even crest the hill!"

"Aha, so now they are as near as that, are they? Go on, then, madam. Bring them round. You are very fortunate I donna hand you over to Hamish's children to be dealt with privately. Robbie, a hand."

"But I haven't any money!" Mrs. Moss cried as Robbie grabbed Jamie around the waist.

"Where are your boots?" Robbie asked.

"Donna know," Jamie said. "Let us go. MacKellan, the horses."

MacKellan disappeared into the garden as Duff began to move with Miss Babcock. The lass screamed so loud that the four men winced. "I am *not* going with you!" she shouted, and began to kick at Duff's legs.

"*Ach,* scream your head off your shoulders, then. No one will hear it," Duff said.

"*No!*" Mrs. Moss shrieked, and threw her weight against Duff. It scarcely moved him. "All right, all *right,*" she said desperately, reaching for Jamie's plaid before Robbie swatted her away, "I beg you, leave my granddaughter and take me! I am the one you want! Give me to Hamish's children, so be it, but leave Daria be!"

Jamie was fast running out of patience. He wanted home, where Rory Campbell, the clan's doctor, could tend him. "I think you will be a wee bit more compelled to return the money you stole if we hold her as collateral."

Mrs. Moss let out a wail unlike anything Jamie had ever heard and sank to her knees, her hands braced against them, her shoulders stooped as she sobbed.

The sight of her sobered Miss Babcock. She stopped fighting and tried to reach out to her, but Duff would not allow it. "Mamie! Mamie, I shall write to Charity in Edinburgh and she will send for Pappa straightaway —"

"If you harm her, I will kill you!" Mrs. Moss shrieked, despair twisting her features.

"I'll no' harm her, madam," Jamie said impatiently.

"But . . . but you can't take her like this!" she argued tearfully, and gestured wildly at Miss Babcock. "She's in her nightclothes!"

"I've a funny trunk we found on the side of the main road. I reckon it's hers," said Duff.

Jamie had had enough. "Bring her, Duff."

He struggled alongside Robbie out of that cottage, Aedus trotting before them, his nose to the ground. Mrs. Moss's wailing cry rent the air, competing with the angry shouting from Miss Babcock as Duff carried her bodily out the door.

With Robbie's and MacKellan's help, Jamie was able to put himself on Niall's back — but the pain was almost more than he could bear. It felt as if the lead were still in him, moving about, tearing tissue and organ from their roots. This ride over the hills would be a lesson in searing pain. Jamie sucked in a deep breath and glanced back.

Duff had a furious Miss Babcock firmly in hand.

"Here, then," Jamie said, gesturing to his saddle. "If we run into trouble, you'll need your hands free." If the old witch was able to summon help, the Brodies would delight in a reason to engage the Campbells.

Duff put the kicking, struggling Miss Babcock before Jamie. He wrapped his arm around her, holding her firmly, while Mrs. Moss shrieked that he would regret this action.

"There will be an army of Brodies at your door!" she shouted.

"Bring whom you like," he snapped. "But bring a thousand pounds." With that, he set Niall to lead, feeling the sickening swirl of pain with each jolt.

"Mamie, don't fret, you mustn't fret!" Miss Babcock cried hysterically. "I shall write to Charity and she will bring help!"

Mrs. Moss sent up another wail of agony to the heavens; it was almost as great as the wail of pain Jamie felt climbing up his throat.

NINE

Daria found it impossible to think, smashed up against Campbell as she was. She was in her bedclothes, for heaven's sake, being *kidnapped* and carried across the mountains of Scotland by a band of rough men. Her plight grew more dire as the landscape through which they moved took her farther from any meaningful society. From *civilization.*

It was the height of indecency. The feel of his body, hard against hers, dwarfing hers, was entirely unnerving. She felt the muscles in his legs move to guide the horse, felt the strength in the arm he had banded around her middle to hold her still. There was nothing she could do — she was entirely powerless against him, his wounds notwithstanding. And what difference would it make if she could somehow fight her way free? There were three more brutes with him. She was barefoot — how far could she run?

Daria alternated between intolerable anger and horrifying apprehension. She glanced to her right, to the man Mr. Campbell had called Duff. He kept his gaze straight ahead, his expression inscrutable. Behind her were the other two men — one of them quite cheerful, keeping up a steady stream of that wretched language they spoke. Behind him, Daria's trunk was being dragged. She could hear it bouncing and cracking against rocks and debris in the road.

For the first time since she'd left England, she could feel tears building. She swallowed hard — she would not, would *not* collapse into a maidenly display of angst. She would let him see nothing but determination to kill him at the first opportunity. He had ruined her with this, had ruined her reputation, her *life.* How would she ever live this down? Any gentleman worth his pedigree would avoid her if word of this abduction got out. The last debutante of Hadley Green would indubitably become the last spinster of Hadley Green! If she hadn't been between a pair of iron thighs and an iron arm, Daria would have kicked herself for having sought this adventure. Yes, she had longed for something other than waiting for life to find her, but *this*?

This was disastrous.

Daria couldn't help but expect the worst. She was reminded of Captain Mackenzie, Lord Eberlin's closest friend and the captain who had brought her to Scotland — and the one who had swept Charity off to Edinburgh, which, incidentally, would give some credence to Lady Horncastle's assertion that Captain Mackenzie was a man of questionable morals, a fact that she averred with the authority of someone who had examined all the sea captains and should know.

Nevertheless, Mackenzie had told a harrowing tale at a supper at Tiber Park one evening of a French heiress who had been kidnapped and held for ransom. She had complained about her accommodations aboard the ship to the point of distraction for all the crew, and when the money was finally delivered, the heiress was returned to her family dead. Fever, the crew said. And they claimed that the bruises around her neck were not from being strangled, no, but the unfortunate effect of their having lashed her dead body down to keep it from rolling about.

Daria shuddered. She would remember to bite her tongue if she thought to complain about her accommodations.

Mr. Campbell's arm tightened a little

more around her.

Why didn't he speak? He was exasperatingly silent! Daria forgot her fear and blurted angrily, "I cannot understand your reasoning for this, in truth. Do you intend to hold me in your cottage? I warn you, it is quite close when a stranger occupies a room. You will find it as tedious as I did; have you thought of that?"

Beside them, Duff snorted and looked the other way.

"You ought to be ashamed of yourself, Mr. Campbell, for taking an innocent woman from her grandmother. I've done no harm to you."

"He is laird," Duff said.

Daria was startled that the big man spoke to her and jerked her gaze to him. "I beg your pardon?"

"Laird. No' Mr. Campbell, aye? *Laird.*"

"At a time like this, you would instruct me on forms of address? Whatever I might call him has no bearing on the fact that he has willfully and unlawfully taken me from my grandmother. It is indecent!"

"It is the fault of your grandmamma," Mr. Campbell — or Laird, whoever he was now — said hoarsely.

His point was rather hard to argue, but Daria did her best. "That may well be, I'll grant you. Yet *you* cannot deny that this abduction hardly improves my situation. Is there no other way, sir? Can we not perhaps negotiate a better —"

"*Uist,*" he said, squeezing her like a plum. "No more talk."

Daria could feel his weight beginning to sag against her. She shifted, but he did not move back; if anything, his body pressed against her even more. He was obviously in quite a lot of pain. Perhaps his pain could be made worse so that he would let her go.

She pressed against his injured leg and heard his sharp intake of breath. "You might have listened to Mamie, you know," she said petulantly. "You might have taken the brew she made you to ease the pain."

"Stop moving," he growled. "I might have taken her brew and died, too, aye?"

Daria shifted again; he jerked her tight against him, his hold surprisingly strong given his state, squeezing the breath from her. She stopped, giving in completely. He relaxed his grip, and with a sigh Daria looked up at the treetops. Her mind raced — she was angry and fearfully determined to escape, in spite of her bare feet. Then she would think what to do next. One step at a time, wasn't that the course people generally took in dire predicaments?

She only had to escape before they reached Mr. Campbell's hovel, for she couldn't bear to imagine where men like these would keep their hostages. She worked to convince herself she could survive almost anything — a night alone in the forest, for example. She could survive anything but a rat-infested dungeon cell. If there were rodents —

Daria shivered rather violently.

"Be *still,*" her captor said roughly.

They continued on, his weight pressing even more against her, his chest, heavy and damp with his perspiration, wider than her back. How far would they go? It felt as if they were riding to the ends of the earth. Perhaps they meant to camp, which would present her with an opportunity to flee. She would take his plaid for warmth. She would tear off pieces to wrap around her feet. She would steal a knife from the sleeping giant.

They crested a rise, then started down a narrow path. Daria could see light sparkling through the dense forest, and as they moved farther down the hill, she could hear water running. A river! They eventually arrived at the river's edge and moved into a small valley where the river widened, turning dark against the gold and green of the hills. Dark green firs rose up to touch a clear blue sky;

wildflowers grew along the worn path. It was ironically picturesque, given that this was the ugliest day of Daria's life thus far.

But then she saw hope — up ahead, she could see two men fishing in the river. Her prayers had been answered!

Duff said something to which no one responded. She guessed he was warning them, telling them that she would attempt to escape. Daria's heart began to pound — this was her chance, and she had to do it perfectly. As they approached the men, one of them turned to look at the party, and Daria seized her moment. *"Help!"* she shrieked.

"Diah," Duff said.

She clawed at Campbell's arm. *"Help me! I've been kidnapped! I do not belong with these men, they have taken me against my will!"*

Campbell reined up, and for a slim moment Daria thought she'd won. But that hope evaporated when he said, "How are they biting, then, lads?"

"Fair enough," the older of the two men said. He trapped his pole between his legs, then doffed his hat, running his fingers through a thick crop of graying red hair.

Daria's anxiety choked the air from her lungs. "Do you not hear me?" she cried breathlessly. "These men have kidnapped me and intend to hold me for ransom!"

"Aye, we heard you," the fisherman said.

Speechless — Daria was completely speechless. What man could turn a deaf ear to a woman's cry for help? And the other one! He squatted down again to continue cleaning a pile of fish as if she'd not even spoken!

"You'll bring some round to Dundavie if you catch more than you can use, aye?" Campbell said.

"There ought to be plenty, Laird." The man returned his hat to his head and took up the pole he'd tucked between his legs.

Campbell spoke in that awful tongue to the others, then nudged the horse to walk on. Daria stared ahead in utter disbelief, sagging against her captor as they rode. "A nightmare," she said in a voice that was dangerously close to a whimper. "I am in the midst of a nightmare from which I cannot wake."

No one bothered to deny it.

Their progress continued at an interminably slow pace, Campbell's warm weight pressing harder against Daria's back. She began to imagine a man like him in a bed, sinking into a mattress. She imagined a man rolling onto his side, his arms going about her — *what in heaven was she thinking?* But she couldn't help herself. With his arm around her, his chin on her shoulder now, she'd never felt a man so firmly against her, thigh to thigh, his sex pressed against her back.

She'd gone mad, that was what. No one could blame her, surely, but only a mad person would imagine such things in this circumstance.

The day had all but passed when they crested another of what seemed like dozens of identical hills. At the top, Daria gasped softly at the sight of the castle and village in the valley below them. It was a real castle, the sort with turrets and battlements. It looked medieval, as if it had not been touched in five hundred years. It was built on a ledge in the hills, its back against a steep and forested incline. A thick stone curtain wall circled the main keep, anchored by the turrets. A wide bailey with a drive and a tended lawn spread out from the keep, and Daria could see the small shapes of people walking across it.

Outside the castle walls was a quaint little village, around which were parcels of land, divided neatly for grazing and crops. Dozens of shaggy cattle ate their way through fields of green grass. In the distance tiny spots of sheep dotted the hills. There was a large stable, and a dozen horses milled about in the fenced pasture around it, their tails swishing lazily.

They started down the path toward the castle, single file, as if they'd done this a thousand times before. They moved into a deep copse of firs that obliterated the sun, then emerged into the sunlight that bathed the clearing around the castle and village.

As they joined the wide lane that led to the heart of the castle, someone in the fields shouted. With his gaze straight ahead, Duff lifted his fist high above his head. More men began to appear, dropping their tools, moving toward the castle, shouting and running alongside the little caravan of horses that carried Daria and her captors.

Daria's heart began to skip. She could imagine being dragged from the horse and . . . and what? *Beaten?* Strung up? Daria tried to push down her fear by reminding herself the year was 1811, not 1611. No one was carrying a pitchfork or scythe. They might be uncivilized here, but they weren't so uncivilized as to harm a defenseless woman, were they?

Be calm, she anxiously told herself. *Be rational.* She did the only thing she could do in the circumstance — she lifted her chin and employed the aloofness young women were taught when entering the ballroom for the first time.

The road curved up to the open gates of the castle, which were held back by thick iron chains. As they neared the gates, Campbell lifted himself off Daria's back, as if he'd found a renewed strength. He was sitting taller, his grip around her tightening. More shouting brought more people running. As the group rode through the gates people began to emerge from the buildings, all speaking the language Daria could never hope to understand.

There was quite a lot of commotion as the horses halted in the bailey. Duff shouted, coming off his horse with surprising grace as he pointed to Daria. Two men hurried forward. Before she realized what was happening, one had grabbed her by the waist and pulled her off the horse; the other helped Campbell down. Everyone was talking wildly, their voices rising, crowding in around Campbell until Duff bellowed above them all. In a moment, everyone had quieted.

He spoke again, his voice calmer but firm. And then, as if the Red Sea had parted once more, all heads swiveled in Daria's direction. The crowd began to step back, clearing a path to the keep. Campbell, whose face bore the deep etchings of his pain, stepped up beside Daria. "Come then," he said, his voice low.

"Come where?" she whimpered.

He grabbed her wrist in his viselike grip and began to limp toward the keep. When Daria didn't move right away, Duff gave her a rough nudge that caused her to stumble forward. She glanced uneasily about her at the angry faces, the dark eyes boring through her, and wrapped her robe even more tightly around her. Her hair obscured her vision somewhat, and for that she was thankful. She imagined a sea of angry Scotsmen, all demanding her head.

Daria considered her options, found them wanting, and moved hesitantly alongside the laird. From the corner of her eye, she saw Robbie and another man dip down and pick up her battered trunk. They fell in behind her.

A movement to her right startled Daria badly — she expected to be struck — but she released her pent-up breath of anxiety when she realized it was the dog. He nudged her hand with his snout, his tail wagging, before loping off to greet a larger dog with coarse brown fur. They excitedly sniffed about one another as if they were well-known to each other.

"Walk on," Duff said.

Daria put one foot before the other and fixed her gaze on the castle's keep. Sitting high on the top of the keep was a row of blackbirds, their heads cocked to peer down at her, too. She tamped down the alarm building in her and glanced at her captor. His face was a sickly shade of gray, and when she averted her gaze, she noticed a dark red stain on the plaid at his thigh. "You're bleeding," she said.

He did not answer.

"Where are you taking me?" she asked, waiting for the word "dungeon" to drop from his lips. She could picture it — iron bars, a room devoid of light. *Rodents.* Alarm began to choke her again; she glanced over her shoulder at the unwelcoming crowd — lest they were following with a length of rope for her neck — and noticed, for the first time, the stain of his blood on her clothing, a dark red patch that spread down her side. His blood, soaked into her night-clothes. Given the amount, Campbell's stride was surprisingly strong.

As they reached the threshold, Campbell paused to speak to a man with bushy brows that matched the untamed nest of hair on his head. He then forced Daria ahead of him into a narrow passageway. She kept moving until she reached a large entrance hall where a row of windows above the passageway door streamed sunlight in, adding to the light cast by candles in a half dozen wall sconces. On the wall overhead, swords were mounted artistically around elaborate body shields. Interspersed between them were portraits of stately men clad in plaid cloths.

"Suithad," said the man with the bushy brows, and pointed to a staircase to Daria's right that marched up alongside more battle armaments mounted on the wall. She glanced around and saw Campbell walking in the opposite direction, his hand pressed to his side as if to stanch the flow of blood, a pair of men flanking him.

"Wait!"

Campbell kept walking. "Campbell, *wait,*" Daria cried, and pushed past the bushy brows. She heard the laird sigh wearily as he turned, with some effort, back to her.

Her heart was pounding; she felt nauseated with fear — he was leaving her with men she did not know. "Am I to be held prisoner here?"

Campbell muttered under his breath. "We are not heathens, Miss Babcock. You are free to roam anywhere you fancy in the confines of Dundavie, aye? But you may no' leave the curtain walls."

Free to roam? This castle was so big, with so many places one might get lost. *Or escape . . .*

"And if you think to escape," he added, startling her, "you willna get far. Do you understand?" He moved toward her, his eyes hard. Daria hadn't realized she'd stepped back until she bumped into a stone wall. "If you think to escape," he said, so close now that she could see the hot glint of pain in his eyes, "you'd best hope I find you first." His gaze drifted down to her mouth. "For if the dogs find you . . ." He shrugged, then slowly lifted his gaze to hers again, pinning her with it. "Do I make myself clear, then, *leannan*?"

All eyes turned to her, waiting for her answer. Daria swallowed. "Exceedingly."

Satisfied, Campbell looked at Duff and said something in their tongue. Then he turned away.

"But I think you should know that I am not afraid of you."

Why she said it, Daria could not say. The words had fallen from her mouth without thought. Inexplicably, it seemed of the utmost importance to let him know that she'd not given up. He stood quite still for a moment, then turned his head to look at her. His eyes were burning. With fever, with anger, with lust — she was too confused to know. His gaze fell to her mouth once more, and he clenched his jaw — in pain? Or restraint? "Are you certain?" he asked, his voice silky and low, tickling her spine like a feather.

Daria didn't answer. She couldn't find her voice to answer. She was suddenly very uncertain about every blessed thing in her life.

A tiny, almost imperceptible hint of a smile turned up the corner of his mouth, and he turned away, his walk halting, his hand pressed to his side.

Daria watched him; her breath was short, her palms strangely damp.

"Suithad," the man with the bushy brows said to her, capturing Daria's attention again. She glanced up the stairwell, then back toward Jamie Campbell, but he had already disappeared into the dark corridor.

There was nothing to be done but follow this man up, with Robbie and her battered trunk trailing behind her. As they ascended, the stairwell narrowed; the walls were damp and cool. The only light came from narrow rectangular windows. She was reminded of the stories Mamie used to tell her when she was a child, of ghosts who would appear in dark and narrow hallways when there was no possibility that the heroine might escape.

They came to a thick wooden door. The bushy-browed man opened it and walked inside.

The room was surprisingly and pleasingly bright, far nicer than anything Daria had imagined or even hoped for. Three small windows of mullioned glass curved around on one wall, and she realized that they were in one of the four anchoring towers. The man opened one of the windows and a cool breeze swept in, ruffling the embroidered canopy over the bed. The smell of summer came with it — freshly mowed hay, the scent of coming rain. There was a cold hearth, a pair of rugs, and a small table with two chairs, as well as a pair of doors on either side of the room that led, she guessed, to dressing and bathing rooms. Against the wall stood a basin and a vanity — everything a woman might need. Daria was so relieved, she wanted to collapse facedown onto the bed and sob.

Robbie and another man entered behind her carrying her trunk, scraping it against the door frame as they maneuvered it inside. They deposited the trunk in the middle of the room, which Bushy Brows did not care for, as he spoke sharply to them. Robbie apparently didn't care for his tone, and they exchanged a few heated words before Robbie and his companion picked the trunk up once more and placed it next to the vanity, then huffed out of the room.

That left Daria alone with Bushy Brows.

"A lass comes," he said cryptically.

"A lass?" she tried, but he apparently wanted no discussion; he was already walking out of the room.

When he'd gone, Daria whirled around, fell to her knees before her trunk, and opened it.

The contents had been jostled and tossed about in their journey to the ends of the earth, but everything was there and intact. Even her bottles of perfume were still in the wooden box where she'd packed them. Daria began to sort through her clothing — silks and fine muslins that seemed almost frivolous in these hills — shaking them out, frowning at the deep wrinkles that had set into the fabrics after a fortnight in the trunk. They smelled a bit musty, a bit briny, and, she thought with a pang of homesickness, a bit like England.

She had most of the contents spread across the bed when a girl appeared at the threshold. She was a tiny thing and eyed

144

Daria suspiciously, toying with the end of her black braid. Her vest, laced up over a white lawn shirt, looked worn, and her black skirt too short — the tops of her boots were showing. She wore a lace cap that reminded Daria of the old women in Hadley Green who refused to acknowledge that caps had gone out of fashion at the turn of the century.

The girl looked as if she were no more than sixteen or seventeen years of age. She did not speak, but took Daria in, from head to foot.

"Ah . . . good afternoon," Daria said uncertainly. "Do you speak English?"

The girl gave her a slight roll of her eyes. "Aye."

Daria folded her arms across her body, feeling rather exposed. "Have you a name?"

"Aye, everyone has a name. Bethia Campbell."

Good Lord, was everyone in Scotland a bloody Campbell? "Are you . . . have you been sent to attend me?" Daria asked. Surely she'd not been sent to stare so disdainfully at her as she was now.

Bethia snorted and folded her arms across her small, thin body. "*Aye,* obviously I have."

"It's not entirely obvious," Daria muttered. She was appalled; an English maid would never act like this. Still, Daria was grateful for any help. "Would it be possible to have a bath drawn?"

"Course," Bethia said. "Everything is possible at Dundavie."

Not *everything* was possible at Dundavie; in particular, her freedom did not seem possible at present.

Bethia yanked on a bellpull three times. She moved to the sideboard and removed the top from a crystal decanter filled with amber liquid.

"What is that?" Daria asked.

"Barley-bree."

"Barley-bree?"

"Aye. To soothe," Bethia added tersely.

Daria picked up the decanter and sniffed. Whisky.

"It's made at Dundavie," Bethia said, a hint of pride in her voice.

"I might develop a taste for it," Daria said wryly. She looked at Bethia. The two of them stood there awkwardly a moment. "I'd like these gowns to be hung," Daria suggested, gesturing to her gowns on the bed.

"Then hang them," Bethia said.

Daria blinked with surprise. "I thought you were sent to attend me."

"I've been sent, aye. I didna want to come,

no' after what you've done, but Duff, he said I should try." She picked up one of Daria's chemises from the bed and studied it, running her fingers over the lace.

It had been a long day, a long *week,* and the edges of Daria's patience were fraying. This was all difficult enough without everyone treating her as if *she'd* done something wrong. After what she'd endured, it infuriated her somewhere in the fog of her exhaustion. "In England, when a maid is assigned to a lady —"

"I'm no English maid," Bethia said sharply. "And you're no' a princess. You canna demand this or that."

Daria was shocked. "Haven't you the least bit of empathy for a woman who comes to you, dressed in her *nightclothes* of all things — which, I might point out, are now soaked in blood — with her hair a mess? Are you not the least bit curious as to why that is?" she demanded.

"No," Bethia said.

"Now you are trying to vex me!" Daria said.

"I donna need to inquire, as I know who you are," Bethia said with a toss of her head.

"Do you really?" Daria said coolly. "Then just who am I, Bethia?"

"You're the woman who stole our money

from Hamish, that's who."

"I didn't!" Daria cried.

"And you very nearly killed our laird."

"I did *no* such thing —"

"That's what is said of you, and everyone at Dundavie knows it now. I suppose you think I ought to take the word of an English-woman over that of a Campbell, aye?"

"I think you ought to give me the benefit of the doubt," Daria said irritably. "I'd do the same for you."

Bethia shrugged. She looked at Daria's clothing, strewn about the bed. She picked up a gown, holding it up with two hands, examining it with a critical eye.

Daria sighed. "If it brings you the slightest bit of comfort, please know that I intend to leave this . . . place," she said, refraining from calling it a pile of stones, "as soon as possible."

For some strange reason, Bethia actually chuckled at that. "Oh, you'll no' leave, miss."

"The bloody hell I won't," Daria muttered, earning an arched brow of surprise from Bethia. "I will leave here, mark me. Once this matter is settled to Mr. Camp-bell's satisfaction, I shall be gone from this godforsaken place and return to the civiliza-tion of England, where ladies are not abducted and held for ransom and maids hang gowns."

"You'll no' leave." Bethia smiled coldly at her. "I've the second sight, aye? You'll no' leave Dundavie."

Daria snorted. "If you had second sight, then you would know it was not me who shot Mr. Campbell."

"Laird."

"Laird, then."

"It may as well have been you, aye? It was your family after all. That's the way it is here."

Too exhausted to argue, Daria just waved her hand at the girl.

Bethia smoothed one gown, then picked it up and disappeared into the adjoining dressing room. She returned a moment later without it, and Daria hoped that she'd hung it in a wardrobe, and not tossed it into a hearth or out a window.

She was in quite a spot, one worthy of legends, wasn't she? It was so fantastic that it bordered on unbelievable. Somehow, someway, she would figure out how she would navigate this predicament. She'd never known anyone quite as difficult as Bethia —

Ah, but she *did* know someone as difficult as Bethia. Mrs. Ogle of Hadley Green could

149

be very obstinate and contrary when she was of a mind — and she was frequently of a mind. Daria had learned how to navigate around women like Mrs. Ogle. She'd learned how to negotiate her way through treacherous ballrooms, too, with people who were far more sophisticated and sly in their loathing of others than this girl. Had Daria met Bethia Campbell in a ballroom . . .

That was it! Daria suddenly realized how she might preserve her head and her sanity. She suddenly sat heavily on a chair. "You're right, you know," she said morosely.

Surprised, Bethia looked at her.

"I'll confess something to you, Bethia. I feel quite lost," she said plaintively. "I came to Scotland only to see my grandmamma, for I have missed her so." She looked at Bethia through her lashes and said tearfully, "She is the one who may have taken Mr. Campbell's money, and I was as shocked to hear it as you all must have been. Can you imagine? My grandmamma!

"But she is no longer the woman I so fondly remember. She is much changed, and oh, how I tried to help her, to shield her from the consequence of what she'd done! But it was no use, of course, for she'd done such a terrible thing — and now I fear there is no return from it."

She buried her face in her hands and waited, hoping Bethia would soften. But a moment passed, and another, and still Bethia had not spoken. Daria resisted a long sigh — she would have to try another tack. She had no idea what that might be, but hopefully a bath and clean clothing would help her think.

And then, Bethia said very quietly, "Aye, it must have come as quite a shock."

Daria nodded and slowly lifted her head. "Quite," she agreed, and with a weary sigh, she stood and prepared to begin the delicate dance of survival. She moved to the bed, picked up one of her gowns, and carried it to the wardrobe in the dressing room as she began to relate the tale of how she'd come to be in Scotland.

TEN

Rory Campbell, Dundavie's doctor, had made Jamie drink something far more foul smelling than what the witch had forced on him, and then had put a salve that burned in his open wounds when they were cleaned. Jamie slept the first night with his dogs, Aedus and Anlan, their backs pressed against the full length of him, Anlan's head resting on his ankle. He slept as soundly as he ever had in his life, his dreams filled with honey-colored hair and golden-brown eyes. Of a quick, bright smile and a quicker frown.

In fact, Jamie slept through most of the next two days, rousing only to eat and to ask a few questions of Duff about matters pertaining to the clan and Dundavie. During one of his waking hours, when he asked Duff if their collateral for ransom was cooperating, Duff frowned down at his large hand. "Aye. She's put her nose into everything, she has."

"What do you mean?" Jamie asked as he slurped down his broth.

"Wandering about the bailey, asking questions."

"About?"

"About?" Duff said, waving his hand. "What they do. Their names, their children's names." He shook his head. "Geordie's been at sixes and sevens since she's come." He lifted his gaze to Jamie's. "She's attempted to befriend him."

Jamie paused in the drinking of his broth to peer at Duff. *"Why?"*

" 'Tis indeed a mystery to us all, Laird."

Jamie had no interest in the mystery, however. He was too focused on his own troubles.

When he awoke the next morning, his dogs were gone. He drank more of the liquid, had more of the salve applied to his wounds, and slept again. He was awakened later by Geordie pacing about his room, his slate in one hand. The moment he noticed Jamie awake, he thrust the slate at him. *She go.*

Jamie gingerly eased himself up. "Go where?"

Hel.

"I grant you it's tempting, but she's our

guarantee against the thousand pounds we've lost."

Geordie's face darkened. He walked in a circle, dragging his fingers through his dark brown hair before writing on his slate, underscoring it several times over — Jamie had learned to recognize when that was happening — and then thrust the slate at Jamie again. *Vxen.*

"Aye, I am well aware how vexing the situation is," Jamie said. "Avoid her, Geordie. It's the only way."

When he awoke the day after that, his stomach was growling fiercely; his head was heavy, but from too much sleep. He sat up and saw Duff sitting in a chair at the foot of his bed, reading.

Jamie looked about, blinking, mentally taking stock. For the first time since being shot, he felt his old self. The pain had receded, and in its place was a dull ache. Dull enough that he wanted out of his infernal bed.

"Back to the land of the living, eh?" Duff said without looking up from his book.

"Aye," Jamie said. "What the devil has happened to my dogs?"

Duff snorted and closed his books. "Donna concern yourself with them, Laird. Two more traitorous hounds I've no' met."

"Traitorous?"

"Never mind them. There's much that needs your attention. Shall I fetch Rory?"

"No," Jamie said, and swung his legs over the side of the bed. "Bring me Young John," he said, referring to his butler.

"Aye," Young John said, appearing from the adjoining dressing room. He held a stack of lawn shirts in his hand.

"Give a hand, then. I want out of this bloody bed."

Duff grinned as he heaved himself out of his chair. "That's about bloody time." Duff was not the sort of man who had much patience for lying about. If Jamie were a betting man, he'd wager that Duff had done a fair amount of pacing these last few days, alongside Geordie.

With Young John's help, Jamie dressed in buckskins, a lawn shirt, and a waistcoat. He shooed Young John away when the butler presented neckcloths and coats to him, as he was ravenous and could think of nothing other than breakfast.

As Jamie headed downstairs, pleased that he could walk without searing pain, he caught the scent of ham. He knew that would be accompanied by haggis, black pudding, and eggs.

His mouth was watering.

"Aye, good to see you up on your feet again, Laird," Mrs. Murray, Dundavie's head cook, called out to him, having spotted him as she made her way out of the dining room with an empty platter.

He smiled and nodded at her as he walked into the morning dining room.

His brother Geordie was present. He wasn't eating but was leaning across the table, his head propped on his hand.

"Madainn mhath," Jamie greeted him.

Geordie sat up. He picked up his slate and wrote something, which he held up to Jamie.

Jamie paused to squint at it. "What is that? Gaelic or English?" He continued on to the sideboard, where he picked up a plate and began to fill it. From the corner of his eye he saw Geordie wipe the slate clean with his sleeve. By the chalky look of that sleeve, he'd done it more than once today. He wrote again, and when Jamie took his seat across from his brother, Geordie held up his slate.

Muny?

"Mooney?" Jamie read. Geordie frowned, turned his hand over, and rubbed his fingers together.

"Money, then," Jamie guessed. Geordie nodded. "I assume you mean the money Hamish lost. I told you, lad, it's in the

156

English lass. The money is tied up in a lady's skirt, so to speak."

Geordie's expression darkened. He shook his head, pushed away from the table, and walked to the window, bracing his arm against the frame and staring out.

It had been like this since Geordie had been rendered mute by the cut of Cormag Brodie's sword across his gullet. Mute for now or forever, no one knew. But since the doctor had forbidden him from trying to speak for a full year to allow any healing that might be done, Geordie had taken to brooding.

Brooding was not something Jamie could easily abide, and it had created a silent rift between him and his brother. He had quite a lot to keep him awake at night as it was, and besides, he missed Geordie's counsel. But Geordie's spelling was so wretched that it made it difficult to communicate at all. Jamie was therefore relieved when his cousin Robbie entered the dining room with Duff. Geordie was better endured with company.

"Jamie, lad!" Robbie said cheerfully. "I'd given up on you." He clapped Jamie on the shoulder and leaned across him at the sideboard to pick up a plate. "You've been set to rights, aye?"

"I am feeling more hopeful that I have." Jamie finished filling his plate and sat at the table. "What have I missed, then? Where is our ransom this morning?" he asked, and shoved a forkful of haggis into his mouth. "And where are the dogs? I've no' seen so much as a hair of them."

Duff snorted. "I suspect she'll be in to join us shortly." He turned his attention to the sideboard.

"I donna need to see her; I want only to know where she is. She is a thousand pounds walking about Dundavie."

"I think you'll no' have much choice. She's rather made herself at home, she has." Duff smiled thinly and sat heavily at the table with a plate piled precariously high with food. "She took your words to heart, she did, and has made herself familiar with every inch of Dundavie."

Jamie could not recall what he'd said to her in the foyer. He didn't know what he'd expected, really — likely nothing, given that he was on the verge of death when they'd ridden into the bailey. And that he was not in the habit of taking a hostage to be exchanged for ransom. Be that as it may, Jamie hardly cared what she did, as long as she didn't leave Dundavie.

And the last thing he wanted to dwell on

was an English rose traipsing about his home. "What else, then? Any trouble from Murchison —"

"What a wonderful sight! You're awake!"

That lilting voice heralded the arrival of Miss Daria Babcock to the dining room. The men all seemed to remember themselves at once, finding their feet as she winged into their midst on a cloud of blue muslin. Her hair was wound up in a style Jamie knew was fashionable in London. Her skin was flushed, as if she'd run to the dining room, and she was smiling broadly. The lass looked very different from when Jamie had last seen her, bedraggled and stained with his blood. Today, she was enticing. She appeared sophisticated, a woman who very clearly had been trained to be a lady.

Jamie realized he was staring at her and instantly averted his gaze — which landed on his dogs, which he hadn't noticed until then. They were trotting obediently along behind her, and now he understood what Duff had meant — the bloody hounds had betrayed him.

"How happy I am to see you at last on the mend!" Miss Babcock cheerfully observed as she came to a halt before him, beaming up at him as if she'd somehow had a hand in it. She absently put her hand down on Anlan's head and scratched him behind the ears. Aedus immediately tried to nose his way in. "I had begun to fret for your well-being, in truth. I begged Mr. Duff to allow me to see you and he would not." She paused to give Duff a withering little look before turning her smile, full and bright, to Jamie once more. "He had me rather convinced that you were not improving as I hoped."

Duff grunted and resumed his seat and his meal.

Geordie suddenly appeared at Jamie's side. He picked up his slate and scrawled, *She leve us.*

"Ah . . . Miss Babcock, if I may, I should like to introduce my brother, Geordie Campbell."

"Yes," she said, glancing down at Anlan, who, Jamie was chagrined to see, was gazing adoringly up at her. "We've met."

Geordie slapped down his slate and took a seat alongside Duff.

She ignored him. "Are you breaking your fast? It smells wonderful." She clasped her hands behind her back and rose up on her toes, then down. "Divine," she added.

No one spoke.

"I slept very well indeed, and I am *famished,*" she added hopefully.

160

Jamie exchanged a wary look with Duff. "Would you care to join us, Miss Babcock?"

"Are you certain I won't be a bother?" she asked quickly, already moving to the sideboard, with Jamie's bloody useless dogs moving obediently with her. Three, four days, was that it? The damned hounds had changed their loyalties in only days?

Miss Babcock helped herself to a sliver of ham and gave a bite to each dog, then poured a thimbleful of ale. She turned from the sideboard and seemed startled to find the four of them staring at her. She smiled, then took an empty seat. Anlan and Aedus slid down on their bellies next to her chair, heads between their paws, waiting patiently.

Jamie gave both mongrels a dark frown before resuming his seat, while Duff, Geordie, and Robbie watched Miss Babcock cut her ham into tiny bites. They eyed her as if they'd never seen a woman eat before, as if they were surprised to find a little blue jay hopping around them and pecking at the food.

She took a bite, chewed delicately, then smiled at Jamie. "I am glad to find you improved," she said as she speared another bite. "I've been thinking that perhaps there are ways we might speed this kidnapping along —"

" 'Tis no' a kidnapping," Jamie reminded her. "You are collateral for a debt."

She gave him a pretty but patronizing little smile that he guessed she'd practiced across dining tables with many gentleman suitors. "You say collateral, I say kidnapped and held against my will. But it's all rather the same thing, is it not?"

Jamie opened his mouth to argue, but she put up a hand.

"Wait, please — hear me out before you disagree. I thought that perhaps we might both return to our preferred state of being — you being a laird of this delightfully rustic castle, and me being an English-woman . . . preferably somewhere far away, say, England — and I thought, would it not make more sense if instead of delivering a letter to my friend in Edinburgh, you deliver me instead? That way I might explain the situation to my friend, who will see to it that your money is returned to you." Her smile brightened. "It should save us all quite a lot of time. It's rather brilliant, do you see?"

"Mary, Queen of Scots," Duff muttered.

"What do you think, my lord?" she asked.

"Laird," Duff said gruffly. "We are no' in England. He is laird."

"Laird," she said with a slight frown for

Duff, then cast an expectant look to Jamie.

"I think," Jamie said, settling back, "that this is a very good idea for you."

She smiled, obviously pleased with herself.

"But I think it a very bad idea for me."

Her lovely smile faded somewhat. "I cannot imagine a single reason why you might think so."

He arched a brow at her. "Can you no' think of at least one or two, then?"

"For heaven's sake, Laird. I give you my word —"

"Ach," he said, taking his turn to throw up a hand. "I have no use for your word. Your grandmamma has no' exactly been true to *her* words, and in the Highlands, the bad word of kin will ruin the promises of an entire family."

She made a sound that indicated she did not care for that at all and put down her fork. "So everyone keeps saying. There seem to be quite a large number of rules in the Highlands. But I have given you no cause to doubt *my* word."

"That is all we will say on the subject, Miss Babcock." He picked up his fork and continued with his meal. He was aware that those big, expressive eyes were fixed on him, and not in an admiring way. He could almost feel them drilling clean through him.

163

"But don't you want your money?" she said, her voice decidedly less cheerful. "Do you not see that mine is a much more expedient way to have your money returned to you?"

Jamie sighed. "Miss Babcock, please do pen your letter. I'll have it delivered to Edinburra straightaway, and far quicker than either you or I would manage it."

She sank back in her chair, her arms folded. "Really, my lord, this all seems so . . . *medieval.*"

"*Laird,*" Duff said through a mouthful of eggs.

"I'm sorry you find it so," Jamie said, and polished off his food, sopping up the juices with his bread.

"Please don't misunderstand me. Your home . . . I suppose it is a home of sorts, isn't it? It is quite lovely, and I cannot complain about the accommodations. I don't mind in the least taking long, winding walks through dark corridors to the dining room, or finding a library in the place where I am certain a dungeon once stood, given the marks on the stone walls. But the fact remains that there is very little to occupy me, and I must be a strain on your coffers."

"You are no strain," Jamie said, and pushed his plate away before turning his glance to her. "No' as yet, that is."

"Well then, what am I to do while you hold me prisoner?"

If she thought she would goad him, she was wrong. He shrugged. "You've letters to write, have you no'?"

"With all due respect, that will require only a few minutes of my time."

Geordie tapped his elbow and showed him the slate. *Shuvl barns.*

Jamie smiled at his brother. It was bloody well tempting. "You seem a resourceful lass. I have every confidence you will think of ways to occupy yourself whilst your family repays its debt to mine."

"You are far too confident," she said sweetly. "It's not as if I am particularly welcome here. Give me some idea of an occupation, please."

How in heaven's name would he know? "I am no' a woman. Try sewing," he said, and looked at Duff. "Someone can give our guest a bit of thread, aye?"

"Sewing! Do you truly expect me to sit about and embroider while I am held against my will?"

"Mary, the queen of all Scotsmen, did precisely that when she was held against *her* will by your English queen, aye? There you are, then, Miss Babcock, something else to occupy your time — you might also hie yourself to our dungeon and read a bit of Scots history."

"Laird!" she said. "There must be *something* I might do. Something I can do to help. In Hadley Green, I am involved in charitable endeavors. Perhaps you might have a charity that could use my services?" she asked hopefully.

He was finding her enthusiastic plea almost amusing. "We take care of our own."

She sighed. "Of course you do. Campbells are entirely self-sufficient in all things, I suppose."

"No' entirely," he said, smiling now. He looked down the table at Robbie. "Have we found a wife for Dougal Campbell?" he asked.

"*Diah,* Jamie —"

"There is something you might do," he said to her. "A wee bit of matchmaking."

Her mouth dropped open. Her fair cheeks pinkened.

Jamie very much enjoyed her maidenly blush. "Find him a wife, then, Miss Babcock. That ought to keep you quite occupied, aye?"

"And why should I, or anyone else, find Dougal Campbell a wife?"

"He is a blacksmith here. His wife died of

the ague last winter."

"What I mean," Daria said impatiently, "is wouldn't this Mr. Campbell want to find his *own* wife?"

"The lad has tried," Jamie said, "but he's no' had the good fortune of finding her."

Daria looked perplexed. "But . . . what has that to do with you?"

"It has everything to do with him," Duff said impatiently. "As the laird, he is responsible for the clan's well-being in all regards. Dougie Campbell has brought this particular problem to the laird to solve."

"And now," Jamie said, "I have solved it."

No, Geordie wrote in rather large letters on his slate, underlining them several times before handing it to Jamie.

"Why no'?" Jamie said. "She has far too much time on her hands, as we've all heard quite clearly. Miss Babcock, Duff will introduce you to Dougal Campbell on the morrow."

"That's not necessary, as I have already made Mr. Campbell's acquaintance," she sniffed.

That surprised Jamie. He gave her a dubious look, to which Miss Babcock smiled, pleased with herself.

"I am not one to mope, sir. I've uncovered the lay of the land — of Dundavie, that is

167

— while you have recuperated, and I have made Dougal Campbell's acquaintance. And he did not seem to me to be in a very big hurry to have a new wife, but if that is your wish, then I will find him one."

Jamie had fully expected her to demur. She was bluffing. He stood up. "To Dougie's happy future, then. Now, if you will excuse me, I've been taken from my duties for more than a week, thanks to your grand-mamma." He started out of the room. "An-lan, Aedus, *trobhad.*"

Anlan was on his feet at once, trotting forward. But Aedus stayed on his belly and began to thump his tail nervously. He looked up at Miss Babcock.

"Aedus, *trobhad,*" Jamie said again, a little more forcefully.

The dog's ears dropped back as he slowly rose.

"Stay," Miss Babcock said airily, without even looking at the dog, and Aedus's tail began to swish nervously along the floor.

"He doesna speak English," Jamie said, and gestured for his dog. But Aedus looked at him as if he were a stranger.

"Good dog," Miss Babcock cooed, and the traitorous Aedus flattened out his ears completely, lowered his head, and slid, like the snake he was, onto his belly beside her.

Miss Babcock smiled coyly at Jamie. "It would seem he speaks at least a little bit of English, wouldn't it?"

Jamie glared at Aedus, who avoided his gaze altogether. He looked at Miss Babcock, who had the most impudent smile he thought he'd ever seen on a woman. Then he whistled for Anlan, who at least had the canine decency to come when his master called.

Jamie stalked out of the room with as small a limp as he could manage.

ELEVEN

A mountain of paper was waiting for Jamie in his study, as well as a list of clan members who required an audience. In his absence, two more clansmen had sold their parcels of Campbell land to Lord Murchison. Their reasoning, Robbie explained, was that they could no longer make a living on the wee bit of arable land. They were bound, as so many Campbells seemed to be bound these days, for Glasgow. If not there, then Edinburgh. Or America. It was conceivable, Jamie thought morosely, that the once mighty clan might be left with nothing at all.

He worked until his eyes blurred and his leg ached fiercely. He stood to stretch it, cursing it under his breath. It had stiffened on him, and he walked to the window with deliberation, willing the injury to heal, to stop distracting him.

It was a fine day from the look of it, and

he cranked open one of the rusty mullioned windows to let fresh air in. He was turning back to his work when the sounds of a very odd laugh and a barking dog caught his attention.

Jamie stilled, listening to the laugh, and turned back, bracing his hands against the cool stone, leaning out the narrow casing to have a look.

He saw the splash of blue muslin in the middle of the bailey, the glint of the sun on honey-gold hair. A boy kicked a ball about the lawn, and Daria chased after it. His dogs were with her, Aedus chasing after the soiled hem of her gown, barking. Anlan, who had left Jamie's side somewhere between the first and second stack of petitions, was curled up in the shade of the wall, watching passively, his tongue hanging from his muzzle.

Daria kicked the ball back to the lad, but it veered off course. He laughed again, and Jamie realized then who the boy was, for it was the sound of a child who cannot hear himself: Peader Campbell, his cousin's son, six or seven years of age, born without the ability to hear. In his short life, Peader had been, to Jamie's mind, shunted off to the side and isolated by his lack of hearing. How had Daria Babcock found him? How had

171

she known how to make the poor lad laugh?

Jamie returned to his desk, the image of her chasing after a ball invading his thoughts. He was grateful that someone had given Peader a wee bit of attention, but what vexed him was that he did not understand her scheme. He had no doubt that befriending the boy gave her some perceived advantage . . . but what? Did she think that by befriending the weak at Dundavie she might somehow sway him to give her freedom? Was she as cunning as that?

Jamie stared at the pages before him, rereading the same words over again. He was surprisingly, and a wee bit alarmingly, plagued with thoughts of a hazy kiss that lived on in his memory, the silky feel of golden hair, of eyes sparkling with ire. He was not thinking of her, his adversary for all intents and purposes, in *that* way, was he? In the way a man might think of an intriguing woman?

"No," he said firmly. It was the pain in his leg, the mountain of work before him. It was a moment of procrastination, nothing more. For Jamie was a very practical man. He did not think of foolish English debutantes in *that* way. Give him a hearty Scottish lass, not some delicate English rose who took issue with the location of Dundavie's extensive library . . .

Even if he might credit her with saving his life. One could make the argument that had it not been for Miss Babcock's arrival, the old witch might very well have succeeded in killing him. But that only meant he might one day thank her. When his money was returned to him. Nothing more.

For he was the Laird of Dundavie.

Dougal Campbell proved no challenge at all for Daria. She'd rather hoped that he might, just for the opportunity to while away a few hours, but when she'd asked him if he was of a mind to marry, he'd said with a shrug and a sigh, "Aye. I suppose I ought."

"Mr. Campbell! If we all did what we ought, life would be so tedious and dull! What do you think, Duffson?" she called out to the young man lurking outside the smithy's covered work area. He had shadowed her every move since her arrival. Daria had deduced, given his large build and heavy brow, that he was the son of Duff, sent to guard her. Like his father, he refused to engage in conversation, or even own to the fact that he was following her. So she had named him Duffson, which had at least caused one caterpillar of an eyebrow to rise.

"Well?" she demanded of him, and Duffson ducked his head and moved out of her sight.

"Do *you* see my point, Mr. Campbell?"

Dougal Campbell, who likewise was as tall as a tree, with a thick crop of auburn hair, rubbed the stubble of beard on his chin, clearly perplexed by her observation. He dusted the soot from his leather apron with his bare hand and examined the small clasp of Daria's bracelet, which he'd spent the past half hour working to repair.

Daria was seated on a table, where Dougal had made a space by moving aside the tools of his trade. Her feet were crossed at the ankles, swinging over Aedus's head. The dog had become her regular companion in the past few days, particularly when she was restlessly wandering about.

"Have you anyone in mind to wed?" she asked the blacksmith.

"No one in particular, no, miss." He peeked up at her shyly. "But I'd like a bonny one, aye?" He handed her the bracelet.

Daria examined it. "Oh, how *lovely,* Mr. Campbell! You are quite skilled, are you not?"

He smiled sheepishly at her praise. "Mind the spring," he said anxiously as she donned the bracelet. When she had fastened it, she held out her arm for him to see, earning a big smile from the man.

"Thank you, Mr. Campbell. Now then, to you — a bonny wife is all you desire? Shouldn't you like someone who shares your interests, as well?"

"Aye," he said, nodding. "But me mum, she saw a faerie when I was born."

Daria blinked. "I fail to see the significance of . . . that."

"That means I shall marry a fair woman."

"Mr. Campbell, there is far too much credence given to superstitions and faeries here. There are really no such things as faeries —"

"Ach, lass, there are," he said gruffly.

"Well. Perhaps," Daria said, a tad bit dismissively, as she admired her bracelet. "But can we not agree that whether or not your mother saw a faerie has no bearing on which young lady you might like to extend an offer of marriage to?"

"But it *does* matter. She ought to be bonny, aye?"

Daria sighed to the exposed rafters. "Very well. Tell me who you think is bonny."

He'd named three young women, all of whom worked within the walls of Dundavie. Daria then set out with Aedus beside her and Duffson trailing behind to pay them each a short visit. Anlan preferred to remain behind and nap in the shade of a cart full of hay.

After introducing herself to the first two — although Daria had already learned that she needed no introduction, as she was notoriously known as "the Ransom" — she learned that both young women had understandings with other gentlemen.

That left Catriona Campbell. Catriona was a kitchen maid, and she bustled about preparing the midday meal as Daria presented the possibility of Dougal as a husband.

"Dougal Campbell, the blacksmith?" Catriona asked, as she chopped onion with rapid-fire precision.

"Yes, him."

She shrugged. "I suppose he'll do as good as any, won't he?"

Daria reached across the scarred wooden table and helped herself to a muffin. The cook had cheerfully pointed them out to her after Daria had cheerfully fawned over her bannock cakes. "Miss Campbell!" Daria cried through a bite of muffin, and quickly swallowed. "Is *that* how you will choose the man with whom you will spend the rest of your life? Wouldn't you at least like to know a little something about him? Aren't you even curious whether you have anything in common with this man?"

"I've something in common with him, aye, miss. We're both Campbells. One will do as well as the next."

"These muffins are *divine,*" Daria said. "I shall leave Dundavie as fat as a pig. As for you, Miss Campbell, that is positively uncivilized. In England, we engage in a period of courting so we might determine compatibility between a man and a woman. A lifetime is a very long time if one is not compatible with one's husband."

"Must have a lot of time for sitting about, then," Catriona said. "In Scotland, we've too much work to be done to determine . . . what was it you said, then?"

"Compatibility."

"Compatibility."

"Interesting perspective," Daria said with a slight shrug. "Well then, it seems that my task here is done. I shall relay to Mr. Campbell that you would welcome his offer, and he may thank the laird for it. Will that suit?"

Catriona smiled. "Suits me well enough, aye."

"Just remember," Daria said as she slid off the stool where she was seated, half a muffin between her fingers, "you've no one to blame but yourself if he proves an unfit husband. I have no reason to believe he will be, as he seems rather amiable, but one never knows, does one?"

"I donna rightly know, miss," Catriona said distractedly as she dug through a barrel of potatoes.

As her one task was completed, Daria continued wandering about Dundavie. If she ventured too close to the gates, Duffson wordlessly shepherded her back into the bailey, ignoring her argument that it was preposterous to think that she might run into the woods in a gown and slippers, and besides, there was an entire village of Campbells waiting to tackle her if she tried to do so.

It *was* preposterous. What would she do if she managed to escape the walls and the village? Wander the woods? No, her escape would have to be more ingenious than that. She would have to persuade someone to aid her. The only problem with that idea was that the Campbells were an unreasonably close and wordless lot. She never knew what they were thinking!

Her attempts to see the laird were expertly thwarted by Duff. "He's got the business of the clan," he said brusquely when she asked why she couldn't speak to him.

"But my grandmother is undoubtedly sick

with worry. And I should very much like to know if my letters were delivered to Edinburgh and my grandmother's house."

"Aye, they were."

"Did you speak with my grandmother? Is she well?"

"I did no' take it, lass. But your grandmamma is fine. The letter was delivered two days past and tacked to her door."

"Tacked to her door! Why did you not just hand it to her?"

"Because she wasna within, lass," Duff said impatiently. "But the letter was delivered, aye?"

Daria didn't know what more to say, so she continued on. She walked the small rose garden, visited a schoolroom where a few children were learning their Gaelic letters and clearly understood when the instructor pointed out who she was, since the five students all turned their little heads and stared at her as if she were the devil himself.

"That's right," she said, lifting her chin. "I'm *English*. Would you like to learn an English song?"

The children did want to learn an English song. So as the teacher stood by, looking confused and suspicious, Daria taught them one. Not the one about a devilish Scottish sailor who left his love behind, which was the first one to come to mind, but a jaunty tune about maypoles and spring.

The children liked it. They particularly liked dancing around a pretend maypole.

As Daria's path became more familiar to her, she worked harder in her attempts to curry favor with anyone who might be inclined to help her — maids, footmen. The butler, whose name was Young John, to distinguish him from Old John, who was at least ten years younger than Young John. Young John wasn't shy about showing his vexation with her, shooing her away with some cryptic mention that the laird needed this or that, and then speaking more strongly to Duffson in their language. He seemed to take great umbrage when Daria rearranged some vases of hothouse flowers in the great hall one afternoon.

And then there was Geordie Campbell, whose handsome countenance was marred by his perpetual scowl. She'd felt sorry for his muteness and wanted to help him, to be a friend. But he'd made it quite clear that he was determined *not* to be her friend, given the injustice done to his uncle Hamish. Or at least that was Daria's interpretation of the things he'd scrawled on that wretched slate of his, things that she thought any self-respecting Englishwoman should find insulting. However, she could not be entirely certain, as the man's spelling bordered on indecipherable.

Daria had found no one who was even remotely inclined to indulge her, save a young deaf boy with an impish smile, who couldn't hear her when she complained that she'd been unfairly imprisoned. Apparently he was the only one who hadn't heard about her. His name was Peter, Dougal said, and he'd been the only sunshine in her week. They'd begun communicating slowly using hand signals. Peter's mother, who had tried very hard to keep from befriending her, began to soften as her son seemed to open up to Daria.

After several days in captivity, as thick clouds rolled in over Dundavie, Daria was delighted to notice Duffson chatting up some girl with a basket of bread braced against her hip. Daria stepped out of sight as he preened for the young girl, then hurried down a narrow mews, looking for someplace to hide before Duffson discovered he'd lost her in the one moment all week he'd been careless enough to turn his back.

She heard Duffson's shout a moment later and opened the first door she came to, jumping inside and whirling about to pull the door shut. She stood a moment with her heart racing, listening for any sign that Duffson had found her. But the voices seemed to be moving away. *Good.*

With a sigh of relief, she turned around to see where she was and started. The laird was standing in the middle of the room, in a shaft of gray light from a row of low windows. He was dressed like a gentleman, in a coat of blue superfine and a dark brown waistcoat. His neckcloth was tied to perfection, and his hair was combed back, brushing against his shoulders. He looked fully . . . recovered.

Daria's heart scudded across her chest, slammed into her ribs, and squeezed the breath from her. She had to remember to smile, and for heaven's sake, to stop gaping. But how could she? If she hadn't known what had happened to him, she would never suspect he'd been shot in the last fortnight. The only evidence of it was a cane he gripped in one hand. He looked every inch a lord. Every blessed inch. But an unrefined lord, and that, more than anything, Daria breathlessly realized, was dangerously exciting.

"Miss Babcock," he said, as if he were expecting her.

"I beg your pardon!" she said breathlessly.

"I didn't know anyone was within."

"Obviously."

She noticed then that he was standing between two long wooden benches filled with plants in various stages of growth.

"And why are you here?" he asked. "Seeking an escape, perhaps?"

She laughed. "No, of course not. I was having a bit of fun with Duffson."

"Who?"

"Duff's son," she clarified. "I don't know his real name, as he has declined to acknowledge he is shadowing me, or even give me his name."

He nodded as if that somehow made sense. "Why do you feel the need to escape him?" he asked as he moved forward, his cane before him.

"I meant only to . . . to divert myself." Another inward wince for sounding childish.

"Mmm," he said, still moving forward with one deliberate step after the other. "You will no' be surprised that I donna believe you are merely seeking a diversion, will you?"

"My lord! Do you truly think I would attempt to *escape*?"

"Laird," he said, so close now that she

could see the twinkle of the gem on his lapel pin.

"Laird," she said with exasperation. "I was not attempting to escape! How could I possibly?"

"I donna think you can," he said with a shrug. "But I understand you are a frequent visitor to the front gates."

"Not true! I've walked by there a time or two, but only because I am out of my mind with tedium, and I should like to see the village."

"Is that why you asked the milkmaid how far it is to the main road to Edinburra, then?"

Well. The Campbells didn't miss a thing, did they? And she'd thought the girl so kind and trustworthy. "I was curious."

He smiled wryly. He was now so close that she had to tilt her head back to look up into his hazel eyes, which, she had to admit, were very alluring. "Miss Babcock, did I no' explain what would happen if you tried to escape Dundavie?" His gaze fell to her mouth.

She wished he wouldn't look at her like a lion admiring the little lamb he would devour for his supper! Because, Daria was vaguely aware, she would like to be that lamb. Her pulse began to race. "Dogs would tear me limb from limb," she said, and paused to catch her breath. "Or some such nonsense."

His gaze lifted to hers. There was a different look in his eyes, a deeply stirring, intent look. "Is that all?"

"No," she said softly. She looked at his mouth, unable to look anywhere else. "I told you I was not afraid of you." Though her knees at that moment would indicate otherwise.

He smiled provocatively. "You *should* be afraid of me. I'm no' a particularly kind man." He leaned closer, bracing his hand against the door, which, Daria realized, she was flat against. "No' at all. I take what I want," he said low, pausing to flick his gaze over her body, "and discard what I donna need."

Take what you want, a tiny voice whispered. "Do you mean to intimidate me?"

"No, *leannan*. I think it would be far too difficult to intimidate you. I am telling you who I am and warning you no' to toy with me."

He was going to kiss her, Daria thought, her heart racing. It was outrageous, scandalous, and disrespectful — but God help her, she hoped he *would* kiss her. Kiss her like he had when he was out of his mind. Just . . .

185

kiss her. And when she thought he would, she heard the click of the door handle.

He was opening the door at her back. "Go now, before I do something I might regret, aye?" he murmured, his gaze on her mouth.

In a moment of insanity, Daria said, "I want to see my grandmother."

That earned a smile of surprise from him, and one brow arched above the other. "Will you make demands now?"

"I am worried about her. I believe there is something terribly wrong with her, and I need to see her."

"You will see her —"

"When?"

"Ach, lass, donna push. You will see her, I give you my word." He pushed the door slightly open; she felt a slight rush of air on her back.

"And I want to dine with you," she added recklessly.

His smile deepened. "Now you are being bloody unreasonable. You are the enemy of this Campbell clan."

"But I am not a prisoner. You assured me I am not." Daria tried not to think about how badly she desired to touch the stubble on his chin. "Yet I am treated as one, forced to dine alone."

"You'll no' be welcome at our table."

"I've endured many difficult tables, I assure you."

"Rather confident, you are. Some might even say brazen."

"I'm not the least bit brazen. But I will own to being rather stubborn."

He suddenly laughed, the sound of it startlingly warm. His gaze swept down her body as he leaned in. "And what shall I ask in return for granting favors to the clan's biggest enemy?" he mused. His arm brushed against her waist. He pushed the door open wider and leaned back. "I shall consider your request. Now, go and find Duffson, and for God's sake, be a good lass." He put his hand on her elbow and wheeled her about, giving her a gentle push out the door.

When Daria turned back, he was pulling the door shut. "There is your keeper, Miss Babcock. Good day."

She whirled around, almost colliding with a red-faced Duffson.

TWELVE

It was the pianoforte that swayed Jamie to invite Daria to dine.

Of course he'd thought of that moment in the hothouse. He'd thought of it as he'd lain in bed; thought of her lips, lush and moist, her bewitchingly sunny smile and glittering eyes.

But it was the pianoforte that decided him.

When morning came round, his mind was filled with the usual business and headaches of managing the holdings of Dundavie. His headaches were made worse by the fact that Hamish had been lost again and found several hours after he'd gone missing, wandering about the woods and talking about his friend, an imaginary English earl.

As if that weren't bad enough, a letter had come from Malcolm Brodie, Isabella's father. He wrote that in spite of everything that had occurred between their families, wiser heads had prevailed, and they believed now that Isabella had cried off too quickly. Malcolm wrote that it was Isabella's wish that he write to propose a reconciliation.

"Then why did she no' write it?" Jamie asked, tossing it onto his desk.

"We should use the opportunity to negotiate a better dowry, aye?" Duff suggested.

Jamie rubbed his forehead. Duff was right — they had the upper hand now; they could seek better terms. "I'll think on it."

Duff cocked a brow. "What is it, lad? Pride?"

Jamie slanted him a look, but he did not answer. He didn't really know what made him reluctant.

It was as he was debating what to do about Isabella that he'd heard the music. He'd not heard the pianoforte played since his sister, Laurna, had died giving birth to her first child only two years past. Laurna had been the musician in the family. Trained in Paris, she had played beautifully, and the notes that came from her pianoforte would echo up and down the ancient flues of Dundavie like a melody from the beyond.

Laurna's passing was hard enough on the clan, and on Jamie in particular, as she and Geordie had been his closest confidants. But the injury to his soul was made worse when she took the music with her. Mr. Bristol, who lived down glen, could be pressed to play the fiddle on occasion, but no one knew how to play the pianoforte, and the clan had resorted to singing in a horrible mismatch of keys and tempos.

There was such a dearth of entertainment, of art, in fact, that Robbie and Jamie had debated hiring a clan musician until one of their own could be properly trained.

They all mourned the music.

So when Jamie heard music creeping in through the vents as he worked one morning, for a few mad moments he thought he was hearing Laurna's ghost. But then the music stopped and started once more, and he knew it was real.

And he knew it was her, the English rose.

He'd walked down the hallway toward the music room, standing just outside to hear her play. Though she was not as talented as Laurna had been, she played well nonetheless, and frankly, it sounded as sweet as anything he'd ever heard.

That was it, then — the thing about her that might appease his family.

Jamie told them that night that he intended to invite her to dine with them.

"With us!" Aileen, Robbie's wife, said, her brown eyes wide with shock.

"With us," Jamie confirmed.

Geordie had picked up his slate and scrawled across it, *Donna keep with inimie,* thrusting it at Jamie.

"She is not our enemy. She is collateral for a debt," Jamie calmly reminded him.

That viewpoint was not held by anyone but him and did not garner any support. Rather, it only served to make everyone more cross. Save Hamish, who seemed quite happy with his meal. "Quite like goose," he said, even though they were dining on salmon.

But in true Campbell fashion, the rest of them flailed their arms and spoke over each other as they voiced their opinions that Miss Babcock was not suitable to sit at their table, that her grandmother had treated Hamish so ill that she ought to be drawn and quartered in the bailey —

"What do you mean?" Hamish demanded. "No one's treated *me* ill. I'm a Campbell, and besides, I've no' left Dundavie in an age!" Forgetting, of course, that he'd been found only a day or two ago wandering about lost in the woods.

The debate continued as port was served: was she or was she not a friend of the Brodie clan, that sorry lot of dung-eating, swill-drinking, grave-robbing cretins who lived on the other side of the hills?

191

"You all seem to have forgotten that I was only recently engaged to be wed to a Brodie," Jamie reminded them. "As I recall, you all thought Isabella quite bonny, aye?"

"We've no' forgotten it, Jamie," Aileen huffed. "But we've forgiven it."

"I would hope so, as our situation is such that she and I might be engaged to be wed again," he'd said crossly.

Geordie gestured to the pinkish scar across his throat and scribbled, *Tuk me hed.*

"Your head is still firmly attached to your shoulders, lad. And the loss of your voice lies with you alone."

Geordie had taken issue with that, slamming his slate onto the table and scribbling so tragically illegibly that even the butler was moved to try to decipher it as he dripped gravy onto the floor at his feet. Alas, he could not, and Geordie did not seem inclined to scrawl again.

"Well?" Jamie demanded of them. "Shall we invite the Ransom to dine?"

No one spoke for a long moment. No one made eye contact. When Robbie cleared his throat as if preparing to speak, all eyes turned to him. "Perhaps . . ." he said carefully, glancing about him, "she's no' as bad as we believe."

That earned him a murderous look from

his wife and a look of surprise from his laird.

"Well, she's made Dougal Campbell happy, aye?" Robbie continued defensively. "And she's reached the lad Peader, though the good Lord knows how she's done it. He's laughing like he's never laughed before, a different boy altogether."

"Nevertheless —" Aileen began.

"She's even taught the wee ones to sing a right cheery song, and if that won't warm your bloody cockles I donna know what will!"

That was followed by a lively debate over whether the children should be singing in English at all.

But then Jamie said, "There is one more thing I should like to add to this spirited debate. She plays the pianoforte."

Now all eyes were riveted on him. Eyes wide with surprise and — dare he think it? — hope.

"Laurna! Where is she, then? I've missed the lass," Hamish said as he examined his sherbet with a critical eye.

"The pianoforte," Robbie said skeptically.

"Heard it myself," Jamie avowed. "She doesna play as well as Laurna, but she plays well enough for us."

Jig, Geordie wrote, his mood brightened by the prospect. He'd always enjoyed a good

Highland dance.

"The tune I heard her playing seemed sprightly enough. The only way to know if she can play a jig is to invite her to do so, aye? Well then, what say you? Shall we have a wee bit of music return to Dundavie?"

The answer was a grudging *aye.*

Jamie summoned Daria the next morning. She swept into his study in a gown of pale green muslin just behind Young John, marching forward like a woman determined to have a word. Aedus and Anlan trotted behind, Anlan's nose to the floor as if they were out on a brisk walk. The dogs almost collided with her when she suddenly drew up short to have a look around at the paneled walls, where the portraits of past lairds hung. She seemed a wee bit caught off guard by the history that his study was steeped in, but then quickly remembered herself and said, "I beg your pardon," dipping a curtsy that he suspected was more out of habit than anything else. "Are these your ancestors?" she asked, peering up at one notorious Campbell, whose tam-o'-shanter sat jauntily on his florid head, his belt sliding beneath a wide belly.

"Aye, they are all Campbells of Dundavie."

"I rather like the look of this one," she

said. "There's a bit of a twinkle in his eye. He might lead one to believe that not every Campbell laird is dreadful." She slanted a look at him from the corner of her eye.

"I'm no' dreadful, Miss Babcock, far from it. If you need convincing, I could demonstrate just how dreadful I could be."

She clasped her hands at her back. "No, thank you. I will take your word on that score," she said pertly. "You sent for me? Should I assume the ransom has come? Or there has been word of my grandmother? Or perhaps you were merely looking for your dogs," she said, and arched a brow.

Bloody useless dogs. "I sent for you because I have considered your request to dine at the Campbell table —"

"Thank heaven!" she said to the rafters, loud enough that both dogs began to wag their tails in anticipation of something great happening. "I will *perish* if I am forced to dine alone one more night —"

"Pardon, lass, but I've no' as yet extended an invitation."

She blinked. And smiled sheepishly. "No, you have not. But I doubt you called me here to tell me you *won't* extend an invitation." She cocked her head curiously to one side. "You didn't, did you?"

He smiled, tossed his quill down, and

stood, moving around the desk. His limp was growing less noticeable every day, thank heaven, and the wound in his side was hardly noticeable to him now. "I intend to invite you to dine at my table, provided we can come to terms."

"Terms," she repeated skeptically. "How odd. I cannot recall another time I was invited to dine under *terms.* Another Scottish custom, I suppose. Very well, what would you like? A fatted calf?" she asked, her hands finding her hips. "Or perhaps you mean to humiliate me in some way. Must I declare some oath of allegiance to my liege?"

"That sounds rather appealing," he said, casually leaning back against his desk.

She gave him a look of exasperation. "What is it about the male sex that requires such adoration? One grows weary from it."

"You sound as if you've done naugh' but adore men, Miss Babcock. If you are practiced, I will no' object."

She snorted. "One can scarcely be a member of my sex and not be practiced, Laird Campbell." She said his name as if he were a wee bit shy of a full brain. "This one must be admired for his hunting," she said, flicking one wrist, "and that one for his prowess at the gaming hells," she said, flicking the other. Aedus and Anlan seemed to think she was tossing scraps and began to dance around, sitting down on their rumps, their heads pointed up at her when she stopped moving, waiting.

"Those are cynical words for an English debutante."

"Practical words," she said confidently.

"I wonder why an English debutante as practical and pleasing to the eye as you is no' married by now," he said.

Her blush deepened and for once, the woman looked entirely at a loss. "That is *quite* inappropriate —"

"You broached the subject —"

"I didn't! You did!"

"Why have you no' married, Miss Babcock? Do you hope for a title? A London townhome? It must be something of the like, for on my word, you are far too bonny to have been overlooked. And you kiss entirely too well."

She gasped. He smiled. She gasped again and whirled around, her hands pressed to her cheeks. "That . . . that's appalling!"

He laughed. "Did you think I wouldna remember, then? Aye, I was a wee bit out of my head, but a man does no' forget a kiss like that."

"Oh dear God," she murmured, looking stricken.

It intrigued him. After all she'd been through, the kiss was the thing to unsettle her? "You didna answer my question," he said curiously. "Why have you no' married?"

"Why haven't *you*?" she demanded, quickly regaining her composure. "You are the laird here. Everyone waits for your heir —"

"Everyone?" he repeated, smiling.

"All of them," she said, sweeping her arm grandly toward them "all."

He must have looked surprised because she cried, "Aha! You would very much like to know who. You undoubtedly think a lass or two who would like the honor of being your wife."

"Are there?" he asked, only mildly curious. He knew very well the speculation about heirs. There had been great hopes placed on his marriage to Isabella, and when that had fallen through, more mothers had hoped for a match with their daughters. He was only surprised that Daria knew it.

"Are there what?"

"Are there lassies who want to be my wife? *Diah,* I will hope they are bonny lassies with wide hips to bear me a passel of children."

She blinked. Her cheeks bloomed. And then she smiled. "Would you like me to find you a wife, Laird?" she asked airily. "It's really rather easy. The only virtue a woman here seems to seek is that her future husband be a Campbell."

He laughed. "I donna need your help, Miss Babcock."

"Don't you?" she asked, folding her arms across her middle, drumming her fingers on one arm. "That's just as well, for I am not inclined to help you, seeing as how you hold me captive here. Even if it would give me a much-needed occupation."

"My marriage," he said, "will be arranged soon enough, donna doubt it. But thank you for your most generous offer to arrange a match for a man whose only redeeming quality appears to be his name."

She put her hand on her heart and inclined her head in acceptance of his thanks. "Well then, you may as well give me your terms for dining with civilization, and I will think on them."

He'd forgotten the start of this conversation. "You'll *think* on them?" He pushed away from the desk and moved so that he was standing directly before her, so close that he could smell the rose scent of her perfume. "You are a clever one, *leannan,* but you have the unfortunate tendency to make demands of me. Donna make the mistake of believing you are in an English salon, aye? I owe you a debt for saving my bloody hide, and for that, I am granting you leeway I would no' otherwise grant. The terms, which you will accept if you donna want to be restricted to your suite of rooms for the remainder of your stay at Dundavie, is that you will play the pianoforte for my family."

She stared up at him beneath the V of her brows. "You want me to play the pianoforte?"

"Aye."

"Why?"

He shrugged. "You do play, aye?"

"Yes, but —"

"Then we will allow you to dine at our table if you will agree to play the pianoforte."

"That's all?" she asked, her frown of confusion deepening.

"That's all."

"Only that," she said skeptically.

The lass hadn't heard a word he'd said about not arguing. He sighed and resorted to cajoling her. "Miss Babcock," he said as he casually pushed a loose strand of her hair from her collar, his finger following the line of her shoulder down her arm, "we've no' heard it played since my sister died two winters past. We haven't anyone who has learned the art and we miss it."

Her gaze followed his hand as it slid down her arm to her wrist, his fingers tangling with hers. She gave a slight shiver and Jamie knew that he could persuade her to allow him to explore more of her. "My condolences," she murmured.

He ignored that — he still found it difficult to speak of Laurna's death. And at the moment, he was far more interested in the small bones he could feel as he wrapped his fingers around her wrist, his thumb stroking the soft underside.

"How did she die, if I may ask?"

"In childbirth," he said simply. "The child as well." His fingers curled around hers, and with his thumb, he traced a line along her palm. So smooth, so soft. So feminine. With his health returned to him, Jamie was remembering with some urgency how much he missed the feel of a woman beside him. He wouldn't mind feeling this woman's body against his in the least, her grandmother notwithstanding.

"My family once employed a maid named Louise. She was my companion as far back as I can recall," she said, her gaze still on his hand. "She married Tom Higgins, and when she carried her first child, she was so full of light, so happy and eager to have the baby. She'd picked out a name, and my father made her a cradle. But she didn't survive the birth." She slowly lifted her gaze to his, looked him directly in the eye. "I still miss her, too. I think it the cruelest irony that the source of so much happiness and life can also be the source of so much pain and death."

He was surprised by her empathy, and surprised even more that it moved him. He remembered his sister every day, remembered the happy glow of her pregnancy and how eagerly she had looked forward to the birth of her child.

"What music would your family like to hear?" Miss Babcock asked as she gently squeezed his fingers.

But Jamie could not escape her gaze. He was caught like a fish by a hook, unable to swim away in the fast currents. "Whatever you like." He had to escape this moment before he did something ridiculous. He leaned forward, his mouth close to her temple, his nose filled with the scent of her. He heard the soft, quick intake of her breath. He felt dangerously close to kissing her, to reclaiming the lips he remembered so fondly from his dream.

"I know a piece that celebrates spring,"

she murmured. "I recall the melody, but not the words. I would wager it has something to do with young love." She smiled sheepishly, lightly laced her fingers with his. "I had a music tutor who was quite fond of the notion of young love." She turned her head to look him directly in the eye. "I think every song he taught me celebrated it in some way. Will that suit?"

Jamie felt himself on shifting ground. "Aye." He brushed his lips against her temple. She stilled; he could feel the fluttering of her pulse beneath his lips. It roused a beast in him, one that would demand to be sated if he lingered. He untangled his hand from hers and walked over to open the door of his study. "We dine at eight."

"Thank you," she said, and began to move toward him. Her hand, the one he'd held, gripped the side of her gown. She glanced up when she reached him. "And I don't think your only redeeming quality is your name." She went out, leaving the scent of roses in her wake, the two dogs trotting after her.

Jamie glared at them as they went past, then shut the door and leaned back against it.

What the bloody hell had just happened to him? He felt as green as a boy with his first infatuation. He didn't care for the feeling it gave him — at sixes and sevens, topsy-turvy, lacking control. All for an English debutante! It went against everything a mighty Campbell laird was.

He limped back to his desk and sat, staring at the paper before him.

Mary, Queen of Scots.

THIRTEEN

Bethia looked stunned. "You've been invited to *supper*?"

"Yes, Bethia," Daria said. "I will dine on haggis yet again, only formally this evening, instead of in this room by myself, as if I were a leper." She paused. "It is formal, is it not?"

"We donna have fancy suppers, as if we are a lot of kings and queens," Bethia snapped, clearly annoyed by this latest bit of news.

"Then I won't wear my ermine cape," Daria retorted. "What do you think, the silk?" she asked, holding up a cream-colored silk gown encrusted with tiny seed pearls. "Or is it too rich?"

"I didna say we dress in rags and animal pelts, did I? The gown is bonny enough."

Daria smiled. "Thank you. That's precisely what I hoped you'd say." She was still determined to win Bethia over, but it was proving a difficult challenge. "Do they gather for wine beforehand?" she asked as she absently sorted through her jewelry.

Bethia's answer to that was stated in rather heated Gaelic. Daria was pleased that she actually thought she made out one or two words, one in particular that sounded like Gaelic for "wench," which Dougal had taught her.

The prospect of the supper — a small but nonetheless important victory for Daria — was wearing on her nerves. The laird had unnecessarily warned her that she'd not be welcome. One need only roam about Dundavie for a few days to know that people were inclined to dislike her. She'd worked very hard to prove she was not the unfeeling beast they believed her to be, and while some had warmed to her, others had not.

Hamish's immediate family was the hardest mountain to climb. They turned their heads and refused to acknowledge her at all.

But it wasn't the fear of rejection that made her feel as if she were a new debutante coming out at her first ball. It was *him.*

The laird. The man who looked more robust and handsome with each passing day. It was ridiculous to think of him *that* way, given that she was his captive, but she'd felt something different between them today. They had gone beyond tolerance of one another, or even friendship. The press of his lips — *his lips!* — to her temple felt like desire. At least in *her* heart it did.

As she dressed for the evening, taking pains with her hair — Bethia was no help, apparently believing that a woman who could not dress her own hair was not much of a woman at all — and applying a bit of rouge to her cheeks, Daria chastised herself for believing in her own fantasies. It was the height of foolishness to dress up for a man who held her captive, and she could all but hear Charity's cackle from Edinburgh.

But there was a force at work that was far more powerful than her usual common sense. It was the rapid beat of her heart this afternoon, the heat of her skin where he'd touched her. She was incapable of dismissing the idea that there *had* been a few moments in which they'd drawn close.

"*Diah,* is there to be a bloody ball tonight?" Bethia grumbled when Daria emerged from behind the dressing screen.

"One never knows, Bethia. That's why it is always prudent to be prepared," Daria said with a wink, and she went out.

At the doors of the great hall, Daria took a moment to square her shoulders and lift

207

her chin, assuming the correct posture for a well-bred woman. *"There is no greater impact than a lady's entrance,"* Lady Ashwood had counseled. So Daria put a smile on her face, put both hands on the knobs of the double doors, and opened them at the same time, stepping across the threshold and expecting to find Campbell and his family —

There was no one within.

Were they truly so uncivilized that they did not come together for a glass of wine before supper? Disappointed in that lapse of gentility, Daria dropped her hands with a sigh and walked into the great hall. Someone might have informed her where, exactly, the Campbells dined. She left the great room and walked down a long, dark corridor lined with armaments, portraits, and tapestries so old and dusty that she sneezed.

As she moved down the corridor, she heard voices coming from behind a closed door at the very end. The voices were raised, speaking rapidly. Daria walked to the door, hoping to hear something that might identify a person to her, but she could not make them out. She leaned closer, her head turned so that she might hear better.

The door suddenly opened, and Daria gasped, stumbling backward with shock.

Standing in the open door, Young John

looked just as shocked to see her there. As he moved aside, Daria saw the Campbells gathered in a loose semicircle, staring at her.

"I beg your pardon," she said breathlessly, and frantically searched for some explanation as to why she was lurking on the other side of the door. "I was looking —"

"Please come in, Miss Babcock."

She hadn't seen him before that moment, standing off to the right. He'd put his hair in a queue, and his square jaw was clean-shaven. He wore a coat of navy superfine and a gray waistcoat. He looked like a king, a highborn English lord, save one small detail — the knee-length plaid wrapped and belted about his waist. His muscular legs were encased in woolen socks. In fact, every man in the room was dressed the same, and the only woman among them, whom Daria did not know, wore plaid draped across her shoulder.

Daria's beautiful gown was woefully underplaided.

"Allow me," the laird said, and moved forward with only a slight limp, his arm extended to her.

Daria put her hand on it; it was wide and as solid as a tree. She found it oddly comforting.

The laird shepherded her into the small

room while everyone else stared at her as disdainfully as one might view a traitor to country and king.

"Allow me to properly introduce Miss Daria Babcock," the laird said to those assembled.

"Isn't she a bonny lass, then?" an old man with a balding head said.

"Aye, that she is," the laird said, and Daria felt a ridiculous swell of pleasure. "Miss Babcock, you've met my brother, Geordie, and my cousin Robbie. May I introduce you to Mrs. Aileen Campbell, Robbie's wife."

Aileen Campbell nodded coolly.

"And of course, my uncle Hamish Campbell. You've heard a wee bit about him."

It was one of those rare moments when Daria really did not know what to do. As she had not been schooled in the proper etiquette of captivity, she erred on the side of caution and dipped into a graceful curtsy worthy of royalty. "It is an honor." She stopped short of saying it was also a pleasure.

No one spoke. No one even moved.

Still in a curtsy, Daria glanced up at the laird — whose eyes, she was not pleased to see, were glimmering with delight. He put out his hand to help her up; she took it, squeezed hard, and rose. "Thank you for the privilege of dining in your company this evening."

"Thank the laird, then," Aileen said, and turned away. "We didna invite you."

"Aileen," Robbie Campbell hissed.

"What?" Aileen said. "She's held for ransom, no' to entertain."

Daria didn't have the chance to be offended, for Geordie scribbled something on his slate and handed it to the laird, who smiled and handed it back. "That's a wee bit pessimistic, Geordie. I feel confident we'll get at least a few pounds for her."

Daria blinked with surprise; the laird laughed.

But the family was not in a laughing mood, and Robbie said something in Gaelic that suddenly had all of them talking at once. Daria stepped back, fairly certain that whisky decanters would begin to fly at any moment. Certainly hands were flying and voices were raised, and Geordie's chalk on the slate grew so insistent that Daria feared he would break it clean in two. She was not welcome at their table, just as Campbell had said, and it was made all the more evident that they were speaking about her when Hamish Campbell squinted at her and said, "But she *seems* rather bonny, aye?"

All right, then. Daria considered herself a

good judge of when one should quit a room, and she was thinking of slipping out the door, but then the laird said something in a quiet voice that made everyone stop talking. He coolly looked at each of them as if expecting a response, and when he received none, he smiled tightly at Daria. "Our supper is served, then," he said, and offered his arm once more.

Daria looked at the family standing behind him, but he shifted, blocking her view. "Donna lose your courage now, lass," he muttered.

He thought she had courage? Surprised, Daria looked up at the laird, but he had already turned his head and was speaking to his cousin as he escorted her.

They entered another chamber immediately adjacent, a small dining room Daria had not yet seen in her wanders. The ceiling was low and held up by beams that were a foot thick. A table that seated only eight stood before a blazing hearth. Across from the hearth was a wall covered with a frayed tapestry that depicted unicorns happily leaping through flowers in what she supposed was Campbell territory. It was a cozy dining room, one where she could imagine the family had gathered to dine intimately for generations.

The butler pulled out a chair and gestured for Daria to sit. She reluctantly took it and sat directly across from Aileen. Daria smiled on the off chance that it might thaw the woman's icy countenance, but she suspected Aileen was determined not to thaw.

To add to Daria's discomfort, Geordie sat on her right, his slate at the ready. Across from him sat Uncle Hamish, flanked by Aileen and Robbie.

Hamish smiled at Daria. "Quite like the mutton."

"We are not dining on mutton tonight, Uncle," Robbie said.

"Quite like the mutton all the same."

Daria smiled at the old man. He was one of the few Campbells who did not seem to harbor any hard feelings for her — he grinned right back.

"Mr. Campbell, I have longed to meet you," Daria said, meaning it quite sincerely.

Geordie scribbled on his slate and handed it across the table to Robbie. Robbie held it out, tilting his head to the right, studying it. "I make out the letter O," Robbie said and looked at Geordie. "The rest of the word is missing."

"Allow me, husband," Aileen said, and reached across Hamish and took the slate from Robbie, studied it a moment, then looked up at Daria. "Owe," she clarified. "I believe he means that you owe our uncle an apology. I agree."

"Aileen," the laird said low.

"I am truly sorry for the misunderstanding with my grandmother, Mr. Campbell," Daria said quickly, wanting to address the issue that seemed to float like a dark cloud above them.

" 'Twas no misunderstanding," Aileen said. "It was thievery —"

"Ba!" Robbie said sharply, and Aileen pressed her lips tightly together and looked away.

"It was not thievery," Daria said evenly. "There has been a terrible misunderstanding, I grant you, but my grandmother believes it was a gift."

Hamish smiled.

Geordie gestured adamantly for his slate, but the laird was quick to take it before Aileen could return it to him. "There is no point in debating it now. I will remind you all that Miss Babcock will be treated as we would treat any guest to Dundavie." He looked pointedly at Geordie. "We pride ourselves on our hospitality, do we no', brother?"

Geordie glowered; the laird handed the slate to Young John, who returned it to

Geordie.

An uncomfortable silence began to thicken around the table. Daria sipped the wine a footman poured for her and thought of Lady Eberlin. When she had assumed the title of countess of Ashwood, as was her right, Lady Eberlin had not been well received in Hadley Green. Before her arrival, her cousin had done some dishonest things in Lady Eberlin's stead, and the people of Hadley Green were slow to forget or forgive. But Lady Eberlin had surely inched her way into the hearts of them all. She'd done it by taking care to speak to everyone, to learn something about them, to make them feel important.

At first, Daria had not trusted her. But then she'd been among the first to fall under her spell. She would never forget how earnestly and sincerely Lady Eberlin had befriended her.

Daria glanced across the table at Aileen, wondering if she could find the fortitude or the patience to do the same. But Aileen was making every effort to avoid Daria's gaze. If she studied the pattern on the china any more closely, she would see nothing but tiny royal-blue flowers for days to come.

Daria looked hopefully at Robbie Campbell, who happened to catch her eye, and before he could look away she said, "Dundavie is a very interesting place, is it not? Have you always lived here, Mr. Campbell?"

Robbie Campbell looked confused and glanced uncertainly at the laird. "Aye," he said. "Where else would I live?"

Where else indeed. Still, Daria forced a smile and turned it on the most recalcitrant Campbell of them all. "I admire your brooch, Mrs. Campbell," she said. "It's quite pretty."

Aileen's fingers went instantly to the brooch at her throat.

"It's a bird of some sort, is it not?"

"A swan," Aileen said. "One of our clan symbols."

"Oh? What does it stand for?"

Aileen frowned. "It means glory, Miss Babcock. The glory of the Campbell name, aye?"

"What a lovely sentiment," Daria said cheerfully. "Did Mr. Campbell give it to you?"

Aileen frowned again. "And which Mr. Campbell would that be?"

Which one! The most obvious one, that was who!

"Just say the name, lass," Uncle Hamish said, very lucid all of a sudden. "Too many Campbells underfoot to be proper about

216

address, I say. Unless, of course, you mean Keith. Wouldn't do at all to call the laird by *his* given name."

"*Jamie,* Uncle," Robbie muttered.

He might have a point, but Daria was not going to let that stand in the way of protocol. "Thank you, but I haven't the right to be so familiar with anyone here," she said, and smiled sweetly.

The laird arched a brow. "No one? But you have seen me at my worst, Miss Babcock."

Warmth sluiced deeply through Daria at the memory of his naked body in Mamie's cottage. "Then you must call me Daria. It seems only fair."

She heard the sound of Geordie's chalk on slate. He handed it across Daria to Jamie so that she could clearly see the chicken scratches he used to communicate. *Donna dress her atol.*

"I think you mean address," the laird said, waving the slate away.

Daria was sympathetic to Geordie's rage — she would be just as angry if someone had used Mamie as they accused Mamie of using Hamish Campbell — but Daria had endured Geordie's wrath for several days now in the form of hard looks and some rather pointed comments to her and about her, the deciphering of which sorely tried her patience.

Geordie wrote something else and showed it to Robbie, who laughed roundly, and finally, Daria lost her composure. "Look here, Mr. Campbell, I have tried to explain myself, but you seem determined not to listen! Or perhaps you did — but it is not *my* fault I can't read your atrocious spelling."

Jamie laughed.

Geordie's face darkened and he jotted, *No me fal you her.*

"There, you see? It would take a scholar *weeks* to decipher that. I am teaching Peter to communicate. Why not you? Yet when I suggested that I might teach you, one would think I had suggested putting you on the rack, so great was your objection." She glared at him. "It is not your doing that I am here, you are quite right about that. But you may as well get used to it. Bethia says I won't leave, and she claims to have the second sight."

Aileen gasped; Robbie looked at her in shock.

Daria looked around warily. "Why are you all looking at me in that manner? You can't truly *believe* her? It all seems rather convenient to me, the second sight. I only meant

218

to make a point to the most intractable among you" — she glared at Geordie again — "not startle you. I hoped you would laugh."

The laird chuckled a little, but Daria had the distinct impression that he was not laughing at Bethia's second sight, but at her.

"Bethia has a gift," Aileen said gravely.

"Now see here," Daria said, bracing her hands on the table. "I have freely admitted that it would appear my grandmother and Mr. Hamish Campbell had a misunderstanding of some sort, and I am as eager as you to rectify it." She paused, glancing at the laird. "Not so eager, mind you, that I would have resorted to kidnapping, but enough to do my utmost to see that reparations are made. *None* of us should fear that this arrangement," she said, gesturing between them all, "is in any way permanent."

"Well then, there you are," Jamie said. "Daria has overruled Bethia and intends to leave just as soon as the debt is repaid. So let us, for once, enjoy our meal in peace." He sat back, allowing Young John to serve a large helping of venison onto his plate.

Another uncomfortable silence fell over the room; there was nothing but the sound of forks and knives scraping against the china plates. Daria had almost finished the few bites of her meal she could manage to swallow when Robbie, bless him, decided to return the favor of polite conversation and took the initiative to speak to her.

"Where in England do you hail from, Miss Babcock?" he asked congenially, ignoring a withering look from his wife.

"Please, sir, you must call me Daria," she said, grateful for the question. "I call Hadley Green home. It is a small village in West Sussex."

"Ah," he said. "And what is your father's occupation, then?"

Her father really had no occupation, but Daria did not think that information would endear her to the Campbells, as they all seemed unduly industrious. "Botanist." It was the first word that came to mind. "He has been working with my mother to create a new orchid."

"Botanist!" Robbie said, suddenly smiling brightly. "Did you hear her, Jamie, a botanist! Aye, miss, the laird fancies himself a botanist," he said to Daria. "He's been trying for an age to improve the yield of our grains. We've no' much room to plant them here."

"You're a botanist?" Suddenly the small shed with the plants made sense, and she was absurdly pleased to find something she had in common with him.

The laird, however, seemed a little embarrassed by the revelation and kept his gaze on his plate. "I dabble, aye."

"Dabble!" Robbie laughed. "It takes up every spare moment, it does."

Jamie glanced coolly at his cousin. "It is a hobby, Rob. Hamish? How do you find the venison?" he asked, changing the subject.

"With a keen sense of smell," Hamish said with a wink, and touched his finger to his nose before handing his spoon to Young John Campbell. Young John quietly returned the spoon to the table beside Hamish's plate.

"Perhaps I could help," Daria offered, in spite of having no idea how she could possibly do so. "I know a thing or two, given my parents' interest." That wasn't even remotely true, but at least it was a start. And it would give her something useful to do.

"You've better things to do than graft grains," Jamie said dismissively, and signaled to Young John to pour more wine.

"What things?" Daria challenged him. "As I've told you, I am entirely without occupation here."

"And as I've told you, your talents would

221

be better used at embroidery."

Daria had done her very best to be a good captive. The least *he* might do was meet her halfway. She put down her fork. "Do you truly believe that women sit about and embroider all day?"

"Aye, he does," Aileen muttered bitterly. "All the men do."

Daria had no doubt Aileen was right. "For the love of England, at least allow me to be useful," she said to Jamie.

He settled back in his chair, his gaze assessing. "For the love of Scotland, I canna help you, lass. I have no children for you to rear, nor a house that needs looking after. You will have to make do." He smiled and lifted his wineglass to her in a mock toast. "But tonight, you may have your occupation and play for us."

"Aye, Laurna, let us hear a wee bit of music," Hamish said.

"Laurna has been gone nigh on two years, Uncle. But our guest has kindly agreed to play."

"I did. However, that does not mean that I have given up on botany, sir; no indeed." She gave him a pert look before she politely dabbed her lips with her napkin and laid it beside her plate. "If you desire to be entertained, then I shall entertain you." She made a show of stretching her fingers. "If you will excuse me, I shall go off and prepare."

Jamie smiled and nodded at Young John, who hurried to pull Daria's chair out for her. She marched out of the room, resisting the urge to mutter unkind things under her breath.

She didn't see Robbie's bright smile or hear him say, "I should like to hear a wee bit of song."

Nor did she see Geordie scribble on his slate, *Jig.*

"Well then," Jamie said as he rose from the table. "Shall we retire to the small parlor?"

He didn't have to ask twice.

FOURTEEN

Daria, with her flowing, sparkling gown and dark golden hair, was already seated by the time Jamie had hobbled into the parlor on his damned leg, his family in tow.

"What would you like to hear?" she asked.

The Campbells merely looked at one another.

"Shall I choose for you?" She began to play. Jamie couldn't help but notice the surprise on Geordie's face — the lad had missed Laurna's playing as much as he had. Robbie and Aileen — who had what some might term a stormy marriage, and he would term a bloody cyclone — seemed to soften as they took seats on the settee. Music had always had a calming effect on the Campbells, thank the saints, and one of Jamie's great regrets was that more of them were not trained in the art. They'd been content to allow Laurna to be their high priestess of music.

Jamie eased himself into a chair and stretched out his leg. He was accustomed to overcoming illness or injury quickly, but he had discovered that lead was a formidable opponent. His recovery was slow, and tonight his leg and side ached. He caught Robbie's eye and gestured to the bottle of whisky on the sideboard.

Jamie was watching Robbie pour two healthy tots when Daria Babcock sang prettily, *"My love is a river that always flows, my heart a seed from which love grows. I cannot remember the words to this tune, and therefore I hope it ends rather soon."*

Even Geordie smiled.

Daria gave them a sly look and played the rest of the tune expertly. When she finished, Robbie clapped loudly, and she graciously accepted his applause with a slight nod.

"Her mother sings like the angels," Hamish said dreamily. "Now, lass, let's have 'The Battle of Otterburn,' aye?"

"Pardon?"

"Ach," Hamish said with a flick of his hand. "You've played it a dozen times if you've played it once. Go on, then."

"Hamish," Jamie said softly, "Laurna is gone."

Hamish looked at Daria, his expression full of confusion as he tried to sort it out. It pained Jamie to see his once robust uncle like this.

"Shall I play a waltz?" Daria suggested.

"A what?" Aileen asked.

"A waltz," she repeated, and looked around at them. "Are you not familiar with it?" she asked, her face lighting with pleasure. "You must learn it! It's a dance that has become wildly popular. Here, allow me," she said, and before anyone could respond, she popped up from the bench and grabbed Geordie's hand, pulling him off the chair. His mouth opened, and if he'd been able to speak, he would doubtless have protested rather loudly. But Geordie was helpless as Daria put his hand on her waist, and placed her hand on his shoulder. With her other hand, she took his and held it out. "On the count of three, we will move three steps to the left, then three to the right. Do you understand?"

Geordie rolled his eyes.

"Splendid!" she said, and began to hum, moving Geordie to the left, and then again to the right, stepping delicately to the count of three. But as Geordie could not seem to follow, she looked at Jamie. "Perhaps you might count it out for us? *One* two three, *one* two three," she said.

"Count it out," Jamie repeated incredulously.

"Yes, just count in threes," she said breezily, and added unnecessarily, "to keep time."

He rather thought it beneath the dignity of a laird and groused, "I do no' keep time."

"We're ready!" she said cheerfully, pretending he hadn't spoken.

He frowned at her lovely smile. "One, two, three," he said.

Daria began to move Geordie about in time to Jamie's counting. Aileen sat up, watching Daria's feet closely, obviously intrigued by the dance, and Robbie, in an unusual show of kindness to his wife, held out his hand. "Come then, *mo ghraidh,* let us waltz."

Aileen looked up at him with surprise. She hesitantly slipped her hand into his, allowing him to pull her up. With their heads bowed together, they began to study their steps.

"No, no, you're missing a step," Daria said to them, pausing momentarily in her instruction of Geordie. "I grant you it is difficult to move when the beat is not precisely to tempo," she said, casting a sidelong look at Jamie.

"What? Am I no' doing as you said?"

"It's *one* two three, *one* two three."

"I know how to count to three," Jamie growled, and began to count again, slapping his hand in time on the wooden arm of his chair.

Daria stood behind Aileen with her hands on Aileen's waist, moving her in the right direction. "There, you see? It's really quite easy." She smiled as she returned to Geordie and began again. "Here we are, *one* two three, *one* two three . . ."

Jamie shifted restlessly in his seat. Though he'd never cared much for dancing, he felt uncomfortably removed from the festivities, as if he were a dog watching from outside a window. He had an almost urgent desire to stand up with Daria, to look at her lovely face and shining eyes as she moved.

Such thoughts were even more disturbing than his desire to dance.

"All right then, with the music. We'll need a partner for you, Geordie," she said, and smiled at the footman. "Would you be so kind as to bring a willing female? Oh, bother, you might be searching all night for a willing one. Any female will do." She sat down at the pianoforte and began to play before anyone could question her, or stop her from bringing in the entire clan. She called out instructions as she played, and after a few false starts, Robbie and Aileen began to move in synchrony. "Splendid!" Daria called from the pianoforte. "*One* two three, *one* two three!"

Aileen, Jamie was surprised to see, was beaming up at her husband. Jamie had not seen her smile quite like that in an age, and he was reminded that he'd once considered her a bonny lass. The footman ushered a maid in, and Geordie grinned at her, took her by the wrist and the waist, and began to dance. The girl protested that she did not know what he was about, but in a few moments she was dancing, her focus intent on her feet.

There was something different in that small parlor that perplexed Jamie. It was vague, intangible, but he could *feel* it. He couldn't name it until he heard the maid laugh, then it suddenly struck him. Since the night Geordie had called Cormag out, there had been no laughter at Dundavie. Not until tonight. Not until an English rose taught them to dance.

They danced until Hamish stood up and clasped his hands behind his back and attempted to dance a jig to the unfamiliar music. But his age and his infirmity had left him without any natural rhythm, and he was soon knocking into the other dancers.

Everyone stopped dancing the waltz to

give Hamish a wide berth. Daria seemed uncertain of what to do and stopped playing.

"Cluich!" Hamish shouted at her, telling her to play on.

"Uncle, it's time we all retired, aye?" Robbie said, putting his hand on his uncle's shoulder.

But Hamish clearly had other ideas and shrugged Robbie off. *"Cluich,* Laurna!" When Daria did not respond, Hamish lunged for the pianoforte.

Geordie stopped him, gently pushing him back.

"Take him," Jamie said, gaining his feet. This was another once unheard of but increasingly familiar side of his uncle — the quick temper, the rash actions.

Geordie linked his arm with Hamish's, urging him to come along and gently pulling him to the door.

Hamish looked confused, staring up at Geordie as if he weren't certain who he was. "Has Laurna finished, then?"

"Aye, she has," Robbie said, and held out his hand for Aileen. He glanced at Jamie, gave him a nod. *"Oidhche mhath."*

"Good night, lads," Jamie said. "Aileen." He handed Geordie's slate to Aileen.

When they had gone, Jamie looked at

Daria. She had stood up from the piano-forte, her expression full of sympathy for the old man. Jamie started toward her, but his leg had stiffened and he limped more than he had all day. When he reached the pianoforte, he eased himself down onto the bench.

She slowly sat beside him. "What happened to Hamish?"

Jamie wished he understood precisely what had happened to his uncle. "I donna know," he said with a slight shake of his head. "It began a few years ago and has grown worse." He touched a few keys, playing a song from a distant memory of his childhood when he'd been forced by his mother to engage in music lessons. *"It will make you a proper gentleman, Jamie,"* she had said.

Daria smiled with delight. "You play!"

"I do no'," he said with an easy smile. "I remember a few things from my music lessons, but I donna play. You, on the other hand, play very well, lass. Thank you for indulging us, aye?"

"Should I take from that you were suitably entertained?" she asked, and playfully nudged him with her shoulder as she began to play lightly, her fingers scarcely touching the keys at all.

"Aye, that I was." He'd been entertained in a way he could not describe. He was softening, he knew it. He did not care to be soft; scarcely anything annoyed him more than giving in to a woman's smile. "When I was a boy," he said, turning his attention away from the curve of her neck, "Hamish was considered the family historian. He would regale the entire clan with tales of heroic Campbell ancestors." He smiled at the memory. "He would act out the more gruesome parts of our history with long swords and descriptions of bloody body parts for the boys, myself included. Now, he canna recall his full name most days."

Daria nodded and played another couple bars. "May I ask you something? Why is Geordie so angry? He may have told me his grievances against me, but alas, his spelling is so very atrocious, I can't understand it."

Jamie couldn't help but laugh. "Aye, in English as well as Gaelic. My brother was never one for the classroom. He wanted to be a soldier, a slayer of man and beast. He is a smart man, a good man, aye? Yet I never knew how poor his writing was until he became mute."

"Until?" Her hands paused gracefully on the keys. "He's not always been mute?"

Jamie shook his head. "It's a recent injury.

In the course of a meal that was intended to bring the Brodies and the Campbells together, no' drive them apart as they've been for two hundred years, Geordie acted rashly. He called another man out," he said to Daria's questioning look. "In the Highlands, there's no' much that can stop two men who want a go at each other, aye? And, as these things generally go when two clans are involved, there is no' much that will stop brothers and cousins and sons and fathers and uncles from joining the fray."

"Oh," she said, nodding.

"And," Jamie added with a sigh, "as these things go for brash, hotheaded young men, Geordie was so badly wounded in the melee that he was made mute."

"How tragic!"

"Aye. Whether or not his voice will return remains to be seen," he said. "But at present, a man who once made better use of his tongue than his hands is now reduced to a slate and a wee bit of chalk. That's what angers him."

She gazed thoughtfully at the keys, playing lightly once more.

If only she knew the whole story of that supper, that infamous, meticulously planned supper, which had been intended to put to bed some of the more egregious complaints the Brodies and Campbells had harbored against each other the last two centuries. Jamie's first thought — when Cormag Brodie had said whatever it was he'd said (his words lost along with the pig that had been roasted for the occasion), and Geordie had flipped the table, sending crystal, china, wine, and pig flying — was that he was right to have wanted a much smaller affair. His second thought — as Cormag had lunged, his hands grasping for Geordie's throat — was that perhaps it would be best if the Brodies and the Campbells never dined together.

The melee had spilled into the old bailey, with Campbells swinging fists at Brodies, and Brodies swinging swords at Campbells. It had ended when Cormag swung his claymore wide, striking Geordie in the neck. If Geordie had not been so agile, he might be headless now. If Cormag had been a little less meaty, he might have lost his life as well, but the knife Geordie managed to stab into his leg had not penetrated so deeply as to drain his life's blood.

As three men struggled to drag Cormag away, Isabella had said, "I canna enter into a permanent union with a man whose brother would wish my brother dead. I'm sorry, Jamie." She'd followed her kinsmen out, daintily holding up the hem of her gold gown so as not to drag it in the blood and muck.

It had been a moment when Jamie could not think of what to say. He was the sort who needed time to think, to mull, when presented with a weighty matter such as the end of an engagement and the crash of dreams for a happy union and a family. He was the sort to choose his words carefully . . . so he hadn't spoken at all.

He had not called her back.

The end of his engagement to the fair Isabella had been a blow to Jamie's heart, and, admittedly, his ego. He'd been quite fond of her, and supposed he still was. She was pretty, with wide green eyes and copper hair. But he was a laird, and women did not cry off from engagements to lairds.

"It must have been horrid for everyone involved," Daria said, as if he'd just told her the story aloud.

"Aye. In more ways than I could ever explain."

"Well," she said, looking at him from the corner of her eye, "I am a good listener."

He laughed. "I've said enough, aye? It was a night for the ages, one that shall go down in the annals of family history; a night in which Geordie lost his voice and I lost my fiancée."

"Your fiancée! How did you *lose* her?"

"In the usual way," he said, smiling a little. "She cried off, since her brother had just been stabbed by my brother."

Daria's eyes widened with surprise and fixed on him, as if she expected him to tell her that he was jesting. Her gaze did not waver, and neither did his. Jamie noticed — and not for the first time, no — that she had long, darkly golden lashes and brown eyes flecked with tiny bits of blue and gray, rimmed with black. Eyes that could live forever in a man's memory.

"You must not tell me any more," she said, her gaze dropping to his mouth. "Or I shall feel quite sad for you and be resolved to help you. I think there can be nothing as dangerous as resolving to help one's captor."

"*Diah,* I could no' bear your help, I am certain of it."

"*You,* sir? I think you could bear nearly anything."

A soft smile played on her lips. He wondered if she was flirting with him now, hoping that he would agree to take her to Edinburgh or give her grandmother undeserved leeway. Daria Babcock might believe she knew the ways of men . . . but Jamie Campbell knew women.

He leaned closer. "And what of you, *lean-nan*? How is it that a woman as lovely as you has descended from a woman who is as mad as a hen?"

She closed her eyes and bent her head closer to him. "You've quite clearly become very fond of my Mamie."

He couldn't help himself; he grazed her temple with his lips. "I assure you, I have no'."

Her smile deepened; small dimples creased her smooth cheeks. "But are you not the least bit curious to see how she fares?" she asked, and tilted her head to one side as Jamie moved his mouth to her jawline.

"No," he said, dipping to her neck.

"But we had an agreement," she murmured.

"We have only one agreement, *leannan*. One thousand pounds in exchange for you." He couldn't seem to stop himself from cupping her face, his fingers splayed against her head. He tilted her head back and moved to kiss her, but Daria quickly inserted her fingers between them, pressing against his mouth.

"You promised me I would see her. Duff said he sent a messenger with the letter I wrote her and she wasn't there. I'm worried, and you promised."

Damnation. She had him. She'd seduced him with her smile and her beauty and her unfailingly spirited nature, and even worse, she knew that she had. Jamie could see it in the dance of her eyes, the curve of the smile on her lips. "You want my promise, lass? You have it," he said, and grabbed her hand, pulling it away at the same moment he pressed his mouth to hers, claiming it, drawing her lower lip in between his teeth.

She was lush, her lips, her body, all of her. He anchored one arm around her and pulled her closer. This woman was irresistible, with her smile and her glittering eyes, and Jamie kissed her with a surrender that surprised him.

Her mouth, as soft and succulent as he'd remembered from that hazy dream in her grandmother's cottage, was warm, and *Diah,* moving erotically against his mouth. The kiss was molten; it had the potential to melt him into nothing.

It wasn't enough — he needed more. He suddenly twisted her about and draped her over his lap, her face between his hands. She gave a small cry into his mouth when he did it, but then she wrapped her arms around his neck, holding herself tightly to him.

He tasted her as if she were some English delicacy, and imagined tasting the more intimate folds of her body. He sank deeper into the sea of longing, riding the wave of pleasure. He cupped her breast, filling his hand and then sliding it down to the hem of her gown, finding her bare leg.

She tried to speak, but he would not allow it. She arched her back, pressing into him, and bent her knee. Something fell off the pianoforte with a crash. He hoped it wasn't a candle, hoped Dundavie didn't burn around him, but in that moment, he hardly cared if it did. He was too bewitched, too engrossed in the feel of her in his arms.

Daria pressed against him, her hands sweeping around his neck, her breasts pressed to his chest. She thrust her fingers into his hair, skirted the top of his ear, then found his shoulders, felt the tension in his muscles. Jamie's body hardened with anticipation. He was only moments from lifting her skirts, from sliding his hand between her legs . . . but his damnably practical head overruled his groin. He did not need this English rose to complicate his life any more than she had already.

She dropped her hand; it hit an ivory key

and the sound roused him completely from his lust. With a strength he would have sworn he did not possess, he lifted his mouth from hers. He kissed the bridge of her nose, then pressed his forehead to hers, cupping her head in his hands, calming his ragged breath.

When he felt his senses return to him, he gazed at her.

She gave him a self-conscious smile that put dimples just below the roses in her cheeks. "When shall we go to Mamie's?"

Jamie sighed. "Incorrigible, you are. When I am assured I can ride, then, aye?"

Her smile broadened; her eyes twinkled with delight. "Aye," she mimicked.

She sat up and tucked a thick strand of hair that had fallen from her coif into the chignon at her nape.

"Good night, then," Jamie said, turning away from her and her captivating smile. "Off to bed with you." *Go out of my sight, leannan, so that I will not be tempted.*

Still smiling, she rose gracefully from the bench. Her fingers trailed across his back and shoulders as she passed him.

He did not watch her leave, but waited until he heard the door shut and then lowered his brow to the top of the pianoforte, his eyes closed, his jaw clenched against a burgeoning physical desire.

FIFTEEN

Nothing in Daria's previous experience matched a man like Jamie Campbell. *Nothing.*

She'd never felt anything as fervently as she'd felt his kiss, had never felt such a burning, untenable desire to press her flesh to a man's flesh — but Lord help her, she'd felt it in every bit of her skin . . . all in the space of a single kiss.

A delicious little shiver shimmied down her spine as she recalled the way he'd kissed her. Like a man who would possess a woman completely, who would lay her down and take her with a lover's determination.

She lay on the bed in the dark cloak of night, her fingers tracing down her abdomen and back up, over and over again. She stared at the crack in the drapery, the soft glow of moonlight spilling into her room, and imagined him, big and bold above her, his hair framing his face, his body, his muscles — all of him sliding into her, filling her.

Lord. She rolled onto her side and buried her face in the pillow. What was this she was feeling? *Lust* for her captor? She was mad, quite mad, to think in such a way! She was not naïve. Jamie Campbell would use her ill and then happily collect his one thousand pounds. But then, had she not used him? Had she not allowed that splendid, truly spectacular kiss so that she might get what *she* wanted?

Daria opened her eyes. There it was. They would each use the other to gain what they wanted. That was the way things were done — in an English ballroom or an old Scottish castle.

How very cynical you've become, she chastised herself. *Now you will invent an entirely new societal rule to excuse being moved by a brazen, unrefined Scottish laird?*

She was far too reckless! What of the damage to her marriage potential? She was being held for ransom, for God's sake — that alone would ruin her chances for a match with a good title. If rumors that she had done something inappropriate with the laird were to reach England, it would destroy any hope of gaining a husband with even the lowest of titles.

It would prevent her from ever getting married at all. Would she risk everything for physical pleasure?

She couldn't bear to become a spinster, spending all her days in her parents' house. Oh, she was playing with fire! She'd walked into the open flame with the ridiculous belief that she'd not be burned. But she had, and it had seeped into her blood and spread indescribable torment through her.

With a sigh, Daria rolled onto her back and stared blankly up at the canopy. She had very few options, really. She needed Jamie Campbell to protect her grandmother. Yet she needed to keep him at arm's length for the sake of her reputation. She must tread carefully, avoiding him where she could, ignoring the way he made her skin tingle and the way her heart beat faster when he was near. *Yes,* Daria told herself as she closed her eyes, *that's what you must do.*

So, given her very firm talk with herself, Daria had absolutely no excuse the next day when she devised a plan after hearing Young John say that the laird was at work in the hothouse.

She gathered up a basket Catriona had loaned her and marched outside. She'd walked past the small garden in the bailey a dozen times, and this time she paused there, turned about to Duffson, and said, "I feel ill."

He blinked and looked nervously about.

"It is a woman's curse," she added, and watched the color rise high in his cheeks. "Would you be so kind as to fetch me some water? I shall be in the garden."

Duffson swallowed so hard she could see his Adam's apple bob. Yet he seemed reluctant to leave her, so Daria put her hand low on her belly and winced. "I can scarcely run, sir. I've such a pain."

The poor young man whirled about and scurried for the main keep.

With a smile, Daria glanced down at Anlan and Aedus. "Stand guard, you beasts." She pushed Aedus's rump away from her knee as she squatted down and pulled several faded spring flowers from Dundavie's ridiculously small garden. Some of them were so rooted that she had to pull with both hands, but she managed to fill her small basket.

Then she hurried to the mews that led to the small hothouse before Duffson could return, the dogs loping alongside her.

"Ridiculous," she whispered as she paused at the weathered wooden door. It was insanity to do what she was about to do, but she very much desired to be kissed again. Who knew whether she would ever have another opportunity? She pulled her shoulders back, lifted her chin, and put her hand on the knob.

A rush of fetid air hit Daria as she stepped across the threshold. It overwhelmed her, causing her to sneeze so mightily that some of her pilfered flowers spilled onto the path between the wooden benches. Clay pots were crammed beside one another on those benches, some of them containing shoots, others empty. It took a moment for her eyes to adjust to the dimness, but she saw a movement at the far end of the little hothouse and said, "I beg your pardon. I didn't realize anyone was within." She smiled brightly.

Whoever responded to her in rapid Gaelic was not Jamie. She squinted and saw a small, wizened man with a scruffy beard, wearing a stained apron. Disappointed, she forgot her basket and dropped her arm. All the flowers spilled out onto the ground. Daria groaned just as the man raised his voice and began to jabber at her in Gaelic, his hands slicing through the air to emphasize whatever it was he was saying.

"Yes, all right, I will go," she said, backing up. "I didn't mean to be a bother." She bumped into the bench and sent two pots tumbling. "For heaven's sake," she muttered as she righted them. "You do realize, sir, that I haven't the slightest notion what you are saying, don't you?" she called out over his blathering as she dipped down to pick up the flowers. "It seems you all believe that if you simply talk louder, somehow I will understand it." She stuffed the flowers into the basket and stood up, dusting off the knees of her gown. "Unfortunately, it's not as easy as that. I wish that I *could* understand it, for the loudness is very unkind to one's ears."

Satisfied that she had removed as much of the dirt as was possible, she folded her arms into the basket handle and looked at the man. She realized then that he had stopped speaking. "There, you see? No harm done," she said, gesturing to the ground. "Good day." She turned about — and collided with Jamie Campbell.

He was standing with his arms folded across his rather broad chest, and while his expression was impossible to interpret, Daria was fairly certain he was not pleased to see her.

"What are you doing here?" he asked, his gaze falling to her basket of mangled flowers. "Where is your keeper?"

"Duffson?"

Jamie waited impassively for her answer.

What had she thought, that he would greet her with open arms? "In truth, I ducked away. I was looking for . . . some shears," she said, relieved to have landed on a plausible explanation.

"Shears," he repeated skeptically.

"For the flowers." She gestured at her basket.

"You might have asked Young John or Duffson for shears, aye?"

"Right you are. But, ah . . . they were occupied."

He arched his brow dubiously. "It must be a busy day indeed at Dundavie."

She would ignore the sarcasm and instead admire the way his voice dripped over her like honey. "This must be where you practice your botany," she said, and averted her gaze from the hazel eyes full of suspicion. "Where is your wheat?"

"Can you no' see it, then, what with your vast knowledge of botany and plant grafting?"

He had her there. "See it? But it's so awfully dim."

"Oh, aye, quite dim," he agreed, glancing up at the noonday sunlight that was streaming in from the windows overhead. "Then allow me to show you." He said something to the old man, put his hand on Daria's back as if he'd done so a thousand times before, and nudged her down the path.

She was aware of him close behind her, aware of the hard length of him, the breadth of him. Warmth began to rise in her. She thought of the previous night, of the way he had so easily stretched her across his lap. She imagined his hand circling her waist now, drawing her back to his chest, his mouth on her neck.

At the end of the row she stopped walking. He leaned over her shoulder. "There you are, then," he said, nodding to the pots on the table.

Daria looked at them and spotted two green shoots with ragged edges in a single pot. "Aha, I see."

"Well? What do you make of it?"

"Looks to be doing very well," she said, nodding thoughtfully. "Impressive."

"Thank you," he said, and leaned closer to her, his mouth at her ear. "But what do you think, Daria? How shall I improve it?"

She loved the way her name sounded when he said it. She smiled, cocked her head to one side as she pretended to consider the little shoots. It was difficult to concentrate with him so near, his cologne

249

clouding her thoughts. "You might use more soil," she suggested. It seemed like her parents were forever speaking of new soil mixes.

"More soil! Aye, that ought to make this little weed grow tall."

Weed? Daria hoped that something had been lost in translation, but when she glanced at him from the corner of her eye, he was grinning. Smirking, really, his eyes shining with amusement.

"For heaven's sake!" She was annoyed with herself for being foolish enough to pretend she knew the slightest thing about botany.

He laughed outright. "You've been quite helpful, *leannan.* Now that Fingal and I know that weeds will grow taller with a wee bit more soil, we might leave him to his work, aye?" He put his hand possessively on the small of her back and began to usher her to the front of the little hothouse.

"You can't blame me for at least *attempting* to be useful," she groused.

"I donna blame you for wanting to be useful, but for dissembling. A wee bit more soil, you say?" He laughed again, opened the door, and stepped through with her into the sunlight. The dogs quickly leapt to their feet, their tails wagging madly. "Come along then, Miss Babcock. I suspect Duffson is quite frantic at having lost you once more."

She snorted.

"I would have thought that the tongue-lashing his father gave him last time would have made for a keener eye. How did you manage it?" He took her basket of mangled flowers, peering at them curiously as they began to walk through the mews.

Daria glanced away. "I suggested that I had a . . . female illness," she said as they stepped into the bailey.

Jamie laughed so loudly that it startled her. "You must no' frighten the lad, *leannan*. I am losing men to Glasgow every day. I donna need to encourage any more of them to flee. Now then, what are you trying to hide?"

"Hide? Nothing! Why must you assume the worst?"

"Ach, I was right, then," he said, winking down at her. He folded his arms across his chest, the basket dangling from his elbow. "You are about mischief."

"I am not."

"Then what is in the hothouse that you wanted so much that you would send the poor lad on a fool's errand?"

Daria gazed up into his handsome face and sighed with great exasperation. "I wanted . . ."

"Aye?" he asked, leaning forward as if she were on the verge of admitting an earth-shattering secret.

"I wanted to see you," she said haughtily. "There you are, Jamie Campbell, you've forced me to confess. Are you happy?"

He leaned back. And then a smile slowly curved over his mouth. "My, my, Miss Babcock," he murmured. "Might I take from this confession that you find me bonny?"

"No." She wasn't particularly convincing, if his overly broad and self-satisfied grin was any indication.

"Aye, I think you do."

"No," she said more emphatically, shaking her head. "At least you speak English. And I am interested in botany —"

"I quite like to see you flustered, for I find the blush in your cheeks very appealing."

"I am not *flustered.*"

"It's quite all right, *leannan,*" he said, dipping his head to look her directly in the eye. "I understand, for I've rather enjoyed our kisses as well."

Daria wished for a chaise where she might collapse with the last bit of dignity she had left to her. Her gaze had drifted to his mouth, and she was debating what to say, how to prolong this ridiculous conversation so that she might ask for one more kiss, when Aedus and Anlan's sudden barking startled her out of her wits.

"Diah," Jamie muttered, and followed that with a string of Gaelic as two riders thundered into the bailey ahead of a carriage.

"I see you have visitors," Daria said, grateful for the opportunity for a clean escape. "I'll take my leave —"

"No," he said, and caught her elbow in his hand.

The first rider slid off his horse and, with a grand flourish, doffed his hat and bowed deeply at the waist. He was an inch or two shorter than Daria and twice her width. He looked to be considerably older, as well. Behind him, a slender young woman with fair blonde hair dismounted gracefully and moved to stand beside him, her riding crop firmly in her hand. Daria had the sense that the woman would not be shy to use the crop at a moment's notice. She did not bow nor curtsy, and seemed entirely too occupied in staring at Daria.

"Good afternoon, Laird Campbell!" the portly man said. He was English, and Daria felt a moment of panic. How would he regard her being held for ransom?

"My lord," Jamie said gruffly. "We were no' expecting your call."

"I can see that," he said jovially, his gaze raking over Daria. "I beg your pardon for the interruption," he said to Daria, "but we were showing some friends about the lovely countryside and I had in mind to slay two birds with one stone, as it were. I had heard of your unfortunate accident, Laird, and came to express my hopes for your speedy recovery. And I thought the ladies should like to see an estate as old and authentic as Dundavie."

A coachman opened the carriage door and lowered the step, and Daria heard quite a lot of nattering. She knew instantly who it was and watched as Mrs. Gant emerged first from the carriage, followed closely by Mrs. Bretton. "Oh no," she murmured, earning a look from Jamie.

"Might we be introduced to your fair companion, Laird?" the fat man asked, eyeing Daria with delight, as one might eye a piece of cake.

Jamie reluctantly said, "Miss Daria Babcock, may I present Lord Murchison and his daughter, Lady Ann Murchison."

"How do you do?" Daria automatically slid into a curtsy. She racked her brain for any knowledge of them, but concluded she had never heard of the lord or his daughter.

"Look here, Mrs. Gant, it's our little

companion!" Mrs. Bretton trilled as the two women bustled forward. "Miss Haddock!"

"Babcock," Daria softly reminded her, extending her hand.

"Yes, yes, of course, *Babcock*. You must forgive me; I have a terrible memory for names. My dear, what are you doing *here*? Does your grandmother live here, in this *castle*? I understood from Mr. Brodie that her abode was quite plain."

"No, she doesn't live here," Daria said, and panicked as she glanced at Jamie. What was she to say? An opportunity to escape had presented itself on a silver platter, and yet she felt an absurd moment of hesitation.

"She can tell us all about her visit and her grandmother over tea," Lord Murchison said, and smiled broadly at Jamie. "The laird will want to impress our guests with that fine Scottish hospitality he's so generously shown me. And besides, I have a small proposition for you, Laird."

"Have you," Jamie drawled, his eyes narrowing.

Lord Murchison laughed. "There's no call to look so stern," he said, reaching up to clap Jamie's shoulder. "A conversation between men, that's all. Ann, my dear, you must engage Miss Babcock and learn all about her visit to Scotland."

"I'll do no such thing," Lady Ann said, and followed her father as he began to walk toward the keep as if he'd been invited in.

Daria did not like Lord Murchison. She'd known a handful of men like him, over-reaching lords full of their own self-importance. Nevertheless, he was her way out of Dundavie, and she had to decide what she must do.

"Doesn't this look imposing?" Mrs. Bretton said, looking up at the keep. "Shall we go in for tea, Miss Haddock?"

"*Babcock,* my dear," Mrs. Gant said. "Miss *Babcock. Haddock* is a *fish,*" she explained as the two women walked toward the entrance, leaving Daria behind with the dogs.

Sixteen

If there was a person on earth whom Jamie could scarcely abide, it was Lord Murchison. He was the worst sort of Englishman, his feelings of superiority quite evident, particularly in the way he attempted to lord over Dundavie as if he had run all the Campbells from the land and taken possession.

That was clearly his plan.

Twenty acres, he said in the privacy of Jamie's study. For twenty acres, he would pay Jamie what he tried to pretend was a princely sum of fifteen hundred pounds. It was a laughable, insulting amount, but Jamie understood the offer. He guessed that Murchison had heard of Hamish's blunder and knew the Campbell coffers needed an infusion of cash if they were to survive the coming winter. That, coupled with the breach between the Brodies and the Campbells . . . it all made Jamie rethink the letter from Malcolm Brodie.

He told Murchison no. He was succinct and to the point, and still, Murchison tried to argue. So did his brazen daughter. "Do you understand what we're offering?" she asked.

He gripped the arm of his chair to keep from speaking unkindly to the young woman. "I was shot in the leg, no' the head, lass. I understand you very plainly — you would steal Dundavie from beneath my feet if you could divine a way. Now then, your proposition has been made and rejected. Shall I return you to your guests?" He stood.

"Very well, Campbell," Murchison said, standing too, tilting his head back to glare up at him. "If you feel you have the luxury of bargaining with the lives of the few clansmen you have left, then who am I to dissuade you? Pay no heed to the predictions of a harsh winter."

"And now you will predict the weather for me, too, will you?" Jamie opened the door.

Murchison scowled as he went out. So did Lady Ann, her face a younger version of her father's. Jamie pitied the man who would one day be bound to that one.

He followed them to the small receiving salon across the hall. Daria was perched on the edge of a settee, her back rigidly straight.

She looked as if she were enduring torture. The two Englishwomen — Mrs. Gant and Mrs. Bretton, "tourists of your fine country," one of them had said — were ogling a very old jewel-encrusted leather sporran that had belonged to Jamie's great-grandfather. Jamie had hung it on the wall to remind him of the days when wearing the Scottish garb had been forbidden by the English. He hung it there to remind all Campbells that the English would never again tell a Campbell what to do.

"There you are!" the smaller of the two old ladies said. "We worried you'd not come back for us." She laughed a little nervously.

"Pardon, Laird." Young John was trying to enter the room with a cart bearing the tea service. Jamie moved so that he could push it into the room, the wheels squeaking loudly. Young John stopped the cart in the middle of the room and began to methodically transfer the tea service to a small table in the sitting area as everyone watched.

"It's quite an impressive castle you have here!" one of the ladies said. "It looks very rustic and . . . *old*. It must require an awful lot of upkeep."

"Aye," Jamie said, clasping his hands behind him. How might he politely send this group on their bloody way?

"Will the work all fall to you?" she asked brazenly. "Lord Murchison explained that your people are all flocking to Glasgow and Edinburgh or even farther afield in search of work."

Jamie could feel himself bristle. "He did, did he? No, madam, no' all my people have flocked," he said tightly. "Most wish to remain here, where their ancestors lived, and their ancestors before them. If we can manage to keep our grazing lands and no' allow them to be overrun by sheep, that is." He looked pointedly at Murchison.

A tense silence followed. Young John poured a cup of tea and offered it to Daria, who shook her head. Her hands were on her lap, curled into small fists.

The taller of the two women sat next to her and waited for Young John to serve her. "Miss Babcock, you *must* tell us what you are doing up here in this musty old castle so far from home!"

Musty? They would call one of the finest examples of a fortress castle in all of Scotland *musty*?

"Ah . . ." The color rose in Daria's cheeks again. Perhaps she was embarrassed to be held in a musty old castle. The lass should consider it a privilege to be held here with her head still attached to her shoulders.

Most English who had landed here in centuries past had not been so fortunate.

"You came all the way from Sussex to see after your grandmother. She must be close by."

"No, she . . . I *did* come to see her," Daria said. "I was with her, but then . . ." She glanced up at Jamie, and he could see the determination in her eye. He suppressed a groan of exasperation — he knew what she was about to do. Frankly, he had expected it, but he didn't relish the thought of explaining to another Sassenach how things were done in the Highlands.

Daria suddenly twisted about on the settee and looked at the woman. "The truth, Mrs. Gant, is that I was brought against my will to Dundavie to be held for ransom."

If Daria had thought there would be a hue and cry, she was surely disappointed, for no one spoke. In fact, they all looked at her as if she were mad — save Young John, who continued pouring tea.

"Ransom!" Lady Ann said with a snort. *"You?"*

"Yes, me!" Daria exclaimed, clearly offended.

Mrs. Gant laughed gleefully. "Oh dear, I almost believed you. *Ransom!*" She laughed again, giving her sister, who seemed confused, a nudge with her elbow.

"I am speaking the truth." Daria looked at Jamie. "He took me from my grandmother's home against my will!"

"Miss Babcock," Jamie said, "you have a delightful sense of humor, I canna deny it. But after last evening's performance on the pianoforte, I say that you are far better with music than with jesting."

"That . . . that was simply a diversion and you know it, sir."

He laughed as if she were teasing him. "A very pleasant one, to be sure. By the bye," he said, turning around to his butler, "Miss Babcock picked some flowers from the garden this morning. I promised her I would have them put in her room. Please see that they are delivered straightaway and replace those from yesterday."

"Aye," Young John said. If he thought his laird had lost his mind of a sudden, he didn't show it.

Daria, on the other hand, gaped at Jamie. He could see the realization dawning in her expression — who could believe that she was being held against her will if she were picking flowers and playing the pianoforte? Her brows dipped into a stormy little frown and her eyes glistened in a way that might have felled a lesser man.

"You've had your fun with us, Miss Babcock, so now you must tell us how you are acquainted with the legendary Laird Campbell," one woman said.

"Legendary," Daria repeated, a little too skeptically to suit him.

"Oh, yes. I am quite certain Lord Murchison will not mind in the least if I am to repeat what he has said of Laird Campbell — that he, more than any Scottish laird, has refused to give over to the new ways of land management and has kept his clansmen very close. You are to be applauded, sir."

"That is true indeed, Mrs. Gant. No one has worked harder for his people," Lord Murchison chimed in, and inclined his head toward Jamie as if he expected to be thanked for his comment.

"You mean that I've worked harder than any other to keep your bloody sheep from overtaking the country."

Daria looked from one of them to the next. "What have sheep to do with it?"

"It's quite complicated," Lady Ann said, and sipped the cup of tea Young John offered her. "I rather doubt you'd understand."

"What I don't understand," Daria said, slowly coming to her feet and fixing her gaze on Lady Ann, "is how a woman — a fellow countryman — tells you all she's being held against her will and no one seems to have a care."

"Goodness, but you're a feisty one, aren't you?" Lord Murchison said, his smile gone. "You needn't say more, my dear, for I suspect we've all guessed the truth. And I rather think *ransom* was not anyone's guess."

The color drained from Daria's face, and Jamie felt something twist inside of him. Murchison was a master at manipulating words, but that remark was a plain insult.

"Have a care, Murchison," Jamie said, moving in front of the smaller man. "Miss Babcock is my guest. Unfortunately, her grandmother was no' able to make the journey over the hills to join her."

"Yes," Daria said quickly. "And we are to return to her on the morrow. That is what you said, is it not, Laird?"

Touché. "Aye," Jamie drawled.

"But I thought the ladies said the coach let her off on the Brodie lands," Lady Ann said. "Is it not dangerous for you to be on Brodie lands, Laird?"

Jamie was on the verge of taking the brash young woman to task, but Daria said, "I think there's not an inch of Scotland that is dangerous to the laird. As your father said, he is legendary. But how kind of you to be concerned."

"You have a good friend indeed in Miss Babcock, sir," the taller of the old women said. "Are we to have the tour? I should very much like to see the castle."

"We really have taken too much of the laird's time," Murchison said.

"Nonsense. You've come all this way, aye? My brother, Geordie, will be delighted to show your guests about, my lord." He looked at Young John and said to him in Gaelic, "Geordie has my leave to make the tour as difficult as he'd like."

With a hint of a smile, Young John went out to fetch Geordie.

"If you will excuse me, then." Jamie looked at Daria and took pity on her. She'd be picked apart by the Murchison vultures. And frankly, it would behoove him to keep her close, lest she manage to convince them that she'd been kidnapped. "Miss Babcock?" He held out his hand to her, wondering if she would take it.

He needn't have wondered — Daria moved so quickly that she accidentally bumped into the tea cart. He smiled and led her out the door.

"You'll think on what I've said, Laird, won't you?" Murchison called after him.

"No' even for a moment," Jamie said congenially, and smiled at the ladies. "Good day."

Once outside, Jamie put his hand on Daria's elbow and steered her out of hearing distance. "That went well, aye?"

Her eyes narrowed. "You think yourself so very clever!"

He laughed softly. "The English lack imagination, *leannan*. They would never believe you are here against your will."

"Well, yes, I realize that now," she said impatiently. "At least *that* group of English lacks imagination. But I will think of something, Jamie Campbell. You can't hold me forever."

"Donna fret. I should like this over more than you." For reasons that were now becoming cloudy.

"In the meantime, I look forward to seeing Mamie," she said pertly. "Don't think you will worm your way out of that promise." She flounced away in high dudgeon.

Jamie had to admit, she was really quite lovely when her dudgeon was high.

SEVENTEEN

Daria fumed for the rest of the afternoon, despising Lord Murchison and his daughter for their inexcusable indifference to her plight, and despising Lady Ann for her inexcusably imperious manner.

She realized that Jamie would likely marry someone just like that wretched woman, and the thought gave her a nauseating little twist. Maybe that was whom he had meant when he said his marriage was all but arranged. Daria shuddered for him.

Her humor wasn't improved when she came down for supper and found only Duff within. He saw her hesitation and gestured for her to enter the room. "I'll no' bite you, lass."

"Where is everyone?" she asked.

"Out here and there."

While she was forced to dine with the tersest man of Dundavie. That, she thought wryly, was quite a challenge.

He glanced up at her as if he knew what she was thinking. "Sit."

Daria sat.

Nothing was said through the first course, which Daria found excruciating. When the main course was served and Duff remained focused on his plate, she said, "I suppose the laird and his family are dining with the Murchisons?"

Duff said nothing.

"Perhaps the Murchisons are frequent visitors to Dundavie, hmm? After all, what other society is available to them?"

Duff merely fixed his gaze on her as he stuffed a healthy portion of potatoes into his mouth.

"If it were me, I would avoid unnecessary society with them. I consider myself a good judge of character, and it strikes me that the laird is quite a bit above that family." She shrugged as if it made no difference to her.

Duff paused and wordlessly looked across the table at her.

She tried to smile. "I realize I am speaking out of turn —"

"Aye."

"I mean well, Mr. Duff. I am speaking to you as a friend who has the laird's ear. It seems everyone at Dundavie is waiting for the laird to marry and produce an heir, and quite naturally, for that is what lords and lairds do. But I would caution him from seeking a match with Lady Ann. I cannot think he'd be happy."

Duff put down his fork. "You are free with your opinions, are you no'?"

Daria shrugged again. "I've never been able to help myself." Nor could she stop herself from imagining Jamie and Lady Ann, shackled for all eternity by matrimony —

"Who he might marry is no business of yours, lass. But I can assure you that he'd sooner take his own life than marry an Englishwoman."

That was a bit of a stinging put-down. "Well, he must marry *someone*," she insisted. "If not Lady Ann, then who?"

An uncharacteristic smile softened Duff's face. "*Diah,* but it warms me heart to hear your concern for our laird's happiness, Miss Babcock. Allow me to put your fears to rest. The laird has held Isabella Brodie dear to his heart, aye? It is likely their engagement will be renewed."

"It is?" she asked, sounding damnably weak.

"Aye." He stood. "Good evening, then, Miss Babcock."

"Wait!" Daria exclaimed as Duff started for the door. He paused and glanced back at her. "Is he . . . Do you mean that he loves her?"

Duff muttered something under his breath and walked out of the dining room.

She stabbed at the food on her plate. The news was oddly unsettling. It should have soothed her, reminded her that she was filled with childish daydreams. But it hardly mattered — she would be away from Dundavie just as soon as she could. Let Jamie marry whomever he pleased. It was nothing to her.

It certainly had nothing to do with her not sleeping well that night. She tossed and turned, feeling every lump in her mattress. She was disappointed that she had been so caught up in a silly little fantasy. She was far too experienced to have her head turned by a mere kiss. Knowing that Jamie would marry Isabella Brodie was exactly what she needed to step back and think clearly. She was a captive here. She couldn't speak the language; no one liked her — *You are a fool!*

She had thought herself fairly awake but was startled half out of her wits by someone shaking her in the middle of the night. Daria came up with a cry of alarm until she saw Jamie standing there, holding a candle aloft.

Her heart began to beat wildly. Several highly improper thoughts scattered across her mind. "What in heaven are you doing?"

"Get up," he said, and tossed something on the foot of her bed.

Daria's skin tingled with foreboding. She looked to the window — it was black as ink out there. "What time is it?"

"It's four o'clock. Don these clothes and meet me in the foyer, aye?"

He set the candle down on the basin. "I'll expect you in a quarter of an hour," he said and walked away, disappearing into the shadows. She heard the door pull shut.

She picked up the first thing she could reach from the items he'd put at the end of the bed: a pair of buckskin pantaloons? What was this? His nocturnal intrusion was scandalous, unacceptable, and possibly even law-breaking in England. Any proper young English debutante would denounce a gentleman who presented himself in such a manner.

But she was not in England. She was in Scotland. And none of the English gentlemen had roused such a heartbeat in her as Jamie had. So she pushed the loose hair from her face, climbed out of bed, and pulled on the pantaloons.

They were short, reaching just above her

ankles, and a little snug, but Daria felt delicious wearing them, as if she were doing something almost indecent. He'd also left her a woolen shirt and a coat, and a pair of boy's boots. The shirt, which she pulled on over a chemise, was quite long, with far too much fabric to tuck into the pantaloons, so she tied the ends at her waist. The coat almost swallowed her whole, but it was warm and smelled slightly of horses. She braided her hair and pulled on the boots. They were a little large, but they would do. Daria picked up the candelabra and made her way down to the foyer.

Jamie was waiting, his feet braced apart, his hands clasped at his back. He was dressed in the plaid, its end draped over his shirt and shoulders and belted at his waist. Daria was so taken up with his appearance that she scarcely noticed how his gaze raked over *her*. "You did as I asked," he said approvingly. "I'd thought there'd be some resistance."

"There was," she said, and smiled. "You might at least explain why I must parade about as a man."

He grinned. "There is no' a person on earth who would ever mistake you for a man, *leannan*. But you canna ride over the hills on an English sidesaddle, aye? The

272

paths are too treacherous; you must ride astride. I thought you'd be more comfortable dressed in this manner."

Daria perked up. "Over the hills?"

"To call on your wretched grandmother, aye."

She beamed at him. "I am in your debt, kind sir. But why on earth must we go in the middle of the night?"

"There is something we must do before we visit your grandmamma."

"What is that?"

"You'll see soon enough, aye?" He took her by the elbow, steering her outside.

Young John was in the bailey, looking a bit bleary-eyed. He handed Jamie a cloth bundle, and the two of them spoke briefly before Jamie continued on, taking Daria with him. In the bailey it was still quite dark, and only one rush torch had been lit. She could see two horses, one gold, one black. Daria glanced around them. "Where is Duff?"

"Sleeping, I would guess," Jamie said. "Did they teach you how to sit a horse in England? Or were you pulled about in wee carriages by wee ponies?"

She snorted. "Every proper debutante has riding lessons, I'll have you know. I am no novice." That was a bit misleading. She was not a novice, but she was not a very good rider, either. Daria had found her dashing riding instructor to be far more interesting than the horse, but she wasn't foolish enough to tell Jamie that. She walked up to the light-colored horse and stroked his neck.

She felt Jamie's hands land on her shoulders. He turned her toward the black horse, giving her a gentle push. "That one," he said, and went about lashing the cloth bundle to the back of his saddle.

Daria eyed the black horse. He eyed her right back, his nostrils flaring as he caught her scent. He was shorter than English horses, which gave her a tiny bit of confidence. She lifted her leg, trying to reach the stirrup, but it was too high. She debated asking for help — she very much desired to do it herself — but before she could speak, Jamie's hands grabbed her waist. He lifted her up and set her on the saddle. The horse danced to one side when he felt her weight, and Daria shrieked as she grasped the pommel of the saddle.

"*Uist, leannan,* you'll wake the dead." He took the reins, gave them a slight tug, then handed them to Daria and eyed her curiously. "You *can* ride, aye?"

Daria clucked her tongue at him as she took the reins. *"Yes."*

He gave her a charmingly lopsided, blatantly skeptical smile, but returned to his mount. He swung up with ease and took the reins from the stable boy, then gave her a wink. "Are you ready, then?"

No, she was not, particularly as they'd be riding into the dark. "Quite."

He smiled, then gave a low whistle. On cue, Anlan and Aedus came racing around a corner, as eager as if they'd been waiting for this moment all night. *"Coisich,"* he said, and the dogs put their noses to the ground and began to trot toward the entrance.

As they rode through the gates and onto the winding village road, Daria gripped the reins with all her might, afraid of falling in the dark. Her feet barely reached the stirrups; she couldn't see more than a few feet by the light of the moon.

Jamie pulled up as they came to the edge of the village. As they moved into the fields beyond, he was somewhere beside Daria, but she dared not look away from the horse or the path. Yet she could feel him near, could hear his horse snorting into the darkness.

"Ease up on the reins," he said, his voice coming from just behind her. "He canna see where he is going with his nose up in the air, aye?"

Daria gave the reins some slack and could feel the horse relax beneath her. They headed toward the forest, Daria's heartbeat rising along with the elevation. The dogs raced ahead, disappearing into the trees. Jamie pushed his horse to a trot, pulling ahead of Daria, and followed the dogs into the forest as if the bloody sun were shining overhead. Daria's horse undoubtedly feared he would be left behind with her, for he quickened his pace and followed without hesitation.

The forest was as dark as a grave, and she couldn't make Jamie out. "I can't see," she called to him.

"Your horse will follow along," he said.

It was so still, so quiet. Daria was reminded of some of the things Bethia had said that she'd deemed nonsensical. Now, she couldn't quite dismiss the tales of faeries and witches roaming about the woods, and a shiver snaked down her spine. She would be more comfortable if she heard Jamie speak. "How is it that your horse can make his way?"

"He has walked along this path many times. He knows where he goes."

"I suppose the dogs know, too?" she asked into the dark, and got no response. A movement to her left — a rustle of leaves —

made her heart skip. She pulled her coat closer about her. "They must be clairvoyant, to see anything in these woods." Her horse jerked his head, giving it a shake, and Daria gasped. "Do you believe in ghosts?" she asked breathlessly as her thoughts began to slip, unguarded, off her tongue. "I knew a girl once who was quite keen to tell ghost tales."

"I suppose she told one or two that took place in dark woods, aye?"

Daria shivered and looked up at the scrap of sky she could see over the treetops. "Bethia says there are faeries and witches in these woods. I don't believe in witches and faeries." At least, she hadn't before she had come to Scotland. "Do you?"

"I'd no' be surprised by anything in these woods."

That gave her no comfort at all. "Dear God," she muttered. She swore she heard Jamie's low chuckle.

They moved steadily upward until at last they cleared the trees and the dark shadows. Daria was pleased to see the sky was beginning to pinken; there was a soft glow behind the hills to the east. She saw a crumbling cairn, the sort that popped up around the rural English countryside. Jamie turned west at the cairn and they began to go down. In the distance, Daria could see the glint of a river. As the sun rose, they rode beneath limbs of junipers and firs, past stands of yew so thick she couldn't see through them. Daria felt foolish for being so fearful. She felt even more foolish for not having appreciated the beauty of the land when she'd first come to Scotland. For finding everything unrefined and coarse by English standards. This was not unrefined or coarse. This was undiluted beauty.

They reached the path that ran parallel to the river. Fresh prints indicated deer had recently wandered through. The dogs had disappeared; she heard Anlan's bark and guessed that he had chased after a hare. The path bent around an outcropping of rock and when they rounded it, the river was there before them, the sound of it soothing in the morning mist.

At the water's edge, Jamie leapt off his horse quite agilely for a man shot only a short time ago. He helped Daria down, then slapped the rump of her horse, sending him down to the river's edge to drink.

Daria took a moment to shake out her legs, which were a bit numb from riding astride. She put her hands on her back to stretch it and looked around her. "It's indescribably lovely," she said, lifting her face to the morning sun, which was beginning to break through the veil of mist that blanketed the trees.

"Aye," Jamie agreed. He walked down a footpath and disappeared into the trees; a moment later, he emerged carrying a fishing pole and a small, enclosed basket.

"What is that?" Daria asked.

"A fishing pole."

"Yes, but . . . where did you find it? Why do you have it?"

He chuckled as he reached into his pocket and withdrew something that looked like feathers. "Because I am going to fish." He walked to his horse and opened one of his saddlebags.

"Here? Now?" Daria exclaimed. "But I thought we were going to Mamic's!"

"*Diah,* we are, in time." From the bag he withdrew a pair of boot coverings that Daria had seen men in England wear when they went hunting or fishing. He eased himself down onto a rock and put them on as Daria stared at him in disbelief.

He smiled. "You will allow me this pleasure, aye? Duff doesna care for it and has the vexing habit of hurrying me along."

"What am I to do while you fish?"

"You have a peculiar habit of inquiring what you ought to be about." He stood up, hoisted the basket over one shoulder, and grinned at her. "Do whatever you like." With that, he started down to the water's edge, wading out until he was standing knee-deep. The bottom of his kilt floated around him as he fit the feather on the end of the fishing line. He then unreeled the line and cast it before him in one fluid motion.

Daria sat on a flat rock beside the river and pulled her legs up to her chest, wrapping her arms around them, watching as he slowly reeled the line in and cast it again. She scarcely knew a thing about fishing, but he made it look artful. He cast the line as if he were painting, then adjusted his hold of the rod to fit the flow of the river. He looked strong and full of vitality, reeling in one fish, then another, putting them in the basket on his back.

It was a peaceful, blissful morning. Daria could imagine herself here, on this rock, painting or reading. She could imagine sun-filled days watching Jamie fish and feeling the warmth of the rising sun on her face and shoulders.

Then she imagined him here with Isabella sitting on that very rock. A slight shudder of revulsion went through her. *He loves her,* she reminded herself.

She pushed it out of her mind and looked

up. There was something magical about the Highlands that she was beginning to appreciate. Not in the way Bethia explained it, but in the sense that it felt good in her soul. Why would anyone leave it if they were born and reared here? "Why are Scotsmen leaving the hills?" she abruptly asked.

Jamie did not take his gaze from the river. "It's complicated."

"Contrary to what you and Lady Ann seem to believe, I am not incapable of understanding complicated matters."

He glanced at her with a smile. "Aye, that I know, lass. Here it is: In the last decades, the Highlanders' livelihood has been cattle and what few crops we might grow, aye? But times have been hard, so land has been sold to enterprising men who put sheep on the land. Sheep need quite a lot of room for grazing and encroach on the land available to cattle. But it's more than that: they encroach on the Highland way of living.

"Some lairds have recognized the opportunity for becoming rich, and have forced their people off their lands against their will so that they might profit from the sheep. Englishmen — lords and rich traders — pay for land, too. The old ways are disappearing, along with families. And there are new opportunities in Glasgow and Edin-

281

burra and America, opportunities for work that is easier than working the land. Work that feeds a family. So, many Highlanders have taken those opportunities."

"That's what is happening with the Campbells?"

He cast his line again. "For some. I've done my best to give the clan a livelihood, yet some have sold to Murchison. Most of our people want to stay, and they will if I can find a way to keep them. It is a fact that the less land we have to produce a livelihood, the less we have in our coffers." He glanced over his shoulder at her. "The money your grandmamma took was to ensure there is food on their tables and roofs over their heads for as long as possible."

Daria felt her cheeks flush warm. She stood up from the rock, picked up a pebble, and threw it into the river, watching it skip twice before sinking. She suddenly remembered a sunny afternoon spent in Mamie's company, throwing rocks into a pond. *Throw them now, my love, for when you are a debutante, people will think it untoward behavior in a young lady.*

She shook her head against that memory. "Perhaps you might grow something," she suggested idly. "Something that might feed them and that you can sell, as well. Lord

282

Eberlin has begun to grow wheat at Tiber Park."

"Would that it were that easy," Jamie said. "There is no' enough arable land in these hills. Most of our holdings are hills or bog."

"There was a bog at Tiber Park. It took up quite a lot of acreage and he wanted it for crops, so he drained it. And now they grow grain there. It was all the talk for quite some time in Hadley Green. No one believed it could be done."

"How did he drain it?" Jamie asked curiously.

Daria shrugged as she picked up another rock. "I don't know precisely how, but they bored a lot of very deep holes."

Jamie paused to look at her. "How large of an area?"

"Let me think — what shall I compare it to?" she asked thoughtfully. "Have you been to London?"

"Aye."

"Then you have surely seen Hyde Park. My guess is it is half the size of the park."

"As large as that, then." He turned his attention back to his line, slowly reeling it in, then casting it again.

Daria walked down the little footpath and squatted down to pick some late spring flowers. "Why were you in London, since you have no love for the English?"

"Aye, the direct result of having spent two years in Mayfair salons among fops and dandies." He winked at her.

"If you feel that way, then why were you there for two whole years?" she pressed him.

"After I completed my schooling at Oxford, my father thought I should live in London and learn the ways of the English."

She grinned. "A painful lesson, no doubt."

He laughed. "It was no' entirely painful. The women are bonny, I'll grant you. But my purpose there was to learn to guard myself — no' ingratiate myself."

Daria frowned lightly. "I don't think we're as bad as all that."

"No? If years of history between our nations doesna convince you, then perhaps you might expound on the virtues of the English for me. Begin with your suitors, if you please, those gentlemen with limp wrists and preening speech that make your heart flutter."

Was he mocking her? She bristled. "I have suitors, if that's what you mean."

Jamie's brows arched with surprise as he cast his line again. "I would never doubt it." His gaze flicked curiously over her. "It would seem I've touched a tender spot."

"You haven't."

"What is it, Daria? What makes you blush at the mention of suitors? Were you bitten by a scandal that has kept you from an offer?"

"Of course not! My behavior is always above reproach."

"Ah, above *reproach.*" Now he was teasing her. "Perhaps *that* is what keeps you from an offer."

It was too tender a subject for Daria to jest about.

When she didn't speak, Jamie smiled. "There now, lass. I meant no harm. I am well acquainted with debutantes, and gaining an offer from a suitable purse is their one goal in life, aye? Donna deny it."

"I won't deny it." She wouldn't try, because it was true. "What else is there for an unmarried woman?"

"Daria, you are bonny. And clever. I'd expect you would have any number of offers for your hand. If you haven't, then the English are even barmier than I'd imagined."

"I've not had *any* offers," she admitted and tossed the wildflowers into the river. "I'll tell you a secret: I am the last debutante in all of Hadley Green."

"The last?" he asked as he began to wade back to the shore.

"Yes, the *last,*" she said. "Everyone else is married but me. There is no one left to offer."

He paused below her in the river, the water rushing around his calves. "Why did no one offer for you?"

She would not confess her deeper, darker fears. The ones that whispered she wasn't comely, or interesting, or was offensive to men in ways she couldn't understand.

"My friend Charity says I haven't the right connections," she said. "It's all about that, you know — where you are seen and in whose company." She couldn't look him in the eye, as if he could see the real reason painted on her shirt. Or worse — he might point out another, even graver reason why. "Unfortunately, my parents are not willing to enter the fray of a London Season."

"No?"

"It's the botany," she said, although she really didn't believe that. She had tried to understand their reluctance to see her properly turned out, and had failed time and again. She'd had her debut, but even then, her Season in London had been cut painfully short by some emergency at home. "I think they are very pleased with their simple existence and they believe that I should be, too. But I can't be pleased with it. I can't live my whole life . . ."

She let her voice trail away, unwilling to say out loud that she could not be a spinster her whole life with nothing more than her parents' interest in orchids to divert her. No children! No family, no society.

"It's why I came to Scotland. I thought I would perish if I were forced to endure one more summer going from this tea to that ball and smiling for all the eligible men with the hope that one of them would offer. It made me feel useful to come and see about Mamie. It made me feel as if I had a purpose. As if my life had some meaning to someone."

"If you dislike your situation so," he said, propping one foot on the rock where Daria was standing, "find another occupation." He stepped up onto the rock, so close that they almost touched.

She snorted at his suggestion. "I am not allowed to have an *occupation,* Jamie. I am to receive callers and take tea and dine when asked. What else could I possibly be?"

"I donna know, *leannan,*" he said softly. "Whatever interests you. But I donna think life will come and rap on your door. You'd best go out and find it, aye?"

"It's not like that in England," she said, her frustration rising along with her pulse.

"That's not what is expected."

"Expected by whom?" he asked, his gaze on her mouth.

"Everyone!" she exclaimed, casting her arms wide.

A smile softened his face. "What do *you* expect?"

"Me?"

"Aye, you," he said, pushing her braid over her shoulder. "What do you expect for yourself?" He put his hand on the side of her face. "I've watched you befriend a boy who canna hear, a man who canna speak. You found a wife for Dougal, and you have endured captivity with grace and humor, insisting that you be allowed into our society. So why, in England, do you sit about and wait for a man to claim you? Make your own way, Daria."

Her heart whispered, *Claim me,* but she folded her arms. "What are you suggesting?" she asked quietly. "That I not marry?"

"Ach, I didna say that, did I?" he asked with a grin. "But I would no' care to see you wait like a lamb for someone, anyone, to find you and know what treasure he holds. Leap, lass. You'll either fall or fly, but if you donna leap, you will waste your time on this earth. Be brave, Daria. Be courageous."

Be brave. It was what she longed to be, and in that moment, with his hazel gaze staring into hers, Daria took his advice to heart. She suddenly rose up and pressed her lips to his, shaping them around his, softly biting his bottom lip. She was brave. She was courageous! And when Jamie responded with what sounded like a growl, she was flying.

He dropped his fishing rod and basket and grabbed her in a tight embrace, returning her kiss with an ardor that surprised and aroused her. A tide of scorching pleasure rose up in her; her mind suddenly flooded with images of him lying naked in her grandmother's house, of that sultry, languid kiss when he'd been half out of his mind.

She threw her arms around his neck and pushed her hands through his hair, causing his hat to fall. He eagerly delved into her mouth, his breath mingling with hers, sending fire racing through her veins. He cupped her face, angling it so that he could deepen the kiss, keeping her anchored to him and the evidence of his arousal.

Daria pressed into him, her breasts against his chest. Jamie suddenly lifted her from her feet and whirled her around, putting her back against a tree and crushing into her, his hips moving seductively against her.

She slid her hands down his hard chest, her hips pushing back against his hardness.

She cared for nothing but the boundless pleasure of that kiss, that arousal of her senses to heights she had never before experienced. He dropped his hand to her waist, spanning her ribs, then sliding up to the soft mound of her breast that filled his palm. His fingers dipped into her shirt, grazing her nipples and sliding into the warmth of her cleavage a moment before he dragged his mouth from hers and dipped down. Swiftly undoing some buttons, he then pulled her breast into his mouth.

Daria gasped at the extraordinary sensation, rising up, pushing into his mouth. He teased her rigid nipple with his tongue and his teeth, sucking and nipping at her as his hands slid down her body, between her legs, driving her past rational thought, past the point of actually breathing.

Then a distant sound suddenly drew Daria back to the present. *Voices.* "Jamie," she whispered, and pushed his head away from her breast. She could hardly hear through her labored breathing.

"Wha—"

Daria quickly pressed her hand to his mouth. Jamie let go of her then, turning to survey the area around them as she quickly straightened her clothing. She was aching for him, her body quivering with unholy desire . . . but also with fear. Someone or something was out there.

She heard it again.

So did he. Jamie held out his hand to her, indicating she should stay where she was, and moved quickly down the path.

But Daria had no intention of being left behind for the faeries and witches to find her. She scurried after him.

He'd climbed up to an outcrop and was lying on his belly. When Daria scrambled up beside him Jamie started and pulled her down, crushing her into his side, his hand over her mouth.

"Uist," he whispered. *"No' a word."*

Daria nodded. He removed his hand from her mouth but kept his arm hooked around her.

Below them was a gorge, and she saw a man on horseback and Mamie standing beside him. *Mamie!* Before Daria could gasp, Jamie quickly clamped his hand over her mouth again, drawing her even more tightly into his side.

Mamie and the man were having an animated conversation, judging from the way her hands flew and the rise and fall of her voice. Daria couldn't tell what she was saying. The well-fed man leaned over his saddle and said something that made Mamie drop her hands and glare at him. Mamie said something else and then whirled about, her cloak flying out behind her as she began to march down the rocky path to the river.

The man watched her go, then slowly turned his horse about. As he did so, he suddenly looked up to where Daria and Jamie were hiding and paused. It seemed to Daria as if he were looking directly at them. Neither she nor Jamie moved.

The tense moment passed. The man turned his attention to the path and spurred his horse, moving up the gorge and disappearing around a stand of trees.

When he had gone, Jamie grabbed Daria's hand and they flew down the hill and up the path. They reached the horses just as Mamie appeared on the path before them.

Mamie cried out in fright, clamping her hand over her heart. "Who's there?" Then she suddenly dropped her hand. *"Daria?"*

EIGHTEEN

"Mamie!" Daria said breathlessly, stepping forward. "What are you doing here? We were just on our way to see you."

"I . . . I was having a walkabout," the old woman said nervously as she eyed Jamie.

"Mrs. Moss," he said, giving her a curt nod.

"You look to have recovered well," she said, her gaze flicking over him.

"Aye, I have. Surprised, are you?"

"Mamie," Daria said, moving between her and Jamie, "how do you fare? I've been so worried about you."

"Me? Oh, my darling, it is I who have worried for *you*. Have they treated you well? Have they fed you, given you a proper place to sleep?"

A proper place? Jamie refrained from pointing out to the old witch that the accommodations at Dundavie were far superior to any she had offered.

"Yes, I have been treated very well. Did you not receive my letter?"

Mrs. Moss blinked. "I did!" she said, as if just remembering it. "Yes, yes I did."

Daria looked perplexed. "Then why did you not send a note in reply?"

"That's very simple, darling," she said as she fidgeted with her cloak. "I haven't pencil or paper. And I thought the money would come soon enough, and you'd be back. Why are you dressed in that fashion?"

Daria glanced down, apparently having forgotten she was wearing pantaloons.

The old woman glared at Jamie. "What have you done? Why is she made to go about in this manner?"

"I am dressed this way for riding," Daria said. "It's a treacherous path over the hills and I couldn't manage it sidesaddle."

But Mrs. Moss was still glaring at Jamie. He returned her look with an impatient one of his own. "Once again, Mrs. Moss, you seem to think I am the one who means harm, when all the evidence points to the contrary."

"Shall we go on to your cottage?" Daria said quickly. "The laird has brought you some fish."

Jamie jerked his gaze to Daria; she smiled at him, her hand subtly touching his. He could see what she was about — she would tread carefully to tease something out of the old bag of bones. But give away his fish? He looked at the basket he'd left on the river's edge and sighed.

"I don't need fish," Mrs. Moss said ungratefully. "I need flour. I've no money for flour."

"But . . . I brought you a banknote from my father," Daria said.

"Times are hard, Daria. A coin doesn't go as far as it once did."

"Let us have some tea and talk a bit, shall we?" Daria gently suggested.

"All right, I suppose." Mrs. Moss ran a hand over her unruly hair. She sounded unhappy at the prospect of receiving them but walked on, her old boots striking loudly against the rocks on the path. Daria exchanged a look with Jamie as she gathered her horse's reins and walked alongside her grandmother.

Jamie returned the fishing gear to the clan's hiding place, then whistled for Niall and followed behind them, his mood effectively darkened.

At first glance the cottage appeared just as it had the week he'd been practically entombed here. But as Jamie dipped his head to step inside, something felt different. He couldn't put his finger on what it was.

Daria had removed her coat and was helping the witch put a pot over the fire, asking questions. The sight of her derriere in the pantaloons distracted Jamie so much, it was a feat of mental strength to keep his thoughts on Mrs. Moss and the strange goings-on.

"Here, then, the water is hot," Mrs. Moss said when the water had boiled. "Let's drink up, shall we? I haven't much time — I am to Nairn this afternoon."

"What?" Daria said, startled. "Why?"

Mrs. Moss shrugged as she placed three biscuits on a chipped plate and set it in the middle of the table. "I have things to do."

"But . . ." Daria leaned across the table in an effort to meet her grandmother's gaze. "But I was taken away from here a fortnight ago against my will, Mamie. I should think you would want to spend as much time in my company as possible."

"Well, I do, dearest, I do! But I assume he'll want to take you back. Where is the fish?" she asked suddenly.

"Outside," Daria said.

"I should clean it before I go," Mrs. Moss said, wiping her hands on her apron.

Daria stared at her grandmother. So did

Jamie. The old woman was strangely distracted, even more anxious than before. And something kept her from looking her granddaughter in the eye.

"I'll get the fish," Daria said, and stood from the table, her head down, her step heavy.

In an effort to avoid conversation, Jamie looked away from Mrs. Moss, to the seating area adjoining the kitchen, and suddenly realized what was missing: the clock. That big, overdone, incessant tick-tock of a fancy cuckoo clock she had kept.

Daria stepped back inside with the basket of fish. "The Brodie boys won't bring the supplies you need?" she asked.

"No. They are . . . engaged in other things. Busy, busy." Mrs. Moss suddenly looked at Jamie. "I hope you have taken the precaution of having a proper chaperone while in my granddaughter's company."

Jamie's brows rose. "Do you think the presence of a chaperone will somehow mitigate the fact that she was carted out of here as ransom against the thousand pounds you stole, then?"

"Mind you keep to yourself, Daria," Mrs. Moss said, wagging a finger at her and ignoring Jamie's valid point. "Do not befriend the Campbells. They would as soon hang you as feed you. Don't forget it."

"That's not true," Daria said evenly.

"They've convinced you, have they?" Mrs. Moss scoffed. "This is the Highlands, Daria. It's naught but a lot of hills and rocks for savages to hide in."

Jamie felt his temper rising. He was trying to remain respectful of the woman, but she made it bloody difficult.

"If that is what you believe, then why were you talking to the man on horseback, Mamie?" Daria blurted.

The question startled the old woman badly; she turned abruptly and collided with the table, knocking a cup over and spilling tea across the surface. "Look what you have made me do!" she said angrily, and used the tip of her apron to clean the spill.

But Daria reached across and caught her hand, forcing Mrs. Moss to look at her. "I am worried unto death about you, Mamie. You don't seem yourself. You say things that make no sense. Your conversation with the man on horseback did not seem pleasant, and you are clearly distressed. How can I not be concerned for you?"

"You have no idea what you are saying," the woman said, jerking free of Daria's grasp. "There is nothing wrong with me. And that man . . . he was — he was asking for directions —"

"No more falsehoods, Mamie. He wasn't asking for directions. You were arguing with him."

Mamie pressed her lips together for a long moment, then admitted, "All right. Yes, we were arguing." She resumed mopping up the spill. "He is a stubborn old man. I've run across him before and he does not listen to reason."

"Why must you reason with him? Who is he? What is his name?"

"I haven't the slightest idea what his name is. He's but another savage that lives in these hills," she said with a dismissive flick of her wrist.

The kitchen shelf, Jamie noticed, was also bare. There were no china plates, no crystal wineglasses. And on the mantel above the fireplace, no silver candlesticks. It looked as if she had packed away anything of value.

"What happened to your clock?" he asked.

Her back to him, Mrs. Moss stilled. "It broke."

"I've a man who might fix it. Ned Campbell is as good with his hands as anyone I've known —"

"It is beyond repair," she said shortly.

"Allow me a wee peek —"

"I sold it!" she snapped. "I sold it to a

299

peddler for food! I don't live in a castle, Mr. Campbell; I am forced to barter clocks for food!"

"But, Mamie, Papa sent you ample —"

Mrs. Moss suddenly whirled about and glared at both of them. "You obviously do not wish to have tea. I ask you, Campbell, do you intend to leave my granddaughter with me?"

"No' till the ransom is paid," he said curtly.

"Well, I don't have it. And I should like to be on my way to Nairn, if you please, so if you don't mind?"

Daria looked shocked and wounded, and Jamie could scarcely blame her. He put his hand on her elbow, but Daria shook him off.

"Mamie, *please* let me *help* you."

And just like that, Mrs. Moss suddenly softened. She smiled sadly and cupped Daria's face in her hand. "My lovely girl," she said fondly. "I do so want you home; you must know that I do. But what I need from you now is to keep yourself well and chaste until the ransom is come. I have every faith that your father will arrive shortly and we will end this ugly business, and perhaps then, perhaps . . . well. In the meantime, I will not have you fretting about

your old grandmother. I am quite all right."
She smiled as she patted Daria's cheek, then
picked up a canvas bag.

"That's it?" Daria asked incredulously.
"That's all you will say?"

"I've said all there is to say, darling."
Looking much older, Mrs. Moss smiled
sadly at Daria and left the cottage.

Daria was speechless. She stood staring at
the open door. When she couldn't see her
grandmother anymore, she turned big
brown eyes to Jamie, blinking back tears. It
pained him to see her hurt, and he put his
arm around her shoulders. "Donna cry."

She sagged into his side, burying her face
in his chest. "She's lost her mind, and I
don't know what to do."

"Aye, she has," he agreed. "Or she is trying very hard to hide something. Here now,"
he said, slipping two fingers under her chin,
forcing her to look up at him. "Let her go
to Nairn, and let us think on how we might
discover what she is hiding."

She nodded, then stepped back and wiped
her eyes. "I *will* discover what she is about,"
she said determinedly. Then she peeked up
at him. "How will I do that?"

Jamie smiled. "First, I'll have a man watch
her, aye? Second, I'll have another man find
the gentleman she spoke to this morn.

Perhaps he might shed some light."

"Yes. Thank you, Jamie," Daria said. "That was no casual encounter. Did you recognize him?"

"No." It surprised him. He knew most men around here, and if he didn't know them, he could identify them by their plaids. But that man was not wearing a plaid. "I'll find him, Daria. And I will see that your grandmamma doesna come to harm."

She smiled gratefully. "Thank you."

He offered his hand to her. "Come, lass."

She slipped her hand into his, allowing him to lead her out of the cottage.

NINETEEN

Somewhere on the road to Dundavie, the dogs disappeared, racing into the forest after prey only they could smell. Their progress was slow, and Jamie had to turn about from time to time to reassure himself that Daria followed. The young woman who had nattered on this morning was silent, lost in thought this afternoon.

At the top of the hill, near the cairn, he drew Niall to a halt and dismounted. Only then did Daria seem to notice him. "I am famished," he said, and took the bundle Young John had given him from the back of his horse. "Are you hungry?"

"A little," she agreed, and slid off her horse.

She followed him up the hill to a flat, grassy hollow between two large, rocky knolls. A lone rowan tree provided a bit of shade, and Jamie spread the cloth open there to find cheese, dried meats, bread, and berries that had stained the cloth blue.

Daria stood looking out over the hills below them. Tendrils of rich gold hair danced around her face on the afternoon breeze. He could picture her looking out over this vista every day, taking stock of the changing landscape. The thought startled him — he'd not thought of her at all past the ransom.

"I think you are right," she said, as if they had been talking. "She is hiding something."

"Aye."

"I am determined not to mope, Jamie. My parents will soon arrive, and together, we will discover what it is she hides." She dropped her arms and looked at him as if she expected him to argue.

He did not. "Come and eat something."

Daria walked over, then knelt to examine the contents of the cloth. "Is it a picnic?" she asked, and made a sound of delight. "Berries!" She popped one in her mouth.

Jamie stretched out on his good side and propped himself up on one elbow. He opened the collar of his shirt, then helped himself to some dried meat. "I'd wager you've no' picnicked like this before, aye?" he asked, glad to change the mood.

"Never." She reached for some cheese. "In England, if one attends a picnic, there are servants to put up the tents and tables and to serve." She laughed softly and put another couple berries into her mouth. "It seems so pretentious now. I think all of England should be made to picnic precisely like this, out in the open, without tent or servant or even utensil to help them."

"Perhaps you will be the one to introduce all of England to the Highland picnic when you return."

"I shall be in high demand, I'm sure." Daria laughed again, then eased down on her side, facing him. "Perhaps you might try the English way of picnicking," she suggested, smiling impishly. "One never knows — it might improve *your* chance of matrimony," she added coyly, and popped another berry into her mouth. "Ah, but yours is all but finalized."

He smiled at her blatant attempt to ask him.

Daria examined the dried meat. "Do you miss your fiancée?" she asked casually.

"Isabella?" He thought about her. Or rather, he thought about the recent blows to the Campbell coffers. There was no denying that a union between them was the easiest way to keep intact the little corner of the world they'd inhabited for more than two hundred years.

But surely it meant more to him than that — he'd been set to marry her, by God. He'd been genuinely fond of Isabella, had he not? Did he not miss her company, if only a little, even now? "A wee bit, aye," he admitted.

Daria dropped her gaze. "What is she like?"

He found the question strangely discomforting. Isabella was everything a man in his position might have hoped for. She was beautiful. She was charming and clever and knew how to manage a very large house. She was the daughter of the Brodie laird, the equivalent of a Scottish princess. She had seemed to care for him — and yet, there was something about Isabella that seemed to pale compared to Daria. She didn't have that same quality of being that Daria seemed to possess — a lightness about her, an ability to greet any situation with charm and grace. Daria was like summer: light, air, warmth.

He could not say the same for Isabella.

That he was even thinking such things about the wee English rose was most disconcerting. It was imprudent, dangerous, and unwise. His fate, his destiny, was Dundavie, and he had a duty to maintain the clan. A dalliance with an English rose would be nothing short of disastrous. Yet he could not seem to think of anything else. She was here before him, her countenance bright and warm, her body a man's fantasy.

"Hmm. You hesitate," Daria said lightly. "I think you do not care to tell me that she has a wart on the end of her nose and eats puppies in her soup."

He grinned. "No warts, no, but I canna vouch for the puppies."

Daria laughed.

Jamie sobered. "In truth, Isabella is bonny and kind."

"Ooh, *bonny* and *kind,*" Daria said with mock gravitas. "It is a wonder that an entire continent of gentlemen have not offered for her."

"What would you have me say?"

"Truly, must I tell you? You were to marry her, Jamie Campbell! Did you not love her? If you did, I think you would say that she is beautiful beyond compare, and that her smile lights the entire northern sky, and her eyes are the source of great poetry, and her lips are the pillows on which yours might rest for an eternity."

He arched a brow in surprise. "I should have said all of that?"

"You loved her, did you not?" Daria asked again, looking him directly in the eye.

"Aye." At least he hoped that he had, in

307

some way.

He noticed Daria's smile was not as bright as it had been, and he dipped his head to catch her eye.

But Daria did not allow her feelings to show. She smiled. "Mark me, Laird, one day you will thank me for my tutelage in love, in dancing, and in managing your vast estate," she said gaily. "I cannot bear to think what you will do without me when I am ransomed."

"I donna know," he said softly. "Walk about in a stupor, I should think. Drink too much of the barley-bree to ease my pain."

She gave him a playful shove of his shoulder and then flopped onto her back, her arms folded beneath her head, her ankles crossed as she gazed up at the blue sky. "What *will* you do when I am gone? Who will play the pianoforte? Who will your dogs adore? What, in heaven's name, will Duffson do without me to follow about each day?"

She was smiling, but the questions made Jamie feel strangely empty. What *would* he do?

"I suppose you shall go about the business of Dundavie," she mused. "You will no doubt marry Isabella, and you will produce the heirs all the Campbells so desperately want, and you will find Geordie a wife, and you will drain your bogs and plant your grains and chase sheep from your fields . . ."

It sounded very tedious to him in that moment. But it was close to the truth — he had a duty to do all of those things, and sooner rather than later. Still, he didn't like to think about it. "And what of you, *leannan*? What will you do when you are properly ransomed?"

"I imagine I shall attend teas and balls, waiting for something exciting to happen and for a gentleman to overlook my dubious summer and offer for my hand." She suddenly lifted up, propping herself up on her elbows, and looked down the length of her body. "I quite like pantaloons," she said, deliberately changing the subject.

He laughed. "I quite like them on you."

"Do you?" she asked, seeming pleased by it as she turned a leg to view it fully.

"Aye. Very much."

She glanced at him with a sunny smile of pleasure, and suddenly something snapped. Apart or together, Jamie wasn't certain, but he could *feel* it, physically feel the draw between them. The moment was charged, full of unspoken questions and possibilities that rose up like a sea around them.

Daria rolled onto her side to face him.

"You are so very different from any gentleman I have ever known," she said softly. "I will truly miss you when I am gone."

That feeling began to pull at Jamie, dragging him down into a desire so great it pulsed in his veins. "I shall miss you as well."

"Will you truly?" she murmured. Her gaze moved to the open collar of his shirt. "You wouldn't say that merely to soothe my wounded pride, would you?"

He leaned forward, reached for the tail of her braid, and tugged her closer. "Never," he said low. "I will indeed and truly miss you, *leannan*."

"What does it mean, '*leannan*'?" she whispered.

"It means . . . sweetheart," he said, and kissed her.

Daria leaned into him, delicately cupping his jaw and sending a thousand tiny little flutters of pleasure through him. He forgot the food between them and wrapped his arm around her waist, rolling onto his back and bringing her with him. Daria wiggled out of her coat, then put her hands on his shoulders, her fingers scraping against the skin at his open collar, and kissed him back.

She was killing him, filling him with powerful desire, the need to feel her body beneath his, to enter her. With a low groan, he rolled again, putting Daria beneath him, and kissed the hollow of her throat, his lips feeling her sharp draw of breath, the slow release of it.

"*Diah,* Daria, you have captured me," he said roughly as he slid his mouth down her neck to her collarbone. "I donna know how you've done it, but you have captured me."

She grabbed his head, forced him to look up, and kissed him on the corner of his mouth. "You captured me first," she said, her voice seductively rough. "You capture me over again, every day."

This woman disarmed him as easily as four men at once. He wanted to feel her tongue against his. He wanted to feel her warm breath on his bare skin, to surround her body with his. He wanted to fill her up, to take her places she'd never been. He wanted to love her.

He wanted to *love* her.

He dipped his head again, his fingers fumbling with her shirt buttons, undoing them. Then he dipped his hand into her chemise and filled his hand with her breast.

Daria sighed longingly and dropped her head back as he pressed his lips to the succulent skin of her neck and kneaded her breast, rolling the tip between his fingers.

Then Daria — brave, courageous Daria

— pulled her shirt and chemise down from her breasts, exposing them to him. With a groan of longing, Jamie gazed down at the perfect orbs, her skin the color of clotted cream. He slid his hand to one, then took the other into his mouth.

A deep sigh of pleasure escaped her; she dug her fingers into his shoulders. She arched into him, her legs moving against his, pressing against his erection, sliding over it until he was aching with need. He slid his hand down her body, caressing the flare of her hip, her leg, and then sliding between her legs.

Daria gasped. She put an arm around his shoulders and found his mouth as he began to move his hand against her, stroking her through the buckskin.

Daria's breath quickened, warm and moist against his cheek. Jamie couldn't bear it; with his thumb he unbuttoned her trousers, then began to inch them down her body. She lifted her hips, helping him, kicking free of the buckskins when he pushed them down to her ankles.

Jamie was beyond rational thought. With his mouth and his hands, he slid down her body, leaving a hot, wet trail. He pushed her thighs apart, kissing first one, then the other. Daria's fingers sank into his hair, anchoring her. But when Jamie closed his lips around her sex, she made a strangled cry. Her legs squeezed against him, but Jamie hooked his hands around her legs and pulled them apart, and began to lave her with his tongue. Her taste and scent were arousing him to madness; her body seemed to throb against him, matching the beat of his own blood. He was adrift on a sea of physical sensation so sweet that a dragon couldn't have pulled him free. He covered her with his mouth, stroked her with the urgency he felt thrumming through him. She pushed against him yet held him tightly at the same time, writhing and gasping.

He felt her release shudder through her body, heard her soft cry of ecstasy, and felt something explode in him. It wasn't physical, although he craved that release like a drowning man craved air. It was something bigger than that, something in the center of him that made him feel tender and warm. Protective. Possessive. Light. *Free.*

He felt like summer.

He skimmed her breast, laid his palm against her heart, and felt its wild beating. She covered his hand with hers.

As the moments slipped by, Jamie became aware of how exposed they were. He shifted out from between her legs and smiled down

313

at her. Her hair had come undone from her braid and lay in a halo of disarray around her head. Her eyes were closed, and one arm lay limp across her middle.

And she was smiling.

Jamie picked up her coat, then leaned down to kiss her as he covered her with it. *"Maise,"* he said softly. "You are beautiful, lass."

She smiled wider, opened her eyes, and gently touched her fingers to his chin.

By the time Jamie had picked up their food, Daria had dressed, combed her hair with her fingers, and rebraided it. She looked a wee bit as if she'd tumbled down a mountainside. It was incredibly arousing.

She glanced at him shyly. "I must admit that I haven't the slightest idea what to say."

"Nor do I," he admitted. So many thoughts, so many strange feelings were rumbling through him that Jamie felt almost incapable of rational speech. He was cautious when it came to women, due to his position and the number of mothers who would like to see their daughters married to him, but this was different. Something had happened to him in the last hour that had never happened before, and he didn't know what it was.

Jamie retreated into his thoughts, choosing to say nothing of what had happened between them until he could sort it out. He held out his hand to her. "Come then, *leannan,* we've been gone too long, aye?"

She nodded and took his hand. He squeezed hers affectionately and slung the bundle of food over his shoulder as he led her back to the horses. When he'd secured their things to his saddle, he helped Daria up onto hers, then put his hand on her knee. He didn't want to leave. He didn't want to return to the reality of his life, which was beginning to seep back into his thoughts like a deep fog overtaking all the light. He would be perfectly content to spend the rest of his life on this grassy hill.

Daria leaned forward and smoothed her hand over the side of his head. "I will never forget you, Jamie Campbell. Not as long as I draw breath will I ever forget you."

Somehow, he managed to put himself on his horse. Somehow, he managed to direct Niall to the path, and saw that Daria followed.

But he wasn't really seeing. He was hearing those words over and over again in his head. *I will never forget you.*

That's not what he'd wanted to hear, not with her scent still surrounding him, the feel of her body still embedded in his skin. But damn the saints if he knew what he *had* wanted to hear her say.

He brooded about it all the way down the hills into Dundavie. Daria seemed not to take notice; she nattered incessantly on. He realized it was her way of putting aside what had happened, filling the air around them with words. She was enlightening him about something — her father's orchids, he thought — as they entered the bailey, but he was lost in his own thoughts, trying to sort out feelings that had sprung up from some hidden, unused ground. His own private bog, now drained, now ready to support new growth. He didn't even notice the others in the bailey — he could see only Daria, hear only his jumbled thoughts.

He dismounted, helped Daria down, and then stood there, his hand on her waist. "Daria," he said quietly, thinking of precisely how he would voice what he was feeling. "I —"

"Madainn feasgar math," he heard a familiar voice say, and it was only then that he noticed the people who had arrived at Dundavie.

Jamie turned his head and looked directly into a pair of green eyes. "Isabella."

TWENTY

Daria, I . . . what?

Daria wanted to catch his arm, twist him about, and hear him say what he was feeling. She wanted to believe it was something profound, something that would help her make sense of her whirlwind emotions. She hoped he would say that he, too, had fallen headlong off that windswept hill, and that, like her, he didn't know if he should stop his fall and claw his way back to where he'd been, or just keep falling.

Daria was still falling.

In the moments after the utterly glorious interlude with him on the hill, she'd seen the hunger in Jamie's eyes and she'd understood for the first time the power a woman held over a man. She'd felt gloriously wicked and desirable, almost giddy with a new sort of lightness.

But as they'd begun the trek to Dundavie, doubts had begun to creep into her

317

thoughts: doubts about what she'd done, doubts about where her morals had skipped off to and what might happen if she continued down this path. *Fall or fly?*

She had looked at Jamie ahead of her, his magnificently robust, utterly virile body. She had looked at the breadth of his muscled shoulders tapering into his lean waist, his plaid spread over strong thighs, and the desire that welled up in her made her dizzy. She craved more of what he'd shown her. She craved the feel of his body above hers, *in* hers.

Lord help her! She'd been so alarmed by her emotions that she'd chattered like a magpie all the way back to Dundavie, trying to force her thoughts down, to cover them up under an avalanche of words, to shut out the cacophony in her head.

And then, when they'd arrived at Dundavie, he'd helped her down, and looked at her with such intensity that she had felt her blood begin to swirl again, and he'd said, "Daria, I —"

But the moment had been stolen away by a beautiful copper-headed woman who spoke to him in rapid Gaelic, her gaze unwavering. She didn't even glance in Daria's direction. Daria knew who she was, and she watched her speak to Jamie briefly, then glide back to the group she'd obviously come with.

When Jamie looked back to Daria, his smile was a little sheepish and a little pained. It had seemed to her that he was eager to be away from her when he'd said, "There you are now, lass, returned to Dundavie. If you will excuse me, aye?" And he'd walked away, his long stride carrying him into the keep. Away from her.

But . . . Daria, I *what?*

Daria retreated to her rooms to stew in private. She barged into her suite, eager for solitude, and almost collided with Bethia, who was removing used linens from her room.

Bethia's gaze traveled down Daria, then up again. She arched one dark brow.

"Stand aside, Bethia, or I will put you aside."

Bethia stepped out of the way and Daria stalked past, shrugging out of her coat and tossing it onto the chaise.

"Have you had a fall, then?" Bethia asked, nodding to the back of Daria's trousers.

Yes. A fall from a very great height. "I have been in the forest," Daria said curtly. She stalked to the window and looked out. There was no one left in the bailey. It was as if the entire day had disappeared.

"You'll be wanting a bath," Bethia stated.

"Thank you. I do," Daria said coolly.

Bethia's second brow rose to meet the first. "Are you wroth?"

"Wroth? Why should I be wroth? No, Bethia, I am not. Not in the *least.*" She began to pull the shirt from her trousers, wanting out of those clothes, especially now with the image of Isabella, looking regal in her blue gown and matching cape, looming in her mind. "But I do not care to be paraded about all of Scotland in pantaloons."

"It's a wee bit too late for that, aye? Mark me, you'll be one of us 'ere you know it."

Daria stopped what she was doing and stared irritably at Bethia. "I will never be one of you, Bethia."

Bethia picked up Daria's coat. "I donna wish it, if that's what you think. I'm only the messenger."

"Do you want to know what *I* think? I think you hide behind that nonsense. Or you deliberately seek to vex me with it."

"I'll no' deny that," Bethia said with a shrug. "But no' in this. As I live and breathe, you will be one of us."

"Enough," Daria said wearily, and sank onto the chaise. It would be just her luck to become one of them and watch Jamie wed

Isabella.

"I'll send a lad up with water now, aye? You'll want your bath before the Brodies settle in."

"What do you mean?" Daria asked, startled.

"If the kitchen is to be believed, Miss Brodie has had a change of heart and wants the laird now. They've come to negotiate the dowry."

Daria's heart began to sink like a stone in a turbulent sea.

Bethia was watching her, but for once, she didn't appear to scarcely tolerate her. She looked as if she pitied her.

The stone that was Daria's heart disappeared into the dark depths of lost hopes. She could feel the blood draining from her face and glanced down to work the buttons of her pantaloons. She felt lightheaded, as if she had been turned round and round. "Good," she said at last. "Everyone at Dundavie wishes for an heir. Perhaps now you will all have one."

"Aye, we'll have one," Bethia said confidently as she walked to the door. "We'll have a stable of them, I'd wager." She walked out of the room.

"One day you will not be so bloody certain of everything, lass," Daria muttered, and fell onto the chaise. She stretched one leg out, closed her eyes, and thought back on her day. On her most glorious, stupendous day. She didn't wipe away the tear that fell from the corner of her eye. After all she'd endured without shedding any tears, she was entitled to at least one.

Jamie had believed there wasn't much that was worse than being shot, but right now, looking at Isabella, he'd prefer the lead to split his skin than have to endure her company.

She was as lovely as ever, her smile as luminous as he recalled. She was speaking to him in Gaelic, her voice melodious, in a way that would soothe anyone, particularly when she placed her slender hand on one's knee, as she had with him.

A month ago, Jamie might have been relieved at her change of heart. But now — today — he only felt oddly detached. "Have I understood you, then?" he asked when Isabella had finished what sounded like a carefully rehearsed speech. "You believe you made a mistake in crying off?"

"Aye, that is what I mean, darling. I was a wee bit hasty. I was distressed after that awful fight, and I thought . . . I thought that I was doing what I ought to do as a Brodie.

You understand."

He wasn't entirely certain that he did understand. He glanced down at her hand on his knee. "That was two months past, Isabella. Has it taken two months for you to realize your mistake?"

"No, Jamie. I understood it straightaway," she quietly admitted. "But it took me that long to overcome my pride." She smiled ruefully.

So did Jamie. He supposed he should have been happy at her change of heart, or at the very least, understanding of it. He guessed she would like him to take her in his arms and kiss her, tell her all was forgiven. He should have averred she was the best possible match for him for so many reasons and admitted that he still had feelings for her.

Yet he said or did none of those things. The only thing he felt with any conviction was cross. With Isabella. With the Brodies and Campbells in general.

Isabella had always been able to read him rather well, and she seemed to now. She leaned across his lap, her mouth next to his earlobe. "I've missed you so, Jamie," she whispered, and lightly bit his ear before fading back to smile at him.

Jamie didn't move.

Her green eyes searched his face for a moment, then she abruptly sank down onto her knees beside him. She covered his hand with hers and looked beseechingly at him. "I was a fool to believe you would forgive me, aye? But will you no' at least think on what I've said? Will you no' at least consider it?"

How could he deny her? He touched her face, recalling the moments he had spent in her company imagining a long and happy future with her. Imagining their children, their robust estates. He waited for the feeling to come to him again.

"I've missed you, Jamie. I *need* you."

The feeling still didn't come.

He wondered why, as he looked at her face, her smile. Her cool smile. *She is winter.* Cool and close and dark. "Aye, of course I will consider it, Isabella." He could see her disappointment, but she was too dignified to cry.

"It's all I might ask," she said, and pushed herself up. "I shall leave you now. Young John will show us to our rooms, will he not?" she asked, already moving to the door.

"Aye, he will."

She paused at the door and looked over her shoulder. She was smiling, but it was not a happy smile. "You should have a bath drawn, *mo ghraidh,*" she said as she walked out the door. "You smell of her."

TWENTY-ONE

Daria desperately needed someone to talk
to, someone who would understand and
counsel her on the wild emotions she was
experiencing — the pangs of regret, the
yearning for more, the need to name this
thing that filled her heart. Her euphoria had
completely dissipated, and in its place was
confusion, uncertainty. She despised that
feeling. Daria was generally confident and
intuitive, but tonight, she hardly knew
herself. Much less Jamie Campbell.

She dressed carefully for supper, unsure
of who might attend, certain it would be a
storm of people, of personalities, of confusion. She wore her best gown, cream and
gold silk and chiffon. She did her best with
her hair, wishing that she could do something more than a simple knot at her nape.
She donned a long strand of pearls and ear-
rings she had been given on the occasion of
her eighteenth birthday — which seemed a

lifetime ago now. Another world entirely. A less exciting, duller, colorless world. She pushed her feet into slippers encrusted with seed pearls, then viewed herself in the mirror.

She tried to imagine herself through Jamie's eyes. She tried to imagine how she looked beside the beautiful Isabella Brodie, with her auburn curls and striking green eyes. It was a bit like standing beside Charity, whose beauty illuminated an entire room. Sometimes Daria felt small and inconsequential beside Charity; she couldn't imagine how small she might feel next to Isabella.

Which was just as well, really. As soon as her parents or Charity came for her, she was bound for England, as she ought to be. And Jamie . . . Jamie would marry and bear many heirs, just as Bethia had said.

"Well then," she muttered to her reflection, "best get on with it. Sooner begun, sooner over." If there was one thing Daria still knew about herself, it was that she could walk into any room and make her way in it. But this would be the greatest test of all. For no Campbell, no English lord or lady, intimidated her quite like Isabella Brodie.

■ ■ ■ ■

Daria heard the voices coming from the great hall before she reached it. It sounded as if the entire population of Dundavie were within, and she slowed in trepidation. She heard only Gaelic being spoken, which reminded her that she was an outsider here. But it also propelled her forward. She needed to see the man who had fueled such deeply stirring emotions in her.

Be brave. Be courageous, her heart whispered.

Daria walked into the great hall and saw at least two dozen people within. No one noticed her. She saw many familiar faces: Robbie and Aileen. Geordie, seated with his slate in his lap. Uncle Hamish and Duff, who was dressed in a kilt and a dark wool coat. Jamie, standing a few inches taller than most, his dark hair brushed back, speaking to someone Daria couldn't see.

And, of course, Isabella.

Isabella spotted Daria at almost the same moment. The woman's gaze flicked over her, then Isabella turned her back and resumed her conversation with a gentleman.

Daria had been in too many ballrooms not to know when she'd been cut, no matter how subtly. And that had not been particularly subtle.

As there was no one to announce her, Daria debated how to enter the room. Then Jamie turned his head and saw her. When his gaze met hers, Daria's foolish heart fluttered like a little hummingbird. Was she mad, or did something spark between them? Had *he* felt it?

He walked toward her, his gaze on her. He was dressed formally in a black coat and white waistcoat, as stately as any English lord she'd ever seen. He was . . . magnetic. Heartachingly handsome. And Daria was aware of a ridiculously big smile on her face as he neared her.

He smiled, too, as he reached her. "Miss Babcock. Welcome."

Daria curtsied from unthinking habit. For some reason it made Jamie's smile broaden. He held out his hand. "Up, lass, before I begin to believe that, at long last, I've pushed you around the bend."

Daria put her hand into his, and Jamie squeezed it lightly as he lifted her up. His gaze slipped over her, lingering on the strand of pearls over her bosom. "How lovely you are."

Daria's heart rose to her throat.

He cocked his head to one side. "We've a

few guests this evening, aye?"

She nodded. She must have looked frightened, for he leaned in and murmured, *"Be brave."*

Daria couldn't help but smile. "I suppose that is your way of warning me."

"Perhaps a wee bit."

"Jamie, I —"

"Will you introduce us to your guest, Laird?"

Daria knew the lilting brogue before she even looked. She turned around to see the beauty standing before her, interrupting her moment with Jamie. Isabella was smiling — or at least attempting to pretend that she was.

"Of course," Jamie said. "Miss Daria Babcock, allow me to introduce Miss Isabella Brodie."

"A pleasure," Daria murmured, and dipped into another curtsy.

"No, the pleasure is mine, Miss Babcock." Isabella extended her hand to Daria. To be kissed? Daria took it and gave it a small shake.

"I've heard quite a lot about you, aye?" Isabella continued pleasantly.

Daria's gaze flew to Jamie, but Isabella laughed. "Not from the laird, Miss Babcock," she said, as if that were preposterous.

"From Robbie Campbell."

She meant that she had asked Robbie about her. That's what Daria would have done if the situation were reversed.

Isabella turned slightly and gestured to the three men with her. "May I introduce my father, Laird Brodie. My uncle, Seamus Brodie. And my cousin, Charles Brodie."

Daria greeted each gentleman as if she were in a receiving line — a slight incline of her head, a remark about the pleasure of making their acquaintance. Young John appeared at her elbow, carrying a tray with filled wineglasses. Grateful for the wine, she turned to take one. But when she turned back, Jamie had moved a few feet away, in conversation with one of the men accompanying Isabella and some other men she hadn't seen before. Isabella had shifted slightly, putting her back to Daria and herself between Jamie and Daria.

Daria sipped her wine, feeling so conspicuous standing there alone that she scarcely tasted it. A touch to her elbow almost sent her glass flying; she turned around to see Geordie.

"Geordie," she said in a release of her breath. "What have I done now? I've scarcely stepped foot inside the room, so I don't think I've had time to offend you."

He wrote something on his slate and handed it to Daria. *Look difernt.*

"Me?" she asked, meeting the hazel eyes that were the twins of Jamie's.

He nodded.

"I don't know what you mean. I am the same as I have been for more than a fortnight." She glanced up at him. "English."

Geordie smiled. He rubbed the slate clean with his arm and wrote again. *Bonny.*

Daria blinked up at him; he gave her a charmingly subtle wink. She smiled. "Geordie Campbell, are you attempting to flirt with me?" she whispered.

Geordie responded with a smile.

Young John rang a bell and announced that supper was served. Jamie glanced back at Daria — a fleeting look — and then offered his arm to Isabella to begin the procession. Of course he would lead her in; she was an honored guest. But Daria's heart sank nonetheless. She stood rooted as people began to file past her, following the Laird of Dundavie into the dining hall.

Remarkably, Geordie tucked his slate up under one arm and offered the other to her.

When Daria looked at him, he arched one brow, as if challenging her.

Daria put her hand on his arm. "I cannot say which of us has lost our mind, sir," she said, smiling, "but I cannot thank you enough."

They were the last to be seated, at the opposite end of the table from where Jamie sat with Isabella on his right. Daria told herself to look at Geordie. To remember that she would leave Dundavie very soon, and for God's sake, whatever she did, to put this afternoon firmly out of her mind.

There was quite a lot of talking throughout the meal — all in Gaelic, of course, and Daria was surprised to realize she had begun to pick up a few words here and there. It had also ceased sounding harsh to her. Jamie tried to converse in English, but the Brodies refused it, responding only in Gaelic.

Halfway through the meal, Geordie slid his slate across to Daria. *Donna lik er.*

Daria studied it a moment, wondering if he was instructing her or informing her. She looked up at Geordie. He nodded in Isabella's direction.

"What do you mean — you don't care for her?" she whispered.

He nodded, then gestured for his slate. He wiped it off and wrote, *evr.*

Why not? Isabella was a perfect match for the laird; even Daria could see that. She glanced down the table and started when her gaze met Isabella's. She quickly slid the slate back to Geordie.

"Miss Babcock, we were speaking of the great number of tenants leaving Scotland for Edinburra or beyond," Jamie said. He had finished his meal and was leaning back, his fingers drumming on the stem of his wineglass. "I told our guests that you had offered a solution."

She had no idea what he meant. "I have?"

He smiled. "Was it no' you who suggested we drain the bog and plant a crop?"

"Oh . . . yes," she admitted, noting the skeptical faces about her. "I am acquainted with a landowner who did that very thing in England. He increased his arable land."

One of the Brodies snickered and said something that had several of them chuckling.

Lord, she felt like a fool, sitting here as if she knew what she was talking about. Had she ever spent a more wretched evening? The infamous supper party at Rochfeld ranked high on her list of wretched evenings, but even suffering the attentions of the drunken Lord Horncastle wasn't as vexing as this.

Time was standing still by the time the meal was concluded and the party adjourned to the great hall. Daria dawdled, hoping to make an unnoticed escape. She pretended to fuss with the clasp of her bracelet and trailed behind the group, lingering at the door.

"Miss Babcock?" Jamie said, turning about as his guests crossed the hall into the great room.

She glanced down the hall. If only she had started in that direction, she might have pretended not to hear him. But he was already walking toward her. Daria said, "Thank you for supper, but if you will excuse me —"

"You donna intend to leave us yet. I had high hopes that you might play again, aye?"

Her heart seized. She couldn't imagine anything more torturous than having to play the pianoforte with Isabella Brodie in the room. "Oh," she said, wincing a little. "I, ah . . . I am feeling a bit —"

"Please, Miss Babcock," Aileen said, suddenly appearing at Jamie's right. "The waltz." She smiled. *Warmly.* Daria had never seen Aileen smile before this moment. "Please," she said again.

Behind her, Geordie and Robbie paused, looking back at Daria.

"Laird Brodie is quite good with the flute. He will accompany you," Jamie said. "It would be a great pleasure for all if you would indulge us."

Feeling trapped, Daria looked around at the Campbells, all of them looking at her hopefully. She could just imagine it — Jamie teaching Isabella the waltz; her having to watch them over the top of the pianoforte.

Geordie thrust his slate before her face. *Plees.*

"Aren't you all quite persuasive." She sighed. "Very well."

"Thank you, Daria," Aileen said. It was the first time she'd ever said Daria's name. Moreover, she sounded truly grateful.

Daria steeled herself and allowed the Campbells to lead her into the great hall, where someone had moved the pianoforte. Aileen hurried ahead, presumably telling them all that there would be dancing.

The Brodies eyed Daria curiously, but someone must have told them about the music, for one of them did indeed produce a flute.

Daria sat down at the pianoforte. She looked at the people assembled, ignored the butterflies in her belly, and began to play a waltz.

Aileen and Robbie were quick to dance, moving with surprising grace and ease around the room. She expected Jamie to stand before Isabella and bow deeply, offering his hand, so she was astounded to see Geordie grab Isabella and begin to move slowly with her around the room. Several others began to waltz, too, to her surprise. The dance was apparently spreading across Dundavie, and she couldn't help a small smile.

The man with the flute quickly picked up the harmony to Daria's song, and before long, everyone was dancing and laughing. When she finished each song, Daria tried to pause, but the people pushed her along. After three songs, a man appeared with a fiddle. There was quite a lot of talk between him and the flute player, and then both looked at her expectantly. "Go on, then, lass," Laird Brodie said. "We'll follow your lead, aye?"

They were remarkable musicians, really. Daria's repertoire consisted of five or six songs, and the gentlemen were gifted enough that they could change them all with tempo and harmony. After a time, though, Daria began to grow weary of playing. Her fingers ached; she wasn't accustomed to playing for so long.

At the conclusion of the fifth song — played for the third time — Daria put her hands in her lap, stretching her fingers.

Jamie walked toward her. "You deserve a rest."

"Thank you!" she exclaimed. "I fear my fingers will fall off."

"Besides, you never taught me," he said.

"Taught you?"

"To dance, lass. Look at them all, waltzing. And here sits their laird, only recently off the cane."

She'd seen him dancing while she played, and she eyed him suspiciously. "You wish me to teach you to waltz."

"Aye."

"In front of them," she said, nodding surreptitiously to the crowd.

"Before all of them, aye." He winked. "Teach this laird to dance. I command it." His eyes were sparkling with gaiety, impossible to resist.

"Well. If you *command* it." She smiled.

Jamie gestured for Malcolm Brodie to begin playing anew, then offered his arm to Daria. As he escorted her onto the dance floor, she was aware that everyone was watching them. In England she would have relished the attention, but here she felt conspicuous.

"Well, then?" Jamie asked.

Daria drew a breath and looked him in the eye. "You should place your hand on

338

my back."

He stepped closer and slipped his arm around her back. "There?" he asked, his hand just above her hip.

"Quite a bit higher."

He smiled. But instead of moving his hand up her back, he pulled her closer, and gazed down at her with those shining hazel eyes. "There?"

Daria swallowed. "Not there, really, but we'll make do."

His smile deepened.

She held out her arm. "You should hold my hand."

He put his hand beneath her elbow, then slowly slid it down her arm to her hand, closing his fingers tightly and possessively around hers.

Daria's heart was beating so rapidly, she feared she might take wing. She put her hand on his shoulder. "All right, then, you will begin to your left. *One* two three," she counted softly.

He was still smiling as he moved to his left uncertainly, and then back again as Daria instructed. He picked up the dance quite easily. Before she knew it, he was moving her about, his lead firm and sure, then spinning her this way and that. He moved so well that Daria began to feel she was dancing on air. The evening slipped away, and she was aware of only the flute, and Jamie. His eyes never left her, his gaze fixed on her face.

"You've waltzed before," she said.

He laughed and spun her about. "Perhaps once or twice."

"Where? Did Geordie teach you?"

"Geordie!" He laughed roundly at that. "No, I learned in London."

"Why didn't you say so?" she laughingly demanded as he twirled her again.

"What, and miss the experience of having the last debutante of Hadley Green instruct me? I'm no' a fool." He spun her to the right, pulling her closer. "You are a very entertaining young woman."

"Because I play the pianoforte? There are squads of debutantes who do."

"I mean *you*, Daria."

"Even though I am English?" she asked.

"Even though."

She smiled up at him. "I think, Laird Campbell, that you hold England in higher regard than you let on."

He shook his head and dipped his gaze to her décolletage. "There is only one I hold in high regard, aye?"

"Then you should reduce my ransom."

He twirled her to the left. "Never."

Daria laughed. "I'd be quite disappointed if you did."

The flute finally stopped, and a smattering of applause went up around them. Jamie's hands slid from her body and Daria reluctantly dropped her hands as well. She was still admiring his handsome face when she became aware of someone beside her. She turned around and looked into green eyes.

"You dance very well indeed, Laird," Isabella said.

Jamie inclined his head in response.

"I beg your pardon, I donna mean to interrupt," she said, then spoke to him in Gaelic.

The smile bled from Jamie's face. He looked at Daria. "Excuse me, please," he said, and moved away.

Daria looked at Isabella.

Isabella smiled thinly. "It is his uncle Hamish. There is a wee bit of trouble."

"Ah." Daria stood restlessly, debating how exactly to make her escape.

"A wee bit of barley-bree, Miss Babcock?" Isabella gestured graciously to the sideboard and touched Daria's elbow lightly.

They moved to the sideboard, where Isabella instructed a footman to pour. She handed Daria a tot, touched her own lightly to Daria's, then sipped. "You'll be away to England soon, I suppose."

Daria wasn't entirely certain how to respond. She glanced down at the amber liquid.

"Jamie's told me about the ransom," Isabella added.

Jamie. They were close, these two. "Yes." Daria looked up. "Perhaps you know my grandmother. She lives on the Brodie lands."

Isabella shook her head. "No." She smiled. "There are so many Brodies, aye?"

"Yes, that is true," Daria said absently. Every time she looked at Isabella's green eyes, she imagined Jamie looking into them. She glanced around, hoping to find a friendly face, someone who might rescue her.

"I think the Campbells will miss you when you've gone. They all seem quite taken with you."

That certainly caught Daria's attention. "Me?"

"Aye, you," Isabella said. Her gaze drifted over Daria. "You're different than we are, are you no'? Rather exotic."

"Me?" Daria said again, stunned by what Isabella was saying.

"In the Highlands, life is simple compared

to in England, I think. It's a wee circle. One is born into the clan, one marries into the clan, one bears children for the clan, one grows old with the clan. Our families are centuries old, aye? It's right hard for a Sassenach to come into that circle."

"Pardon?"

"Foreigner," Isabella said, smiling a little. *English,* she meant.

"Jamie and I will carry on the tradition as our parents did before us. Only this time, we'll unite two powerful clans."

So it was decided. Daria tried to ignore the painful, tiny twist in her belly.

"You will return to England to regale salons with tales of your journey to Scotland," Isabella said lightly. "You'll undoubtedly attend balls and marry one of your own, aye?"

This was no show of friendly interest. This was a message.

Isabella smiled and sipped again from her drink. "Well, I may no' see you 'ere you go, so I will wish you God's speed to England, Miss Babcock."

That was a dismissal if ever Daria had heard one. "Thank you." Daria forced a smile and put her untouched whisky on the sideboard. "Good evening, Miss Brodie."

Having delivered her thinly veiled message, Isabella glided away.

Daria walked in the opposite direction, out of the great hall, without looking at anyone. She walked away from Scotland and Campbells and Brodies, and summer kisses and mammoth castles.

She wished she had never seen the naked man in her grandmother's cottage. The image would haunt her all her life, for she had fallen in love with Jamie Campbell.

In her rooms, Daria began to pace. She had to leave Dundavie before she lost her mind. She had found such joy these last few days, and tonight, such desperate pain. It hurt everywhere; it pressed against her chest and her head.

She had fallen in love with her captor. She couldn't imagine anyone else that she might ever love like this. But what did it matter? Her spring in Scotland had ruined her. No one would have her now.

She was alone.

Once, when she was a girl, she and Mamie had seen a bird with a broken wing. It had lain on the lawn, still very much alive, its wing at an odd angle. Other birds flew down and hopped around the poor thing, looking at it, but eventually they all flew off.

"But who will come to save the bird?" Daria had asked Mamie.

"No one," Mamie had said sadly. "She has a broken wing. She cannot fly, and if she cannot fly, she cannot remain with her family. They've gone on without her."

In despair, Daria collapsed onto the window seat. The full moon cast a milky glow around the castle. Daria glanced up at the moon, wishing that someone, anyone, would come for her.

Then a movement caught her eye. She looked down to the battlements and saw Jamie and Isabella walking arm in arm.

A broken bird. Daria felt like a broken bird.

TWENTY-TWO

There were moments in a man's life when he no longer knew the things he thought he knew. Jamie had believed he knew what was best for the Campbells and for himself, but he was no longer certain that was true.

Why could he not seem to be rid of the image of her? He could see her now, lying on her back, her arms behind her head, her legs crossed at the ankles, smiling up at the sky. He could see her as she'd appeared tonight, in a beautiful silk gown that hugged every feminine curve, her hair loosely knotted at her nape, her skin luminous, her eyes at once sparkling and shrewd.

And yet, here was Isabella, her green eyes fixed on him, shining in the candlelight as they had moved around the dance floor. He had cared very much for Isabella. He still did. But something had changed in his feeling for her. Everything felt a wee bit off.

It wasn't because she'd cried off; he would

have done the same. It wasn't that there was anything less appealing about her.

It was him. It was all in him. He could feel a sea swell of change in him. It felt as if his heart were turning over, end to end. Everything he'd thought he'd known was upside down.

The evening was winding down, and the Campbells and Brodies, most now well in their cups after an evening of forced reconciliation, were staggering off to their rooms. That was where Jamie wanted to be — in his rooms, enveloped in silence so he could *think* — but Isabella had led him out of the great hall and outside, up to the old battlements. From here, the view of the glen in which Dundavie sat was spectacular. The full moon cast a glow so bright that Jamie could see cattle grazing next to a stream.

Isabella stood next to him, her head resting lightly on his shoulder. "You've not said much this evening," she said in Gaelic. Jamie kept his gaze on the view below, of the land his family had overseen for two centuries. "I think you are not as happy to see me as I am you."

"That's not true," he said instantly.

She lifted her head and gave him a skeptical smile. He couldn't escape the fact that she knew him rather well. She rested her

347

head again on his shoulder. "You are a fortunate man, Jamie Campbell," she said. "You've managed to keep your clan together when others have failed."

"I've tried," he said. "I made a promise to my father that I would." He'd promised that he would keep the clan as close to him as if they were his own children, that he would do everything in his power to keep them intact. But a question had dogged him of late. Did the clan want that, too?

"I have long admired that about you," Isabella said, turning to face him. She rested her chin on his shoulder, gazing up at him. Jamie draped his arm around her, but the closeness felt forced. There had been a time when he'd been eager for her touch, but tonight, he found it cumbersome. He wasn't the sort of man to take pleasure with one woman in the afternoon and then kiss another that evening.

"Your clan admires you, too, Jamie. They look to you for strength and guidance in all things. I don't think they would like to see you sell land to the English. Or worse."

He looked down at her. "Worse?"

She shrugged and looked down. "Marry one."

Jamie snorted, but his dismissal felt false. Hadn't he thought of Daria in that way today? He'd rejected the foolish notion, of course, but he'd thought it all the same. "That's ridiculous. Of course I won't."

"It gladdens my heart to hear it," she said, and smiled. "She *is* quite bonny."

"So are you," Jamie said, noting the lack of conviction in his own voice.

Isabella noticed it, too. Her smile grew cool. "I risked my heart coming here today, Jamie. I wouldn't have blamed you if you'd refused to see me. But I think — I have always thought — that we are destined to be together. Haven't you? For the sake of our love, and for the sake of our clans — you and I both know the Campbells and Brodies can only be made stronger with our union."

Jamie glanced away. What she said was true.

Isabella cupped his chin to make him look at her again. "You and I can be made stronger, too. I've never believed otherwise, even after all that has happened between our families. But the Brodies are ready to forgive it for the sake of our clan. The question remains . . . will you?" She rose up on her toes and kissed the corner of his mouth. "I still love you, Jamie Campbell, I do," she whispered. "I hope you still love me." She kissed him fully.

Her lips were soft and warm, and the male in Jamie responded. She was right; of course she was his future. She was the natural, logical choice. He closed his eyes and kissed her back.

Apparently he *was* the sort of man to take pleasure with one woman in the afternoon and kiss another that evening. Why, then, could he not rid himself of the image of Daria lying on her back, her arms folded behind her head, smiling up at the blue Scottish sky?

Jamie slept very little that night, his heart warring with his head, his body feeling as if a good part of him had gone missing. He was up well before dawn, staring into the cold hearth, thinking. He had no idea how long he'd been sitting there — hours, maybe — when the sound of a barking dog filtered into his consciousness. He roused himself, shaking out his injured leg, and walked to the window, yawning as he pushed it open. The barking caught his attention again, and he leaned out to look.

He saw the red head of the boy first, racing across the expanse of green of the bailey, Anlan and Aedus at his heels. The boy reached for something in the grass, pushing Anlan's snout away from it, then turned and held it up. From that distance, Jamie couldn't make out what it was.

He was about to turn from the window when Daria suddenly appeared, the train of her day gown trailing in the grass behind her, leaving a path in the morning dew. She took the thing from the boy, and together they examined it. A moment later, the boy stepped back and Daria threw the thing, very poorly, across the lawn. It scudded and fell into a pond.

The dogs raced for it. Aedus reached it first and bounded away with it, Daria and the lad, Peader, chasing after them. Aedus jumped into the pond with the thing held between his jaws, then trotted out, his tail held high, proud of his victory.

Just as Daria and Peader reached him, Aedus and Anlan both shook out their coats, spraying them. Peader squealed with harsh laughter. Daria draped her arm around his shoulders as the two of them headed back to the keep, leaving the dogs with the toy.

And Jamie stood at the window for a long time after they had disappeared from view, thinking.

After breakfast, he went to the throne room for a standing Friday morning discussion of clan business with Duff, Robbie, and Geordie.

"Are you ill, Laird?" Duff said as Jamie walked in, and glanced at his pocket watch.

"I am well," Jamie said, and sat heavily in his chair. He had no desire to hear the clan business this morning. No desire whatsoever.

Duff put his watch back into his pocket. "I had a wee chat with the Brodie laird this morning before they took their leave —"

"They've gone?" Jamie interrupted, surprised.

"Aye," Duff said. "Said they never meant to stay as long as they had, but they quite liked the dancing."

Jamie nodded, dubious. He hadn't exactly settled things with Isabella or her father. He'd left her last night with a question still twisting between them. Were they reconciled, or not? "What news, then?" he asked, and absently rubbed his thumb along the gash in the chair's leather.

"The Brodies have proposed a devil's bargain," Duff said. "They want a renewal of the betrothal, aye? But if we canna come to agreement on the terms, then they'll agree to sell land to Murchison."

"What has one to do with the other?" Jamie asked as his muscles began to tense.

"Nothing but satisfaction," Duff said.

"Meaning?"

"The land borders ours in the east."

Jamie stared at Duff, understanding then what they had done. Either he agreed to renew the engagement with Isabella, or the Brodies would work with Murchison to squeeze him out. The land meant nothing to the Brodies — they couldn't graze cattle in those hills or farm it.

But Murchison could put dozens, if not hundreds, of sheep there. It would be only a matter of time before they encroached on Campbell land and began to compete with the cattle for grass. With the tenants in the west agreeing to sell, and the Brodies selling in the east, the Dundavie lands would be surrounded by sheep, with no escape but through a marsh. "I see," Jamie said. "They intend to extort a marriage, aye?"

Before Duff could answer, Geordie scribbled on his slate. *Hav care.*

Jamie looked curiously at his brother.

Geordie wiped the slate clean and wrote again, holding it up to Jamie. *Yur hart.*

Jamie shook his head, confused.

Frustrated, Geordie slapped his hand on his slate.

"What have we to lose?" Robbie said with a shrug. "We were set on the marriage before Geordie raised a bloody hand, aye?

It was to our advantage, we said. It was our fault that she cried off. No' a bloody thing has changed — it's still the best arrangement for us."

"Aye," Duff agreed. "I canna think of a better option for us."

"Neither can I," Jamie said, and Geordie huffed impatiently. "But if I were to say no," he added carefully, eliciting a gasp from Duff and a wide-eyed look of surprise from Robbie, "we might drain the marsh. They may surround us with sheep, aye, but we could drain the marsh and farm it."

Duff's eyes narrowed. He placed his beefy hands on the table before him. "Beggin' your pardon, Laird, but are you suggesting that you *no'* marry the Brodie lass?"

"I'm no' suggesting that, no," Jamie said calmly, and rubbed his thumb along the gash in the chair. "But we must consider all our options."

"Draining the marsh," Robbie repeated skeptically. "You would take the suggestion of a slip of an Englishwoman with no more experience than a mockingbird?" He clucked, waving a hand dismissively at his cousin.

"No experience, aye," Jamie agreed. "But you must admit it makes a wee bit of sense."

I, Geordie wrote.

Duff looked at Jamie as if he thought he'd lost his mind. "We need heirs, lad. Draining the marsh might make a wee bit of sense, but it canna give you heirs."

Jamie shrugged and looked out the window.

"What in blazes are you thinking, then, Jamie?" Robbie demanded.

"I donna rightly know." It was the honest truth. "But I've a lot to think about," he said, and walked out of the throne room.

There were times in a man's life that no counsel, no friend, no one could answer the questions that were burning in his head. No one but him.

He'd go to his hothouse. He did his best thinking there, when his hands were buried in rich Scottish earth. He made his way there, looking neither right nor left, not wanting to speak with anyone or hear any complaints about this or that. He wanted only to think about what he would do about the Brodies' offer to settle the betrothal. What he would do with his bloody life.

But when he turned toward the mews he saw Peader walking toward him, his head down as if he were searching for something.

Then Daria appeared, the dogs trailing behind her. Her face was bright, her cheeks rosy, the signs of exercise on a brilliantly

355

bright day. She went up to the boy and touched his hand. The boy opened his palm, and Daria put something in it. They both bent over it, not noticing Jamie's approach until he cast a shadow on them.

Daria looked up, and her beguiling eyes lit when she saw him. "As I live and breathe, Laird Campbell has come to enjoy a glorious spring day," she said cheerfully.

He could feel a smile warming his face. "Miss Babcock. How do you fare this morning?"

"Quite well," she said, and touched the boy's arm. "Peter and I have had a walkabout." She looked at the boy and pointed to his hand.

The boy instantly held out his hand to Jamie. In the center of his palm was a piece of agate, polished to a high blue sheen. Agate was plentiful at Dundavie; Jamie's father had crafted his mother a necklace of such stones when Jamie was a boy.

"Quite bonny."

Peader beamed at him.

Daria bent down to the boy, smiling at him. She folded his fingers over the stone, patted them, and then touched his pocket. The boy put his stone away. Daria nodded, then wiggled her fingers at him, and Peader took his leave, running a bit, then hopping on one leg before doing it all again.

"He's bright," Daria said as she watched him go. "I think he could learn to communicate rather well if given the proper attention. We've been teaching each other."

Jamie had never considered it, really. The deaf and mute were generally kept from society, and the Campbells were no different.

"He is very fond of your dogs," she added. "Were I you, I'd put him in charge of their care."

"Would you? Have you any other advice for me?"

"I do. I think Duffson should be given his freedom. He has far more important matters on his mind than my wandering about." She leaned forward, peeking around Jamie. He followed her gaze and saw the younger Duff chatting up a chambermaid.

"Aha." Jamie sighed. The lad had the same important matters on his mind as Jamie had on his.

"He is easily distracted." She folded her arms across her middle. "You need a better guard."

"Aye, it is clear that is so. I ought to hang him for leaving his post." He looked at Daria. "What other advice have you for me? More bogs that should be drained? Perhaps you've had more thoughts on botany? Or dancing?"

She pretended to think hard, then shook her head. "Nothing comes to mind. But if there is any advice you would like, you need only ask." She cast her arms wide. "I am here, ready to advise, my liege."

Jamie could feel his smile reaching out through his limbs. "Walk with me?"

"Of course."

They began to walk, each with their hands clasped at their backs, as if to keep from touching one another. Or so Jamie wanted to believe. A yellow wildflower Daria had put in her hair bobbed around her cheek, slowly working its way free. Jamie imagined her picking the flower, then slipping it into her hair, pleased by the result.

"Did you enjoy the rest of your evening?" she asked.

The mention of last evening shook him from the pleasant rumination. "I did." He glanced away, unable to look into her eyes and think of Isabella. "I would that you had stayed to enjoy it as well. There were quite a lot of tall tales and lies bandied about." He smiled at her. "A typical Scottish evening."

"Tall tales happen to be one of my favorite pastimes. What tale did you offer?"

"Me? Why, I could scarcely manage a

word among the lot of them."

Daria laughed. "I wouldn't have understood the tall tales even had I stayed, you know. Gaelic is a very difficult language to comprehend."

"Aye, I suppose it is," he conceded. He didn't like the reminder of the differences between them, language being the most glaring of them. "I hope you will keep my confidence if I tell you that I find English a wee bit easier for conversation than my native tongue."

Daria feigned a gasp. "Scandalous, Laird! But I swear I will not utter a word." She smiled up at him. "At least not in your presence."

"Of course no'. You've no one to tell here," he teased as they reached the hothouse.

"That is not entirely true!" she protested. "Bethia has, on rare occasion, accidentally listened to what I have said."

He chuckled as he reached for the door. "I would strongly advise against saying a word of my preference for English to Bethia, for she will surely see it as a portent of some great calamity to befall the Campbells."

Daria tossed her head back and laughed as they stepped into the hothouse.

There was no one within, for which Jamie

was grateful. He wanted this time with Daria to himself. As he walked down the narrow path, examining his experiments, it occurred to him that he rarely *had* moments alone. That he'd rarely felt a *need* for moments alone before now. He couldn't recall a need to be alone with Isabella bubbling up in him like a thirst.

He thirsted now.

He paused at two pots of barley, examining the thickness of the stalks. He thought about how many iterations of barley he'd tried, seeking a greater yield per stalk. He would have sworn to anyone, to God Himself, that he was thinking of barley and only barley when he opened his mouth to speak. But instead, he said, "Isabella wishes to resume our engagement."

He was as surprised as she that the words had tumbled out of his mouth. But there they lay, and he could not bring them back. For a moment, he dared not look at Daria. He couldn't guess her reaction, and he suddenly realized he didn't want to be disappointed. So many other things in his life had let him down; he didn't think he could bear for Daria to be a disappointment to him.

She did not speak right away, and the silence began to press against his throat. He

360

shouldn't have said it. What purpose did he think it would serve?

"Is that what you wish, as well?" she asked quietly.

"It ought to be, aye," he said flatly, and finally risked a look at Daria.

Her cheeks had bloomed and she was looking down, as if she were intently studying a strain of wheat. She nodded, as if she'd expected him to say yes.

"But I canna say that it's what I wish any longer."

Her head came up, her eyes searching his. "What *do* you wish?"

He wished for things he would never have guessed he'd wish for. He wished for things far beyond anything he would ever admit to himself, much less out loud.

He touched the flower in her hair, then brushed his fingers against her collarbone.

"I know what I wish," she said. "I wish I had come to Scotland before Mamie shot you."

He arched a brow as he stroked his fingers up to caress her earlobe. "So do I," he said with a wry smile.

"She wouldn't have shot you had I been there, and I never would have come here. I wish I had never come to Dundavie."

Jamie's hand stilled in surprise. And disappointment. He had thought that perhaps she liked it here. "It's no' a bad place," he said, perhaps a wee bit defensively.

"No," she said, her eyes locking on his. "It's the very best place. And I shall miss it more than you will ever know."

His mind was racing, his questions looming larger. He moved his thumb to her lips, brushing against them. One thought was crystal clear. "Stay," he said. "Stay at Dundavie. As my guest, as my —"

"As your friend?" She smiled sadly and pressed her hand against his heart. "You know I can't do that."

But Jamie wasn't going to stand for that, or the meaning behind it — not in this moment. He abruptly grabbed Daria in a tight embrace and kissed her. It wasn't a gentle kiss; it was one brimming with confusion and hope and want.

He loved her. Everything suddenly seemed crystal clear to him: he loved this English rose.

He moved without conscious thought, picking her up and setting her on the wooden bench. He kissed her mouth, her cheeks, her brow. He playfully bit her neck and kissed the hollow of her throat as he filled his hands with her breasts. He was slender moments from losing control, from making love to her, and damn it all, he *wanted* to lose control. He wanted to take her. His mind and heart warred, his thoughts telling him that he couldn't abandon his principles to satiate his burning need, and his heart insisting that he could.

When Daria slid her hands down his arms and to his waist, then intentionally brushed against his cock, Jamie sucked in a breath. He moved over her, drifting down with her onto the low table, Daria on her back beneath him. He groped for the hem of her gown and slid his hand under her skirts, touching the smooth skin of her leg, sliding in between her legs, pressing against her sex, his self-restraint holding by the thread of a spider's web.

Daria's breath was shallow, her skin flushed, and he thought she had never looked more beautiful. He kissed her again as he pressed himself against her. It was all too much. The desire in him was bubbling like a witch's cauldron. He had never felt so incapable of restraint — but Daria had done something to him, had sunk down into his skin, her person knitting with his.

He abruptly lifted his head and closed his eyes. *"Mi Diah,"* he said, emotion raw in his voice, and he held himself above her, his arms taut with his restraint. "I canna be so careless with you, *leannan.*"

Daria's lashes fluttered; then she rose up, grabbed his jaw with one hand, and kissed him with as much passion as he'd just shown her. "Be brave." She wrapped her arms tightly around him and kissed the corner of his mouth.

It was a delicately small kiss, but it rocked Jamie to his depths. He had no defense against her. He was hopeless, hopelessly in love. He stroked her hair, kissed her mouth, her temple. *"Daria,"* he whispered into her hair. *"Tha gaol agam ort."*

"What?" she asked laughingly, and kissed him, her hands stroking over his body, exploring him as he moved against her.

Jamie was lost in the feel of her body, the scent of her skin. He wasn't certain how or when he'd freed his cock from his trousers, but the tip was pressed tantalizingly against her damp folds, and he could feel himself spiraling to the steady beat that was coming from somewhere . . .

Something made him focus on that beat.

It was not a siren call. It was coming from the door.

He rose just as Daria did. He stood up, pulled her from the table, and quickly adjusted his clothing as Daria turned her back to the door to adjust hers, smoothing the hair from her face.

"Stay here," he said low and stalked to the door, his mood gone black for having been interrupted, and perhaps even blacker for having found himself in such a compromising position.

He threw open the door and glared down into the face of one of the young footmen. The young man spoke in rapid Gaelic, pointing toward the main keep.

"Aye," Jamie said when the lad had delivered his message. He shut the door and turned around, pressing his back against it.

Daria was standing on the small path, her color still high. "What is it?" she asked, her voice full of trepidation. "Has something happened?"

"Aye, something has happened," Jamie said. "Your rescue has come."

TWENTY-THREE

The words didn't make sense to Daria. She did not want to be rescued. What she wanted, with a strength that squeezed the breath from her, was for Jamie to make love to her. *Madness.* She was filled with madness. She stood on the edge of ruin as it was, but to invite the final push off the cliff?

"Who?" she asked angrily.

"English." Jamie shoved a hand through his hair. "He knows only that they are English and they've come for you."

Her parents? Of all days, of all moments, they came for her at *this* moment? She should be overwhelmed with gratitude, happy that she would at last be rescued from her captivity. But she was neither of those things. She was disappointed, recalcitrant, cross. She pressed her palm to her forehead as she tried to gather her thoughts.

This is an omen, she tried to convince herself. An omen that she had gone too far, that she had to stop before she did something she would never recover from.

She lifted her gaze to Jamie's. His eyes were dark, his demeanor suddenly distant. He knew it, too. "My parents, surely," she said.

He just held her gaze.

Daria looked at the door. "I can't . . ." She couldn't do so many things, she thought wildly. She couldn't be with Jamie the way she wanted to be with him. She couldn't linger here, and yet she couldn't imagine herself beyond this day —

"Come, Daria." He looked at the table where they had come so close to experiencing what she suspected would have been the most brilliant thing she had ever felt; a tiny shiver ran down her spine just thinking of it. But then he turned his back to it. "Let us discover who has come to rescue you."

The conflicting swirl of emotions was a nauseating mix in the pit of her belly. She walked stiffly beside Jamie. She thought she should say something, anything meaningful, but she was completely numb.

As they reached the end of the mews, Jamie said, "Daria."

She stopped and looked into his eyes. She could feel the pull between them, as strong as the moon pulled the tide. His gaze drank her in, his brow furrowed. There was so much she wanted to say — *You astonish me time and again, I adore you, I want you,* any number of things. But she couldn't find her tongue.

"I should go," she whispered.

He pressed his lips together and nodded. His hand slipped from her elbow, and the tide ebbed between them.

She turned away and walked, then ran, to the keep's entrance, slowing as she rounded the corner and saw the polished black-and-red post chaise coach, and the coachmen standing attentively around it.

That was not her parents' coach.

Daria walked cautiously forward.

"There you are, Miss Babcock, and looking quite bonny, I say. It would seem Scotland agrees with you, aye?"

Daria whirled around. Captain Robert Mackenzie was standing just outside the small entry to the castle's keep. He was dressed in a fine coat over an elaborately and richly embroidered waistcoat. His dark hair was combed away from his face and his jaw clean-shaven. He looked different than he had the few times Daria had seen him at Tiber Park. He looked like a wealthy English lord, not a sea captain with a reputation for running blockades.

He pushed away from the wall. "You are a wee bit surprised to see me, aye?"

"Yes — did Charity send you?"

He smiled and the warmth of it, the pleasure in it, was striking. His blue eyes shone as he said, "She didna send me, no. I brought her here. I'd no' allow her to make a journey into the Highlands alone."

"Madainn mhath."

Captain Mackenzie shifted his gaze from Daria to Jamie as the laird strolled into their midst. *"Madainn mhath,"* the captain answered easily. "Captain Robert Mackenzie at your service, Laird," he said, and bowed low. "I've come to fetch the wee one."

"Did you think it necessary to bring an army to do it?" Jamie asked, eyeing the men around the chaise.

"One never knows what one will find in the Highlands, aye?" Captain Mackenzie said cheerfully.

"Spoken like a Lowlander," Jamie muttered. "Come in," he said, gesturing to the keep.

"Where is Charity?" Daria asked breathlessly.

"She's just inside, lass. Waiting for you."

Daria flew past him.

Charity was standing in the middle of the small foyer with Duff and a young woman in a drab traveling grown. Charity was dressed in a lilac gown and coat with a matching bonnet. Her blonde hair was fastened artfully to the back of her head with crystal pins that winked at Daria.

"You came!" Daria exclaimed as she burst into the foyer.

"Of course I came," Charity said. "How could I allow my dearest friend to be held for ransom?" She held out her arms.

Daria hugged Charity tightly to her. "Thank God you've come. I worried no one would ever hear from me again —"

"Nonsense. Had you not come to Edinburgh when I expected, we would have searched for you." Charity took a step back to study Daria closely. "Hmmm. It seems Mr. Duff is right. He assured us that you were in excellent health, and that you've been well treated."

"I have," Daria agreed. "My parents — have you sent word?"

"They arrived in Edinburgh only yesterday. They had some . . . financing to arrange," she said carefully. "But I expect we shall see them any day. One of Mackenzie's men is waiting to bring them here." She looked past Daria and smiled.

Daria turned; she hadn't heard Jamie and Mackenzie enter the foyer. They were conversing in Gaelic, their polite smiles gone.

Mackenzie gestured to Charity and Jamie paused, bowed his head. "Madam."

"Miss Charity Scott," Captain Mackenzie said. "The sister of Lord Eberlin of Tiber Park." And to Charity he said, "Laird Campbell."

"How do you do," Charity said, sinking into a graceful curtsy. "I hope you will forgive our unannounced arrival, but my dear friend's letter made it seem rather urgent."

Jamie looked at Daria and said, "It was. You are most welcome, Miss Scott. If you will excuse us?" He said something to Mackenzie, and the two of them began to walk down the narrow corridor leading to the throne room.

Charity watched them go and then smiled at Daria. "Captain Mackenzie has graciously offered to negotiate the terms of your release, then we may be on our way."

Daria felt a physical pain at the mention of leaving. "We can't leave without Mamie."

"Of course not. We'll fetch her straightaway tomorrow." Charity smiled at Duff in the way she had of smiling at her brother to get what she wanted. "We've come such a long way, sir. Is there a place we might rest and talk privately?"

She would not charm Duff, judging by his dark expression. "Never mind, Duff," Daria said, linking her arm with Charity's. "I'll show her around."

"Lydia, dearest, be a help to Mr. Duff in bringing the bags in," Charity said to the girl, and if she heard Duff's grunt of displeasure, she gave no sign of it.

"This way," Daria said, escorting Charity up to the suite of rooms she'd lived in for more than a fortnight. She was grateful to find it empty and closed the door.

Charity walked into the middle of the suite and looked around. "My. This is rather quaint, isn't it? Very . . . castle-ish."

Daria lost her train of thought for a moment as she looked around, too. She rather liked this room. It was cheerful.

"You seem quite at ease here," Charity remarked as she tossed her bonnet and gloves onto the chaise and sat beside them. "Perhaps you like being captive," she said, and arched a brow over a devilish smile.

"Don't be ridiculous, Charity," Daria said sternly. "What was I supposed to do, curl into a ball and sob day in and day out? You abandoned me to this fate." She stalked to the sideboard, poured two tots of barley-bree, and handed one to Charity.

"I didn't abandon you." Charity's second

brow rose to meet the first. "What is this?"

"Barley-bree. Some sort of whisky. I know only that it is quite soothing."

"Oh," Charity said, and lifted it to her nose. "Do you need to be soothed?"

Daria looked at her friend with astonishment. "Wouldn't you, if you were held for ransom?"

Charity shrugged. "If I were held for ransom by a man as virile as the laird? I am not certain. Tell me, how in heaven did you come to be held for ransom? Your letter was lacking in details."

"There were too many to write." Daria sat next to Charity. She was relieved to be able to speak about it at last to someone she could trust completely. "It is quite a fantastic tale. It began with that wretched coach ride from Nairn."

"Wretched! The ladies seemed very nice."

Daria gave Charity a withering look. "They dropped me on the side of a road. The only living being was a dog, who followed me through the forest to Mamie's cottage."

"Then you found it easily enough?"

"Oh, I found it," Daria said, nodding. "A rather charming little cottage in the woods. Nothing around for miles. Well hidden from the road. And Mamie wasn't there. But do you know who was?"

Charity shook her head.

"An unconscious man. An utterly *naked* unconscious man."

Charity blinked. She put aside her glass and leaned forward. "I'm all ears."

"He'd been shot." Daria told Charity what had happened then. That Mamie had returned to the cottage and claimed she'd found the poor man. That she didn't know who he was but had saved him. She told Charity that Mamie had seemed anxious and erratic, and really, a bit mad, but that she'd attributed it to the devastation of finding the man in such a state.

"The man was the *laird*?" Charity asked, her eyes lighting with delight. "Goodness, Daria! What an education for you!"

"Quite," Daria said.

"That causes my heart to race —"

"Mine as well."

"Well? Go on!"

Daria told her how it appeared that Mamie was not trying to save the poor man's life, but perhaps trying to hasten his end. "She's mad," Daria said flatly.

"Or hiding something," Charity offered.

"That's precisely what Jamie said," Daria said thoughtfully.

"Is that indeed what *Jamie* said?" Charity

echoed, nudging Daria with her shoulder.

Daria frowned at Charity. "Your imagination is working far too hard. Every person you see here is a Campbell. It's impossible to distinguish them if one does not use given names."

"Or 'my lord,' " Charity said with a shrug.

"Not lord. *Laird* —" Daria sighed. "May we please return to the reason I am held for ransom?"

"Yes, please do," Charity said.

Daria told Charity how Mamie had finally admitted that she'd shot Jamie, but quite by accident, and Jamie had accused her of stealing from his addled uncle Hamish. She related how Mamie had adamantly denied it but finally admitted that perhaps she did indeed owe the Campbells money, but she did not have it. Then Jamie had threatened to have the authorities brought round, but had settled on the ransom instead, and brought her here.

"Perhaps she's gone barmy from living in solitude, do you suppose?" Charity asked.

"I don't know," Daria said morosely. "But something is very wrong with her. No one here will believe it, of course."

"At the very least, Jamie Campbell sounds to be a chivalrous man. That is, taking debutantes for ransom aside." Charity smiled coyly.

"He is," Daria agreed. "He's really been very kind, considering what my grandmother has done to him."

Charity put her arm around Daria. "Don't fret, darling. Your parents are on their way, and I am here to help you. Now then, tell me what happened after you came to this charmingly rustic castle."

Daria thought back to the days she'd been here. "Nothing, really. I taught them to waltz."

Charity's face lit with a rare smile. "To *waltz*?"

"They were not the least bit familiar with it!" She told Charity about the dancing, and how she'd demanded a suitable occupation and made a match for the blacksmith. She told her about Peter, and how eager the lad was to learn. She talked about Geordie, about Bethia and Duffson. About the muffins the cook made her, the dogs who followed her, the children who sang songs about spring.

Charity was rapt, listening to every word, smiling at some things, frowning at others. When Daria had told her everything, Charity studied her for a moment. "You've not said a word about the laird."

Daria averted her gaze. "What is there to

say?" She stood up, moving to the sideboard. "He's to be married soon."

"Is he? That's unsettling, as I think you've come to esteem him," Charity said.

"That's not it at all, Charity," Daria said impatiently. "You've misunderstood me completely." But maybe it was impossible for anyone to understand her. The Daria who had set foot on that ship so many weeks ago was nowhere to be found.

"I hope I have," Charity said. Surprised, Daria glanced at her friend. "While he may be a man to be respected and esteemed, he is a Scotsman yet."

Why did the hair on the back of Daria's neck stand up? She turned slowly around to face her friend. "What are you trying to say?"

Charity rose. "Only that I hope you have not come to esteem him *too* greatly. Your future is very bright. But your future is in England."

"I did not say —"

"No, you said not a word. But I know you rather well, Daria. I see the look in your eye when you speak of him. I would not like to see you compromise your future because of a charming captor."

Daria couldn't help but laugh. "Perhaps you should take your own advice. Your feelings for Mackenzie are quite obvious, Charity. Worse, you willingly went off to Edinburgh with him. What do you think that will do for *your* happy future?"

She regretted the words the moment she'd said them. Charity's future had been compromised beyond repair years ago, when she'd borne her daughter out of wedlock.

But Charity merely smiled with deep satisfaction. "I may have found my happy future," she said. "But if I have not, it is hardly the same case, is it? I was never capable of making a great match. But you are, Daria. You could marry a titled man."

Daria shook her head. "I doubt that is true. I have been kidnapped and held for ransom."

"But don't you see?" Charity said, crossing the room to take her hands. "That makes you exciting! The circumstances were beyond your control. One cannot dare to question *your* character in being kidnapped. When word reaches Hadley Green, you will be quite sought after to tell the tale of your adventure. Women will envy you and men will admire you."

Daria thought of all the lords in London she had long wanted to attract, but felt no stir of excitement.

"Shall we go and find what Lydia has

done with the bags?" Charity asked. "I brought you two new gowns from Edinburgh that are very lovely."

TWENTY-FOUR

Captain Mackenzie was the antithesis of who Jamie imagined would come for Daria. He was a Lowlander and, Jamie suspected, something of a scoundrel. Nevertheless, Jamie liked him; he had a certain charm. Yet he did have one habit that Jamie found vexing, and that was his insistence on naming Daria's highborn connections.

Jamie thought it entirely unnecessary, as Mackenzie had readily agreed the ransom ought to be paid and did not question the facts surrounding the kidnapping. He was a fellow Scotsman, after all. So why, then, did he feel compelled to present to Jamie that Daria was a "close and personal confidante" of Lord Eberlin of Tiber Park, as well as Lord Ashwood, and therefore, by extension, of the powerful Duke of Darlington?

Darlington was the only name familiar to Jamie in the list of lords who would, to hear Mackenzie tell it, take up arms against

Dundavie if a Campbell so much as gazed in Daria's general direction.

Jamie wasn't intimidated by Mackenzie's remarks; they amused him. "Do you honestly think your words strike fear in me, man?" he asked, after Mackenzie had talked about Darlington's power in the House of Lords.

Mackenzie chuckled. "I had hoped," he admitted. "In the event you have any thoughts of keeping her," he added with a sly smile.

Jamie's gut tightened and he looked down at his tot. "The lass will be free to leave Dundavie when her ransom is paid."

"It will be paid," Mackenzie said as he helped himself to another tot of whisky. "If her parents haven't raised it, Miss Scott and I are prepared to remit." He offered the decanter of whisky to Jamie, who shook his head. "But there is one condition," Mackenzie said, returning the decanter to the table.

"Aye? And what is that?"

"I should like to accompany Miss Babcock to her grandmother's house. To see with me own eyes that she is well."

Jamie considered that. "My man will accompany you."

"Aye, of course," Mackenzie said with an

easy smile. "But you need no' waste a good man on us. I give you my word as a fellow Scot that she will be returned so that you may collect what is owed to your family." He inclined his head as if he had just offered something very noble.

Jamie grinned. "Then you will understand, as a fellow Scot, that I donna trust you completely."

Mackenzie laughed heartily and lifted his glass in a toast. "Aye, that I do." He tossed the whisky back.

Duff had spent the better part of the day finding the mysterious man Mrs. Moss had met in the glen.

"English," Duff said, his distaste obvious.

"Another one." Jamie sighed.

"Aye. Lives in the old MacKreegan fortress. I had thought it long abandoned, but he's done a bit of repair to make it habitable."

Jamie had thought the place long abandoned, too. Once a military outpost, it was far back in the hills. There was nothing else there, and the land was unsuitable even for cattle. "Anyone else?" he asked curiously.

"Didna see another."

"How long has he been there?"

"That, he wouldna say. He was no' the

welcoming sort, aye?"

An Englishman who kept to himself. Jamie thought of Hamish and his claims of befriending an English earl. Was it possible? When his guests had left, he'd ride over and have a look himself.

"And what of the Brodies, lad? What do you intend to do about their offer?" Duff eyed Jamie closely as he awaited his answer.

But Jamie didn't have an answer for him. He felt as if he'd left something unfinished in the hothouse today. It wasn't the physical satisfaction, although he had felt that rather keenly. No, it was something else, and Jamie was at a loss to understand it. He looked away. "I'll call on Isabella on the morrow, aye?"

That seemed to satisfy Duff.

It did not satisfy Jamie, however. He couldn't shake the restlessness in him. Later, in the throne room, as he listened to the complaints of his clan, that feeling of something missing grew, pushing against his thoughts. As Gwain Campbell presented the latest complaint — his neighbor had stolen a goose — Jamie stared at the rafters, trying to find his bearings.

"Well then, Laird?" Gwain demanded. "What say you?"

The two men stood below him, waiting.

Jamie looked at the both of them. "I'll tell you what I think. I think that this is an awful lot of bother for a goose."

The two men exchanged a look of surprise.

"Let us delay judgment until next week, lads. I've no patience for it now." He came off the laird's seat and walked through the small crowd, ignoring their looks of astonishment.

He didn't realize Geordie was hurrying after him until his brother caught him by the shoulder and forced him around. He held up his slate. *Ill?*

"Ill? No," Jamie said.

Geordie wiped the slate and wrote, *Mad?*

Everyone waited for his words, and yet Jamie couldn't find them. He knew only that the words he needed to say, to *hear,* were missing.

In honor of the English guests — or, as Robbie said to Aileen, to keep an eye on them — supper was served in the formal dining room.

"I am waiting for King Arthur to sweep in with his mighty sword at any moment," Charity said wryly. She and Daria, along with Mackenzie, were seated across from Robbie and Aileen Campbell and some other Campbells Daria had not met before tonight. Geordie, Hamish, and Duff flanked Jamie at the head of the table. The laird was looking a little glum, Daria thought.

"It's positively medieval," Charity muttered.

Daria made herself look away from Jamie and to the room. The people gathered to dine were laughing loudly, eating game, and drinking barley-bree and beer. "I find it interesting," Daria said with a shrug. "It's not as stuffy as a formal supper in England."

Charity gave her a look. "It's easy to see why you are an Original here. You are the most beautiful woman here."

"No, *m'annaschd,* you are," Mackenzie said. He leaned around Charity and smiled at Daria. "You, lass, are the only one who might compare," he added smoothly.

Daria rolled her eyes at him. The gown Charity had brought her was stunning — a summer-green silk with an overlay of a sheer silver silk. When she walked, she looked as if she were moving in water.

"You should have seen the laird's face when you walked in," Charity whispered. "You could not see him, as every man in this room was standing before him, eyeing you like a sweetmeat."

"They were eyeing *you.*" Charity was

dressed in a simple white silk, but with diamonds glittering at her throat and her ears, she looked as elegant as a queen.

"No, you silly goose, it was you. Think of it, someday you will be seated in a grand ballroom — your *own* ballroom, darling — surrounded by fine things. You will think of this old castle in the wilds of Scotland and be thankful you escaped."

"Will I?" Daria sighed. "I rather think I shall miss it."

"At first you will," Charity agreed. "But the memory will fade away once you are back where you belong. I know; I have experienced something quite similar."

A young footman placed a large platter of fish and potatoes before them, then bowed low before hurrying off. Mackenzie graciously took Charity's plate and filled it, then Daria's.

"Look there, aye?" Mackenzie said, nodding up at the dais. Geordie was scribbling something on his slate, handing it to Jamie. "I saw him earlier today, scratching on that thing. Was he born mute?"

"No," Daria said. "He was injured in a duel."

Mackenzie's eyes lit with interest. "*Ach,* if that's what it is, I know a surgeon in Edinburra who might help him. One of me deckhands was hit right across the gullet by a rogue boom. Cut him deep, it did. Dr. Elgin gave him back his speech." He suddenly put down his fork. "I'll have a word," he said, standing.

"Now?" Charity asked.

"What better time? We're in Scotland, lass. We donna make much of social rules, aye?" He leaned down and said softly, *"Tha gaol agam ort."*

Charity smiled as he sauntered off.

Daria tried to remember where she'd heard that phrase. It sounded rhapsodic to her. "What did he say?" she asked.

When Charity didn't answer, Daria looked at her. The woman who could always be trusted to have the most inscrutable demeanor was suddenly blushing. "Charity! What did he say?"

A soft smile brightened Charity's face. "He said, 'I love you.' "

Daria gasped.

Charity's blush deepened and she said, "Did you truly not suspect it? Yes, Daria, he loves me. And I love him."

Of course Daria had suspected it, but that was not the reason for her gasp. It was because she had heard that phrase in the arms of Jamie Campbell. Jamie had said that to *her.*

Daria's heart began to flutter. Her gaze flew to the dais, but Jamie was listening intently to what Mackenzie was telling him.

She drew a shallow breath. *He'd said that he loved her.* Not in English, the way she could understand it, but he had said it — and Daria allowed herself to believe that he did. Or hoped that he did. She hoped so fiercely that her head hurt.

"He was right glad for the information," Mackenzie said when he returned. "He said he'd send his brother as soon as he was able, but that he had business with the Brodie clan on the morrow."

Daria's pulse began to pound. That was it, then. He would accept their terms. What other option did he have? Her heart ached. It was really no different here than in England — he loved her, but duty called. Duty always called.

She had no right to interfere in the course of his life, of this clan's life. She had no right to try to persuade him to turn his back on Isabella for her. She had no business in Scotland, and once her parents arrived, she would be gone.

Charity was right — her future was in England. It was obvious.

So why did it hurt so badly?

■ ■ ■ ■

The evening had grown raucous, thanks in part to an endless supply of barley-bree, courtesy of Ian Campbell, who had made it his life's work to perfect the brew. After supper they'd retired to the great hall, and Jamie's injured leg was stretched out before him, aching a little, even after a few tots. He watched Daria across the room. She was with Geordie and her friend Miss Scott, the three of them engaged in some sort of diversion having to do with Geordie's slate.

He'd hardly spoken a word to her this evening, other than to ask her how she enjoyed the meal. He was brooding, pondering what, if anything, he ought to do about her. But he'd come to the painful conclusion that he had no other option than to marry Isabella.

He could not marry Daria, as much as he desired to. The clan would not approve of his taking an English wife. And in truth, there were so many things to consider beyond that. She didn't meet any requirement that had guided the matches of Campbell lairds for years. She couldn't bring him wealth, or an alliance of any sort. She couldn't stand in his stead should something happen to him, since she was English. And there was the matter of what her grand-mother had done to Hamish.

Yet Daria brought him joy and happiness.

Wasn't that what a man should desire? But he wasn't free to follow his heart. He was laird. He was the sum of all the people gathered tonight. They owned him.

He stood. To hell with the clan.

He walked across the room to where Daria was writing on Geordie's slate. "Miss Bab-cock, a word?" he asked.

She looked up with surprise. "Of course," she said, and handed the slate to Geordie.

He offered his arm and led her away from the ears of the others. "I have news," he said.

"Oh?" Her smile suddenly disappeared.

"We have found your grandmamma's acquaintance. He is also English."

"English!" she exclaimed, and smiled again. "What in heaven are so many English *doing* here, I wonder?"

Jamie couldn't help but laugh. "If you determine what, you must promise to en-lighten all of us poor Scots."

She fixed her gaze on him and absently bit her bottom lip. "It appears I should have ample opportunity to survey all the English travelers. Charity says I shall be in high demand when I return home."

"Will you?"

"Mmm," she said. "I've had a very grand adventure, apparently, and everyone will want to hear about it."

"Aha. *Diah, leannan,* where will you begin?"

"That is a very good question, sir," she said with mock seriousness. "I rather doubt I will have the time I need to tell it all. I shall touch upon the highlights. An unconscious, naked man." Her smile broadened. "The kidnapping, of course. That was dramatic at the time, but naturally I shall endeavor to make it seem *very* dramatic."

"I think you must. Daggers drawn, that sort of thing."

"Yes! Thank you!" She laughed. "I shall make myself appear brave and courageous."

He covered her hand with his and squeezed it. "You should," he agreed. "You were."

Her eyes softened. For a moment, she looked sad.

He stroked the back of her hand with his thumb, running over delicate bones and silken skin. *Diah,* how he would miss her. "I can well imagine your return to England with the tales of your great adventure. And before you know it, you will no longer lay claim to being the last debutante."

Tears filled her eyes, but Daria smiled. "Do you know that I've not even thought of it recently? Things are so different here, Jamie. Things that I thought were of great importance now seem to have no importance at all."

"Aye," he said. "I've noticed the same."

"I'm going home, aren't I?" she whispered.

She was not asking if the ransom would be paid or if he would release her. She was asking if he would keep her. To love, to cherish.

Jamie swallowed down a lump of bitterness and looked at her hand.

She continued, "If I don't have the opportunity to thank you before I go — not for kidnapping me; it seems rather ridiculous to thank someone for holding one for ransom. But for being so kind about it — well, I don't really mean that, either," she said, frowning. "I realize of course that things could have been much worse than they were, and for not making them worse, I thank you."

He brought her hand to his lips before she could say anything else that would destroy him. "Perhaps it is best if you donna speak of it, aye?"

"Right you are," she muttered. She pulled her hand free from his, as if she intended to walk away, but then suddenly poked him in the chest. "Promise me you will see to it that Peter has someone to talk to. And Duffson. You must keep an eye on him, for he is far too enamored with the young ladies at Dundavie."

Jamie smiled.

"Well," she said, squaring her shoulders, "I should get some rest. I suspect a visit to Mamie's will be grueling. Good night, Jamie."

"Good night, Daria." He bowed low and watched her walk away.

She was far braver than he.

He was ready to quit this feast himself and turned about, almost colliding with Geordie.

Geordie held up his slate. *Donna low drea go.*

Jamie squinted at it, sounding it out. "Donna low drea go —" He suddenly looked up at his brother. "Donna allow Daria to go," he said.

Geordie nodded.

But Geordie knew as well as he did that he had no choice.

Twenty-Five

Daria spent another night tossing and turning in anguish, her heart breaking. But she was smiling the next morning as she waited for her horse to be saddled. God help her, she would be brave and courageous. She would not allow anyone to see how her heart had shattered.

Only she, Mackenzie, and Robbie would ride to Mamie's. Charity had declined to join them. "I refuse to wear trousers," she said, gazing down at Daria's.

"They're really very comfortable."

Charity shook her head. "I think your parents will arrive today, and I will be here to explain to them that all is not lost. I think I've never been so eager to see anyone leave a place as I am to see you leave Dundavie. I fear if you don't leave soon, you will be shearing sheep."

Shearing sheep sounded almost idyllic to Daria this morning. She strode out in her pantaloons to ride with the men.

On the way to Mamie's cottage, she discovered why Charity was taken with Captain Mackenzie. He rode with Daria, chatting easily, complimenting her profusely. She was one of the bonniest women he'd ever met, et cetera, and he'd long thought so. He enumerated the various bachelor gentlemen he had met through Lord Eberlin and assured her that she would be found quite desirable by them. "I can make the necessary introductions, if you'd like, lass."

"You?" Daria asked laughingly.

"Aye, me," he said confidently. "You might be amazed, then, how many men have a secret desire to be a sea captain. I am well-regarded company in most circles."

Daria laughed at him. "How modest you are, Captain!"

"I know my worth, Miss Babcock. Perhaps you are no' as certain of yours, aye?" he asked jovially, and rode ahead.

His words echoed in Daria's head as they made their way to Mamie's cottage.

When they reached the cairns and started their descent into the little glen where Mamie lived, Mackenzie had another piece of advice for Daria. "It is my experience that a man who spends weeks on a ship will do what he must to be free of the sea, aye?"

"The sea?" Daria repeated, confused.

"What I mean, lass, is that your granny might very much like to be free of her sea. Go in there, then, lock the door, and donna let her out until she tells you what she's hiding, aye? The truth may pain her greatly, but it will set her free of her sea."

Yes, Daria could see why Charity was taken with Mackenzie.

When they reached Mamie's cottage, Daria was alarmed to see the door standing open. The flowers that used to grace the windows were gone. There was no smoke at the chimney. Panic began to spread through her — the cottage looked abandoned.

Daria threw herself off her horse and hurried to the gate.

"We've the right cottage, have we no'?" Mackenzie asked.

"Aye," Robbie said gruffly.

Daria pushed through the gate. "Mamie!" she called out.

"Daria?" Mamie's voice filtered out from the back room.

Daria strode to the dark room where Jamie had spent a week.

Mamie met her at the door, looking slightly dazed. "Oh dear, is something wrong?" She rubbed her hands on her dirty apron. She was entirely disheveled.

396

"What are you about, Mamie?" Daria asked, peering past her into the darkened room.

"Just sorting things," she said absently.

Daria whirled about and went to the front door. She waved to Mackenzie and Robbie, then shut the door and bolted it. When she turned around, Mamie was staring at her warily.

Her grandmother looked so small and so . . . *old.* Daria grabbed her up and held her tightly, burying her face in her neck. "Mamie, what has happened to you?" she asked tearfully.

"I am glad you have come, darling." She pulled away and tried to smile, but Daria scarcely noticed it. She couldn't look away from the dark circles beneath Mamie's eyes.

"I'll just put the kettle on," Mamie said, and moved to the hearth.

Daria watched her. Something seemed different about the kitchen. She glanced up at the shelf. "Where are your china plates and the crystal?"

"Only things," Mamie said, with a dismissive flick of her wrist. "Tell me, darling, how have you been at Dundavie?"

That was Mamie's way of deflecting questions, Daria realized. The moment Daria asked her something she didn't want to answer, Mamie would respond with a question for Daria. She wanted the old Mamie back, the grandmother who had taken her for long walks in the garden, and had ladies to tea, and allowed Daria to play dress-up in her silk gowns and pearls. She wanted to tell Mamie about the knots in her belly, the butterflies in her veins. "Actually, I . . . I have come to esteem the laird very much," she blurted.

Mamie whirled about, her eyes wide, her mouth gaping in shock. "*No,* Daria! No, you mustn't! God help me, when will my daughter come?" she cried to the ceiling.

"What is wrong?" Daria cried, taken aback. "What have I said?"

Mamie lurched forward and grabbed Daria's face between her hands. "Daria, *listen* to me! You *must* leave here! You must go to England as soon as you are able, do you understand? You should never have come to Scotland! I don't care if that man has granted you a kingdom, you will not ruin your life with such talk!"

Daria pushed her grandmother's hands away from her. "Stop it," she said angrily. "There was a time when I could speak to you about anything, Mamie."

With a groan, Mamie sank onto a chair and pressed her hand to her forehead.

"Dear God, I am so weary. I have done all that I could — I swear that I have. But I cannot keep you from ruining it all."

Daria's heart began to beat wildly. "You are mad," she said, her voice shaking. "My parents will be here today or tomorrow and my ransom will be paid, and they must deal with you. For I swear, I cannot bear this a moment longer."

"Then please, do not bear it," Mamie said, lifting her head. "Just promise me you will return to England at once. I want your word that you will! I want your word that you will not be charmed by that Scotsman and ruin everything I and your parents have tried to do for you!"

Daria's heart had been beating so hard that she could scarcely catch a breath, but those words stopped it altogether. "What you and my parents have *done* for me? What have any of you *done* for me, Mamie? I have put *myself* into society! In spite of all of you, I have done all that I could to make a decent match. Even my debut was at the behest of Lady Horncastle, and yet my parents brought me home from London as soon as the debut was made! For what? So that I might spend my days watching my parents create orchids?"

"You cannot imagine how difficult it has

been," Mamie moaned.

"Then *tell* me!" Daria pleaded. "For God's sake, Mamie, tell me something that is the *truth*. Tell me why you dislike the laird so, or why you would shoot him, or why you didn't tell me that the man you met in the glen that day was an Englishman! Do you truly expect me to believe you don't know him? That you hadn't gone to meet him?"

Mamie burst into tears, covering her face with her hands. Daria hurried to her side and fell to her knees, her hands on her grandmother's knees. "Please, Mamie — what is happening?"

Mamie gulped back her tears. Her hands shaking, she wiped the tears from her face. "I have tried to spare you, darling. Oh, how I have tried. But I always knew you would learn the truth one day."

"The truth," Daria repeated. "So that man *is* known to you?"

Mamie nodded.

Daria stood and pulled a chair close, sitting directly in front of Mamie. "We will not leave this cottage until you have told me everything, do you understand? Begin with that man. Who is he?"

Mamie drew a deep breath. "It's quite an involved tale —"

"I don't care! For God's sake, *tell* me!"

Her expression pained, Mamie said, "Do you recall when, a few years ago, the old Earl of Ashwood went missing?"

"Yes," Daria said. "He drowned. But what has that to do —"

"The truth begins there. You recall he'd gone fishing on a swollen river, and he was never seen again. The only things they could find were a mangled fishing pole and his tackle on the shore. His body was never found. Well, the earl didn't drown. He duped everyone into believing he had, and he escaped to Scotland.

"He had sizable gambling debts that he couldn't pay without dismantling Ashwood completely. But if he were dead, his gambling debts wouldn't be pursued. He had no heirs, and the sort of men to whom he owed money couldn't legitimately make a claim against Ashwood. So the earl emptied his coffers, staged his death, and disappeared."

Daria shook her head in disbelief. "Even if that were true — and I can hardly believe that he might have accomplished such trickery — what has that to do with *you*?"

"The earl's thirst for gambling did not end with his supposed death. He continued to gamble here, and he began to lose more money. When he had lost almost all that he had, he needed someone to bring him more. So he chose us," Mamie said bitterly.

" 'Us'? Who is *us*?" Daria cried in frustration.

"The Babcocks."

Daria blinked. Nothing made sense. "What do you mean? How could he choose us from Scotland? And choose us for *what,* pray tell?" She felt exhausted, emotionally drained.

"Because we have the means to bring money to him —"

"Absurd," Daria said angrily and stood up. "I won't listen to more of your lies, Mamie. If you won't tell me the truth, I'll go —"

"He chose us to do his dirty deeds because he knows our devastating secret."

Daria threw her arms wide in disbelief. "Yes, of course! If this isn't *enough* madness, then we'll add a devastating family secret! What is it, Mamie? What possible secret could we have?"

"Oh, Daria," Mamie said sadly, and gazed at Daria as if she were about to walk up on the gallows. "I never wanted to tell you this. I — we — had hoped there would never be a need. But as you've grown up and wanted more from life . . . I *told* Beth that this was inevitable, and she wouldn't listen to me!"

"What?" Daria snapped. "Say whatever it is now, or I will walk out the door for good. I have been held for ransom because of this secret! You shot an innocent man because of it! You will tell me, or I will walk out the door and you will never see me again." She angrily swiped at a tear that was sliding down her cheek.

"I am telling you the truth now, Daria." Mamie slowly gained her feet and reached for Daria's hand. "Have you ever wondered why your parents came to live in Hadley Green? Why your grandfather and I followed?"

"Mamma said they came to Hadley Green for the air."

Mamie swallowed. "They came to Hadley Green to escape an awful scandal, and the earl was happy to help them. Your father was a jeweler, did you know? He had helped a broker sell some of the countess's jewelry for the earl. And when scandal came to your father, the earl offered your parents refuge."

"Refuge," Daria repeated.

Mamie swallowed again, as if the words were stuck in her throat. "He knew that your father was married . . ." She looked away. "He was — he *is* — married to someone else."

It took a moment for Daria to understand what Mamie was implying, and then she gasped. "Good God, have you any idea what you are saying?" She tried to pull her hand free of her grandmother's, but Mamie tightened her grip.

"Listen to me. I was very unhappy with their relationship, obviously, for he was a married man. I didn't care that he was trapped in an unhappy union with a wife who refused to agree to a divorce. I cared only that my daughter — who was younger than you are now — was throwing her life away by courting such a scandal. Oh, but she was stubborn. She said that she loved him.

"But when Richard's wife found out that he esteemed Beth and had been meeting her privately, she threatened to ruin him. Your grandfather and I wanted to send Beth away, to spare her such a ruinous scandal, but it was too late. She had already conceived you."

Daria sank onto a chair, suddenly unable to breathe.

"That's when your father sought the help of his friend the earl, and the earl brought him to Hadley Green and established him there. It was awful — Richard and Beth left in the dead of night, slipping out of their homes, out of his marriage, out of society. Out of even his name! They chose the surname Babcock from a grave marker! All these years, they have lived as man and wife, while his true and lawful wife was living not one hundred miles away."

"I don't believe you!" Daria cried.

"That is the reason they have kept to themselves, my love. They thought you would be content to live in that house with them, but I told them you were far too spirited, and sooner or later they would have to tell you the truth —"

"That I am a bastard?" Daria said, nearly choking on the words.

Mamie did not deny it. "We protected you all these years . . . but then the earl began to blackmail us. That's why I came to Scotland. I tried to reason with him, but he is *relentless*. He wants more and more until he has taken everything, and then he wants even *more* —"

"So it's true, then! You stole from Uncle Hamish."

"No! The earl befriended Hamish Camp- bell at the horse races. When he understood how addled the poor man was, he asked for the money, and Hamish agreed. I met Hamish in Nairn to receive the money and deliver it to the earl. I suppose he forgot that he agreed to give it to the earl."

"It was not his to give," Daria said flatly. "Nor was it yours to take, Mamie."

"I haven't sought more from him; I just delivered it! I've sold things — Oh, what is the use? The truth is that there is not enough money to satisfy that beast. He bets it all on the ponies."

"But why have you allowed it?" Daria demanded. "Why have you not told the authorities?"

"Because your father's wife is still alive," Mamie said bitterly. "If she knew where he was, she could bring about criminal proceedings for abandonment."

"Let Pappa face what he has done," Daria said bitterly.

"But it's more than that now, darling. You would be ruined, your chances at a match destroyed. Even if you had married before now, such news would give a man grounds to claim fraud if the truth were to come to light. Don't you see?"

Daria felt light-headed. She drew a shallow breath, and then another. She had almost single-handedly worked her way up in Hadley Green society without any help from her family, all with the hopes of marrying and having children one day. That was what she wanted, and this — this was devastating. She couldn't imagine how they could keep the truth from coming out.

She turned away from her grandmother, her thoughts racing, nausea building. She thought of Charity, surrounded by opulence but imprisoned by society's conventions, a path she'd been put on when her father was falsely accused of stealing the Ashwood jewels. Daria's family *had* actually stolen, had lied and dissembled — and she would be completely disgraced. No self-respecting man would have her.

She suddenly thought of Jamie. A laird, an upstanding man of honor. She couldn't bear to look at him, knowing what she knew now.

Daria turned away from her grandmother and walked to the door.

"Daria? Where are you going? Come back!" Mamie begged her.

"I've heard enough." Daria couldn't look at her grandmother. She could scarcely even breathe. She walked out into the yard as Mamie rushed to the door behind her. She was aware that Mamie called her back, that Mackenzie was asking her if she was all right.

But all Daria could manage was, "I should like to go."

"Aye. Where?"

An excellent question. There was no place where she might escape this disaster.

TWENTY-SIX

Malcolm Brodie was quite pleased to see Jamie. He walked out to greet him with a hearty clap on the back. *"'S e do bheatha,"* he said in greeting. "Come and we will talk, the two of us, aye?" He gestured to the door of his home.

"Thank you, Malcolm. Would you mind if I spoke to Isabella first?"

"Aye, aye." Malcolm smiled as he opened the door of the house. Isabella was coming down the stairs.

"I'll leave you alone for a wee bit, aye?" Malcolm said. "No' too long, mind you, or the lass's mother will have me head." He laughed heartily.

Isabella smiled indulgently at her father and gestured to the salon. They entered, and she waited with her hands clasped tightly behind her back until he'd closed the door. "I havena said that I am gladdened to see you so recovered," she said as she moved forward.

Was he recovered? He wasn't entirely certain he would ever fully recover. From the gunshot, yes. But not from the engagement, the crying off.

When she stood before him, she rose up on her toes and kissed his cheek. "Thank you for coming, Jamie."

Ah, but she was a bonny lass. She would bear beautiful children. Life would go on, winter turning to spring and summer turning to autumn, and Jamie would sit in his chair, rubbing the gash in the leather. He would determine whose goose it was, and the river of life would flow on, cutting deeper and deeper into its bed.

He took Isabella's hand, pressed his lips to her temple.

Isabella was still smiling. "What are you thinking, *mo ghraidh*?"

My love. Those words clanged emptily about Jamie's breast. "Do you love me, then, Isabella?"

She smiled at him as she had smiled at her father. Indulgently. Patiently. "Of course I do."

He stroked her knuckles thoughtfully, then let go of her hand. "Do you truly?"

She sighed impatiently. "What is it you want, Jamie? Aye, I am quite fond of you."

"As I am fond of you," he said. "But I donna love you, Isabella."

He expected her to be offended, but Isabella merely blinked at him. Then she smiled sympathetically. "Is that what is on your mind? Jamie, it will come. There is no reason it will no'. We are compatible in every way; we have a fondness for one another. One day, we will love each other." She smiled reassuringly and stroked his cheek.

Jamie wrapped his hand around her wrist and pulled it away. "Two months ago, that would have been enough for me, lass. But it is no' enough for me now."

Isabella's smile faded. "What are you saying?"

"I think you know," he said quietly. "I canna marry you."

The news clearly stunned her. "Are you mad?" she whispered incredulously. "We have a perfect match, Jamie. And you would throw it all away, risk your clan and your lands, because you do no', in this moment, *love* me?"

Those were the words. Those were the words he'd been trying to find in himself these last two days. It all came together now. Yes, he would risk all. But not because he didn't love Isabella. He would risk it all

411

because he loved Daria. She was worth the risk.

"Jamie?" Isabella said, demanding an answer.

He sighed helplessly. "Aye. That is precisely what I would do."

She took a step back, her eyes wide with shock. "Do you love the Englishwoman?" she asked.

"Aye."

"But she is *English*!" Isabella cried. "You scarcely know her! How could you, Jamie? How could you do that to your clan? To Scotland? Is an *English* woman worth everything that will befall you and your clan if you donna take the offer we've made you?"

He pressed his lips together. He didn't believe Isabella truly wanted to hear his answer.

"*Mi Diah,* Jamie, think of what you are doing," Isabella beseeched him. "Your people will no' stand for it, aye? She canna protect you from Murchison. No good can come of it. You are infatuated, and one day you will regret that you did no' marry the Campbells and the Brodies, and it will be too late."

"I canna help what is, Issy. It's more than my feelings for her. It's my honor as well, can you no' see it? If I married you, loving someone else, I would no' be true to either of us. Is that truly what you want?"

"I donna care about your bloody honor," she said angrily. "*Ach,* you Campbells are all the same! My father warned me I should never trust you, and I defended you! First your brother, and now *you,* Jamie. You have just deepened a rift between the Campbells and the Brodies that will never be repaired. Were I you, I would say farewell to my people and begin to study the farming of sheep, for that's what you and the English whore will be doing." She strode quickly from the room, throwing the door open and running out.

Jamie sighed, then closed his eyes. *It was done.* He'd just made life harder for the Campbells, all for the sake of his heart.

He waited a moment for his head to clear. When it did not, he walked out before a Brodie took it from his shoulders.

He rode as fast as he could through the hills to Dundavie. He knew that Murchison would hear of this and gleefully dive into the rift between the Campbells and the Brodies. He was equally certain that the Brodies would sell as they had threatened to do. He fully expected that Isabella would mourn a day or two and then be on about

413

the business of the Brodie clan. So he had best see about draining the bog as quickly as possible, and even then, he wasn't certain it would be enough.

Duff greeted him in the bailey as he rode in, a hint of a smile on his fleshy face. "How did you find the Brodies?" he asked hopefully.

Jamie came off his horse and looked at his old friend. "I did no' accept the offer, Duff."

A range of emotions instantly flitted across Duff's fleshy face. He clenched his jaw and shook his head. "Might have avoided a lot of trouble if you'd accepted the betrothal."

"I am painfully aware, aye," Jamie agreed. He didn't say more; he didn't know how to tell a man like Duff that he could no more marry Isabella than he could marry Duff. And Jamie was certain that Duff would not approve of Daria as his choice for a wife. Yet he was helpless to stop himself. Everything about Daria, from the moment he'd awoken in that opiate haze and seen her, had been beyond his control. He did not want to love her, he did *not*. But God help him, he did, with everything that he was, and he felt at his core that he could not live without her.

The Campbells would accept it, or they would choose a new laird.

"More English have come," Duff said.

"*Diah,* are there none left in England, then? Who is it now?"

"The lass's parents."

Jamie stilled.

"In the throne room," Duff added, and turned about, moving for the door of the keep.

Jamie pulled his saddle off Niall and handed it to the stable lad. "Rub him down," he said, and removing his gloves, he walked into the keep.

Jamie had expected Daria's parents to be strong and spirited, as she was. He was not prepared for the couple who looked so uncertain when he entered. Miss Scott was with them, but she remained seated.

"Good afternoon," he said. As he approached, the couple seemed to take a small step back. They reminded him of a pair of hares who would, at any moment, hop off and hide in their hole.

Jamie paused before them and looked directly at the balding man.

"Ah . . ." The man cleared his throat and took a small step forward. "Mr. Richard Babcock at your service, sir," he said, and fixed his gaze on Jamie's neckcloth. "Thank you for receiving us," he said softly. "We came as soon as we received Daria's letter."

Jamie nodded. He thought the man might introduce his wife, but he said, "We brought the ransom," so softly that Jamie wasn't entirely certain he'd heard him. Mr. Babcock glanced at his wife, who opened her reticule and removed a bundle wrapped in vellum. She handed it to her husband, who in turn held it out to Jamie. "It's all there, you have my word."

Jamie arched a brow. "One would think that a man might first have a question or two for his daughter's captor, aye? Such as why it is I found it necessary to hold her for ransom? Are you no' a wee bit curious?"

"Yes, yes, of course," Mr. Babcock said nervously. "But we are quite concerned for Daria and should like to make the necessary arrangements to have her back."

"Aye." Jamie nodded at Duff, who stepped forward to take the bundle from Mr. Babcock. He handed it over hesitantly and swallowed hard as Duff's hand closed around it.

"Will you no' sit?" Jamie asked them, gesturing to chairs. The Babcocks chose a bench and sat as one, their hands clasped. Miss Scott sat across from them.

"I thank you for returning my uncle's money to us," he said as he took his seat.

"Pardon?" Mr. Babcock asked.

"The ransom," Jamie said. "It is the sum

of what your mother took from my uncle."

Mrs. Babcock made a sound like a moan, then closed her eyes and dropped her head.

"I see," Mr. Babcock said.

Jamie looked from one to the other. "Did Daria no' explain in her letter what had happened?"

"Ah . . . not in great detail," Mr. Babcock said.

Jamie looked at Miss Scott, who shrugged as if she couldn't guess, either.

"Allow me to enlighten you, then," Jamie said. "Some weeks ago, we'd determined that —"

He heard a door slam and Daria call, "*Charity!* Charity, are you here? Where are you?" She sounded frantic.

He rose to his feet, as did Miss Scott. She and Jamie exchanged a look, then the four of them hurried to the foyer.

Daria stood with her legs braced apart, her riding crop beating a steady rhythm against her calf. She stared at them all, her chest rising and falling with each hard breath. Her eyes were red, as if she'd been crying. But Daria was not the sort to cry easily.

When she saw her parents, she whirled about and stalked to the stairs.

"Daria!" her mother cried.

Daria jerked around. *"No,"* she said, her voice shaking. "Don't say my name. I never want to see you again." She ran up the stairs.

"Daria!" her mother cried again with anguish.

Miss Scott looked helplessly at them, then hurried up after Daria.

"What are we to do?" Mr. Babcock asked.

Jamie glanced back at them, wondering the same thing. And he was wondering something else — who exactly had Daria been speaking to when she declared she didn't want to see *you*?

Because she'd been looking right at him.

Daria could scarcely relate the entire nightmare to Charity between her gasps of outrage and pain and her occasional pounce on the pillows to pound out her fury. "All is lost," she said. "All is *lost*!"

"All is not lost," Charity tried, but it was clear she didn't believe it. She paced as much as Daria, her brow furrowed. "He must be brought to justice. My father *hanged* because the earl accused him of thievery, when he himself was the thief! He has ruined too many lives, and I will *not* stand by whilst he lives in leisure in Scotland!"

"And my parents — my *parents* — have

abetted him!" Daria cried angrily.

She was in the midst of a harangue about the duplicity of her own flesh and blood when Bethia slipped into the room. Daria was in such a state that she very nearly paced right over the wisp of a girl. "Bethia! What in blazes are you doing?" she exclaimed impatiently.

"The laird sent me. He would have you come and see after your parents," she said. "He does no' wish to entertain them."

"No."

"He has accepted a ransom from them, Daria. It would not do to sup with them and talk about the bloody weather!" Charity snapped. Her nerves were obviously as frayed as Daria's.

"I can't speak to them yet," Daria said. "I simply cannot bear to look at them." A clap of thunder just overhead startled all three women; Daria stalked to the window and peered out. The skies had opened and were pouring down on Dundavie.

"Bloody hell, we're trapped," Charity muttered.

"What shall I tell the laird, then?" Bethia asked.

"Tell him . . ." Daria closed her eyes. *Tell him I am so terribly sorry. Tell him I wish he'd never met me. Tell him I wish I had never come to Scotland, for I will spend the rest of my life missing him.* She turned to Bethia, her gaze beseeching. "Please, I need time. Divert him — tell him something, anything."

"He'll only send me back again," Bethia said with a shrug.

Daria wanted to throttle the girl. She was the most obstinate female she had ever met —

"Aye, I'll think of something," Bethia said.

"Thank you," Daria said. "Thank you so much, Bethia."

Daria grabbed Charity's hand as Bethia went out. "Help me. Help me think what to do."

"There is only one thing you can do," Charity said. "You must go to your parents and force them to tell the truth. It is the only way *my* family will ever have justice."

"That would mean . . . that would mean returning to England with them."

"Is there any other way?" Charity demanded angrily. "Do you know how many lives the earl has ruined? And *continues* to ruin, clearly! By your own admission, your grandmother has been made mad by him. Do you not want to see her avenged?"

"Even if it means turning on my parents?"

"You are not turning on them, Daria. You

420

are the only one who can help them now."

Tears began to burn in the back of Daria's throat. She did not want to return to England.

"It's maddening, I understand," Charity said earnestly. "You must think you will never be in society, but that is not true. You'll always be welcome at Tiber Park —"

"That's not what saddens me, Charity. It's Jamie."

"The laird? Oh, poor Daria."

"You don't need to persuade me to leave, if that's what you think. I could no more burden him with who I am now than I could you. I am a bastard child with criminal connections," she said bitterly.

"Just like Catherine," Charity responded, referring to her daughter.

"Charity, I didn't mean —"

"But it's true," Charity said curtly.

Daria thought of Charity's daughter, that sunny little girl, her future so hazy because of the circumstances of her birth. And that finally opened the spigot of her tears. She'd finally found the excitement she'd sought, the taste of living beyond the ivy-covered walls of her home. She'd finally found the man who sparked her imagination, who had captivated her on first sight.

And in one afternoon, she'd lost the only

love she'd ever really known, lost her name, her parents, and her future.

Charity wrapped her arms around Daria, weeping, too. They held tightly to each other for a long moment until Daria sucked in her breath and lifted her head. "No more," she said. "There is too much to be done."

"Perhaps," Charity said, wiping the tears delicately from beneath her eyes, "perhaps your parents don't need you so?"

"What are you saying?" Daria cried. "You've said the very opposite for two days."

"Yes, I know what I've said." She winced as if the memory pained her. "Do you know how I have envied you?"

"What are you talking about?"

"You are the darling of society, Daria, the one everyone wants at their table. When I first came to Tiber Park, I was envious of you. No one wanted me, not with a bastard daughter. And that's why I have urged you to go home, Daria. I thought perhaps you didn't understand how fortunate you were." She shook her head, and closed her eyes a moment.

"I endured a family tragedy which colored everything. *Everything!* My brother and I lived in squalor. I was forced to learn about the ugly side of life at a very young age. It made me a very lonely woman, Daria. I can't tell you what I would have given to have had love in my life — any love, if only that of a friend. I wanted desperately what you have found here at Dundavie, and yet, I've advised you against it. What sort of friend am I?"

"The very best of friends," Daria said tearfully. "You were right all along, Charity. I could never fit in here. I don't belong with these people. And my parents' deception, the ordeal they have put my grandmother through? I could not dishonor Jamie so."

Charity sighed. But she did not agree that Daria was right.

TWENTY-SEVEN

Jamie could not make sense of what had happened. He couldn't grasp what had put up a stone wall between him and Daria so suddenly. He'd come back for her. He'd risked all for her. And now, he couldn't even see her.

Robbie told him some of what had happened at the cottage. There had been a heated argument, and Daria had fled from her grandmother. He told Jamie how ragged the old woman had looked, her decline evident since the last time they'd seen her.

It was Mackenzie who told him what Mrs. Moss had said, having learned it from Charity. Mackenzie told him that long ago, Charity's father had stood accused of having stolen priceless jewels from Lady Ashwood, and had hanged for it. Years later, it was discovered he'd died an innocent man, that Lord Ashwood had made it appear as if the jewels had been stolen. And he'd allowed the woodcarver to be accused and hanged for the crime. The earl had disappeared, presumed to have drowned in a swollen river — but the secret the old woman had been keeping was that he was very much alive, living in an abandoned Scottish fort.

Jamie ordered four men to go and bring the earl to Dundavie at once.

But he still did not understand why Daria would not see him.

He brooded, pacing before the hearth in his study.

He brooded until Geordie entered the study with his slate, which he put under Jamie's nose. *What?*

Jamie didn't want to try to explain his heart — he could scarcely understand it himself. He shook his head. "It's quite complicated, aye?"

With a dark frown, Geordie erased his slate and wrote, *Mut. Na dum.*

Jamie sighed. "No, you are no' dumb. All right, then, brother. I have fallen in love. But no' with Isabella Brodie."

Geordie's brows lifted and he gestured for Jamie to go on. So Jamie told him what he was feeling for Daria. That he'd refused the Brodies' latest offer. That he expected to be squeezed mightily between the Brodies and the Murchisons.

Geordie nodded. He wrote, *Good.*

That surprised Jamie. "Good? Have you heard a word?"

Geordie nodded.

Jamie studied his brother. "You like her, then?"

Geordie smiled. *I,* he wrote. And then another word that Jamie thought was Gaelic for "spirited," although it was impossible to be certain. He also wrote *Sasnak.*

"Sassenach, aye, that she is," Jamie said, and shrugged helplessly.

Geordie erased the slate. *Good for Dundavie.*

Remarkably, the words were as clear as if Geordie had spoken them. Jamie smiled. "Thank you. I needed to hear a bit of support."

Geordie nodded, then frowned. *Hast,* he wrote.

"Haste?" Jamie shook his head. "I am paralyzed as long as she remains locked away from me."

Geordie grabbed his elbow and pulled him to the window. Jamie looked out to see his footmen loading bags and a trunk on the back of Mackenzie's coach in the rain.

She was leaving him. *No, no!* Jamie whirled around from the window and dashed from his study, Geordie at his side.

He reached the foyer just as Mackenzie stepped inside.

"What are you doing?" Jamie demanded.

Mackenzie's demeanor changed slightly, and he squared off in front of Jamie. "The ransom has been paid, aye? We are leaving."

"And who would *we* be then?" Jamie demanded.

"If you are referring to Miss Babcock, she has spoken with her parents and they want to leave at once."

"No," Jamie said.

"Aye," Mackenzie said calmly. "As I said, the ransom has been paid."

Jamie had waited long enough, and he intended to demand answers. But when he turned for the stairs he saw Daria slowly coming down, her parents and Miss Scott behind her. She was dressed in a heavy cloak, her step leaden and her face drawn.

"What is this?" he demanded of her, gesturing to the door. "What are you about, lass?"

She looked at him with dark, lifeless eyes. "What it seems. I'm to England."

"Daria —"

"Now that the ransom has been paid, I am free to go, am I not?"

He would not deny that; he had given his

word. "What of your grandmamma, then?" he demanded a bit frantically.

"Captain Mackenzie is sending his men —"

"The hell he is." Jamie looked at Geordie, who knew instantly what he needed and quietly walked out the door to the bailey. "No one is going anywhere, as it happens," Jamie said. "I hold all of you for ransom."

Daria gasped. "You can't do that!"

"No, you canna," Mackenzie said, his voice deadly calm.

"No? I am laird here; I can do as I please. Do you intend to stop me?" he asked Mackenzie, just as calmly.

Mackenzie braced his legs apart. "If I must."

"Assuming you can, which I doubt, you'll have to stop them, too," Jamie said, nodding at the Campbell men who were filing in behind Geordie.

Mackenzie's face darkened. "You are making a grave mistake, Laird."

"Aye, well, I'm no' alone." Jamie looked up at Daria. "Come here, Miss Babcock. We must speak —"

"No," she said. "We are leaving, Laird. You must honor your word." Her mother put her hand on Daria's shoulder, but Daria angrily shook it off. "You said that I was

free when the ransom was paid; you promised. And if *you* don't honor your word, if *you* betray me . . ." She choked back a sob.

"If I donna honor my word, what?" he challenged her, stepping up onto the stairs. "What will you do?"

"I will lose all hope." She whirled about, pushing past her parents and Miss Scott and retreating up the stairs.

Jamie looked at Geordie. "No one leaves. No' until Miss Babcock and I have resolved a thing or two." He started up the stairs.

"What do you intend to do, Laird Campbell? Force her to your will?" Miss Scott asked as he moved past her.

Jamie paused to look her directly in the eye. "If necessary, that is precisely what I mean to do."

A smile spread across Miss Scott's face. "Best of luck, then," she said softly, and stepped back.

"Mr. Campbell, please," Jamie heard Daria's mother say, but it was too late. He was running up the stairs, his mind made up.

The door to her suite banged open with such force that it hit the wall. Daria whirled around with a start; she opened her mouth to protest, but Jamie didn't give her an op-

429

portunity. He strode across the room, grabbed her face between his hands, and kissed her. Hard. He kissed her until her body softened, until he could feel the tension seeping out of her.

He softened his kiss, then slowly lifted his head. "You meant to board that coach and leave without a word? Bloody hell, *leannan,* what do you mean to do to me?" he asked softly.

She sighed wearily and dropped her head against his shoulder. How could she possibly explain it? "What I mean to do is spare you the dishonor that will soon be associated with my name."

"You'll have to be a wee bit clearer than that."

A tear slipped from her eye. "I learned something quite horrible today. I am . . . I am a *bastard,*" she whispered.

Jamie stared at her, his brows sinking with his confusion.

"Mamie told me the truth at last," she said, and reluctantly, tearfully, related the full story.

Jamie listened, his expression reflecting the horror of her words. She knew it was the worst sort of news for her. And for him.

She waited for the inevitable, for him to say he needed time to think — or perhaps he would be more blunt than that.

"Daria," he said, and she closed her eyes, unable to bear the weight of the words if she looked at him.

"Daria, I donna care," he said softly.

Daria opened her eyes. "You're *mad* not to care."

"Aye, well I know it. But I donna care. I love you, *leannan.* It doesna matter to me."

She quickly pressed her fingers against his mouth. "Of *course* it matters. Your clan —"

He jerked her hand from his mouth. "My clan will accept it or they will no'. And if they donna, they may answer to Geordie as their laird."

Her breath caught. "You don't *mean* that," she pleaded. "You have the opportunity to marry a lovely Scottish —"

"God in heaven, lass, listen to what I say!" He slid his hand to the nape of her neck. "Today I told Isabella I'd no' marry her. I told her I loved someone else. God as my witness, I've never felt this way about anyone before, and I'm no' losing you. I donna care if you were born of faeries, or are English, or have a barmy grandmother — you're mine."

She gaped at him in shock. "You didn't! You *couldn't*! Isabella Brodie is a perfect match for you, Jamie. Don't be a fool — I

431

am so *damaged.*"

"I'll marry you here and now to prove it."

"*Jamie . . .* how can you give up all for me?"

"Donna make it sound like a fairy tale, Daria. I tried no' to love you — God knows I tried, but I failed miserably. I've been plagued with wanting you since I first saw you."

"Oh dear God," she whispered, her heart filling with happiness, with hope.

"You said that you thought I could bear anything, aye? Well I canna bear losing you."

She grabbed his head in her hands. "I love you, too. Fiercely. Completely."

He wrapped his arms tightly around her and lifted her up to kiss her deeply. Then he picked her up into his arms, walked to the door, and kicked it shut. He went to her bed, falling with her onto it. His hair fell over his brow as he searched her face, his hand lightly caressing it. Then his fingers slipped down to the neckline of her gown. "Aye, lass, I do love you," he said again, and his knee slipped between her legs as his mouth found her ear. "I didna demand enough ransom for you, I think."

"I love you," she whispered and smiled up at him.

Jamie growled his appreciation and moved

down her body to her breast, mouthing it through her gown while his free hand found the hem. He slid up her body, rough skin over smooth, setting her skin on fire where he touched her. There was no need for words — their touch was born of bottled-up desire and ravenous need for one another.

Daria was surprised by her willingness to explore him. She felt brave and courageous as she pulled his shirt over his head and put her mouth to his chest. He groaned, then quickly undid the buttons of her gown, pulling it over her head and tossing it aside before standing up and removing his trousers. He was beautifully built, as she knew, his body tall and erect in all aspects.

He gazed down at her and shook his head. "How is it possible for one woman to be so irresistibly enticing," he said roughly, and came over her again. He took her breast into his mouth, sucking and nipping. He explored her with his hand, his fingers finding every crevice, sinking deep into them. Daria could scarcely draw a breath when he rolled her over onto her stomach and kissed her hips, biting playfully at her flesh.

But then he rolled her onto her back again and slipped in between her legs, his cock brushing against her sex. Daria was wild with desire, and she smiled up at him as she pushed his hair from his face.

She cared about nothing but Jamie. She wanted to love him, to be loved by him, to know this exquisite moment in his arms.

When he whispered *"Tha gaol agam ort"* in her ear and thrust into her, Daria felt nothing but lightness. As her body adjusted to his, she marveled at how a man and woman could fit together so completely, how a man could move so seductively inside her, tantalizing her with the breadth and the depths to which he smoothly stroked, and she was amazed at how bottomless was the intimacy in this act between lovers.

Now that she understood what it meant to belong to someone, she couldn't imagine belonging to anyone else but Jamie Campbell. Ever.

Her body seemed to inherently know how to respond to him; her hips lifted to meet his thrusts, her knees squeezing around him. Jamie groaned as he moved deeper inside her, and he slipped his hand between them, stroking her folds as he stroked inside of her, stroking and stroking until Daria felt the tidal wave crashing through her, drawing from her toes and exploding deep within her. Jamie covered her cry of ecstasy with his mouth and quickened his strokes. She heard his moan in his chest, felt his strangled cry as he found his release. It was hot and potent; he filled her completely. And then he collapsed beside her, gathered her tenderly in his arms, and kissed the top of her head.

"Ah, Daria. I love you, I do," he said breathlessly, and wrapped her in a tight embrace against his chest.

She would have sworn it was impossible to be this happy. She traced her finger across his jaw, but a thought suddenly occurred to her. "Shouldn't we say something to all those people waiting downstairs?"

"Mary, Queen of Scots, I forgot them!" He laughed.

TWENTY-EIGHT

No one waiting in the great hall was surprised when Jamie and Daria appeared hand in hand and announced their intentions toward one another. Daria's parents seemed to be more relieved than shocked, and Jamie could guess that it was a solution to their fears about their daughter returning to English society. Duff scowled, as Jamie knew he would do, and whispered to Robbie about the trouble they would face. But Robbie and Geordie were quick to congratulate Jamie.

The mood was festive as they dined that evening, all the troubles they had been through and were facing forgotten for the time being. The clan would learn soon enough of their laird's decision, and no one knew how the news would be received.

The next morning, Mackenzie's men fetched Mamie. She arrived that afternoon in the midst of another downpour. Beth

Babcock cried out when she saw her mother and fell to her knees with grief, her arms around Mamie's legs.

There wasn't much her parents could say to Daria to appease her. One needed only look at Mamie to see the toll their deceit had taken. Daria's father especially seemed to have no words; he sat with his head hung as his wife begged their daughter for forgiveness.

"Don't ask for my forgiveness," Daria said. "It's Mamie's you want."

"It's impossible for you to understand," her mother said pleadingly. "I know that it is. We knew we were wrong, so wrong . . . but, Daria, we were in love and there was nothing that could keep us apart. No law of man, no force of nature. I know how very hard it must be for you to hear."

"No, Mamma, that's not hard to hear. What *is* hard to hear is that you had so little regard for your mother. For *me.* That you chose to lie and help a wretched man instead of face the truth."

"Don't be too hard on them," Mamie said sadly. "Hindsight can be so much clearer than the view of the present."

Daria wasn't convinced of that. "Well, now you must face up to what you've done. You can't hide any longer."

"We'll all be ruined," her mother said tear-fully.

"Beth, dearest," Mamie said, "we already are."

"What of you, Mamie?" Daria asked. "Will you stay here in Scotland?"

She shook her head and took Daria's hand. "I am returning to England. Whatever they face, I should like to be there with them."

Her father's head sank even lower.

"You are all welcome at Dundavie," the laird said.

"Here!" Mamie said. "But . . . I *shot* you."

"That was a wee bit hard to look past," Jamie admitted. "But I am willing to let bygones be bygones, Mrs. Moss, if you will give me your word no' to shoot any Camp-bells."

Mamie smiled ruefully. "Thank you, Laird, but I think it safer for us all if I return to England with Beth and Richard. They will need me as they've never needed me before. And I confess, I am eager to go home."

Young John entered and said something to Jamie, who nodded, then looked at the group. "Our English ghost has arrived," he said.

"Ashwood?" Charity asked.

"Aye."

Charity and Daria looked at each other, then hurried out the door before the others.

The man they brought into the foyer with his hands bound at his back did not look like an earl. He'd lost all the hair on the top of his head, and the buttons on his waistcoat strained. While Mamie had scrimped for food, he had feasted, judging by outward appearances.

He looked at all of them, an angry scowl on his face. "What's this about?" he shouted angrily, as if he didn't know.

Charity walked to where he stood, halting directly before him. "Do you recognize me, sir?"

"Why would I?"

"My name is Charity Scott," she said, and slapped Ashwood across the cheek with such force that his head was knocked round. *"That,"* she said, "is for my father, Joseph Scott." She turned and left.

The earl was still stunned when Daria slipped up to him. She dealt his other cheek a slap. "That is for Mamie," she said, and walked back to where her parents stood.

"That's the least of what you deserve," Jamie said. "We'll keep you until the English authorities arrive in Nairn."

"You can't keep me!" Ashwood shouted,

but no one listened. Jamie directed his men to take the monster from their sight, then looked at the Babcocks.

He was glad they were returning to England to face their own crime. Daria deserved much better than the two of them.

EPILOGUE

After much consultation with Duff, it was decided that Jamie and Daria would be married by week's end. It seemed unwise to wait any longer, given their close proximity and their obvious desire to marry. They couldn't keep their eyes from one another, their hands straying to each other at every opportunity.

"It's indecent," Aileen complained, but she was smiling when she said it.

As Duff predicted, there was quite a lot of opposition among the clan to the laird marrying an Englishwoman, much less the granddaughter of one who had shot him.

But there was also a surprising number of clansmen who were in favor of the marriage. Daria had found her way into the hearts of more than one Scotsman. She'd done it just as Lady Ashwood had done it, one person at a time. Most still called her the Ransom, but some called her friend as well.

Daria understood her precarious position. The clansmen might accept her in time, but the test would come in weeks and months and years ahead, and in how they would perceive her support of Jamie. She understood it would be a difficult road, but she felt quite strong with her hand in Jamie's.

Jamie and Daria decided the first thing they must do was drain the bog, and the following spring, the ransom her parents paid was used to do precisely that. As many guessed, there was a lot of grousing about it. Not many of the Campbells were believers . . . until the first green shoots of grain began to grow there.

Jamie and Daria's wedding was inherently Scottish, which meant that it hardly mattered that it had come with a special license in a few short days. It was a reason to celebrate, a reason to drink and dance, and Campbells came from miles around. Even a few Brodies saw fit to attend. Cormag Brodie, Isabella's brother and Geordie's nemesis, sent a sheep as a wedding gift, with a note thanking Jamie for not marrying his sister.

Three days of games and dancing marked the celebration of the laird's marriage, and at the end of it, there was scarcely a Campbell who didn't know how to waltz.

Days later, the Earl of Ashwood was handed to the British authorities at Nairn on a warrant for deception, thievery, and possibly even the murder of his wife. Shortly after his departure, Daria, her parents, Mamie, Charity, and Jamie set sail on Mackenzie's ship for England.

Daria spent most of the time in her bunk as before, but this time she had her grandmother to tend to her. Jamie spent most of his time on deck, relishing the feel of being at sea. The Babcocks remained belowdecks, away from everyone, and Charity Scott and Mackenzie . . . well. No one knew precisely where they were, and no one was brave enough to inquire.

Charity had written to her brother to tell him what had happened and when she might be expected, so there were quite a lot of people waiting to give Daria a hero's welcome when they arrived in Hadley Green. She was credited with having found the Earl of Ashwood, and while she swore to all assembled that she had *not* found him, they wouldn't listen.

Just as Charity had guessed, Daria was quite sought after at supper parties and salon parties. Even some of the Quality came down from London to hear of her adventure. More than a few ladies were quite keen to meet Daria's ruggedly handsome husband with the charming brogue. More than one remarked behind painted fan that they could not believe Daria Babcock had managed to land such a virile figure. More than one speculated that there were other dashing lairds tucked away in Scotland, and as it was quite in fashion now, perhaps it was worth a trip to have a look about.

But Daria's improved social standing was, unsurprisingly, short-lived. Once word began to circulate that her parents had known the earl was alive and where he'd been, the invitations began to wane. What would become of her parents, no one could guess; their future looked uncertain.

There were, however, spots of very bright news in the midst of the latest Ashwood scandal. The current Earl of Ashwood, the bastard son of the disgraced earl, was confirmed by the Crown as the rightful earl. Charity and Captain Mackenzie were treated to a wedding befitting of royalty at Tiber Park. Charity's daughter, Catherine, was thrilled. She'd long adored the handsome captain, and in fact aspired to be a sea captain herself one day.

Very soon after, Charity announced she would be adding to the crop of Hadley

Green babies the following spring.

Mamie thrived in her return to England. Very happy to be home, she looked healthier each day. She dressed elegantly and delighted in the commission of new gowns. She hosted teas to tell *her* ordeal. Mamie was a fine storyteller, and her tale, embellished as necessary for the sake of drama, had her friends and acquaintances on the edges of their seats. She had been through quite a lot, but as she cheerfully said to Daria, she would do it all again for her darling granddaughter.

Jamie soon grew restless. Dundavie called to him, the business of the clan first in his mind. There was also the matter of the surgeon Mackenzie had pointed them to; Jamie very much wanted to be in Scotland when the gentleman called at Dundavie. They had great hope that Geordie's voice would be restored, for many reasons, being spared his awful spelling just one of them.

There was one more spot of bright and happy news that Daria kept to herself, until her husband confronted her.

"I know what you're hiding, lass," he announced casually one morning as they shared breakfast in bed at Tiber Park.

"Hiding!" Daria exclaimed. "I am hiding nothing!" But she could feel the traitorous blush creeping into her cheeks.

"Aye, but you are," Jamie said sternly, and rolled onto his side, his hand on her belly. "You've that look about you."

"*What* look?"

He smiled. "The look of a fat cat who's had all the milk, that's what."

"Ridiculous," she said. "I don't even care for milk."

"I think you are carrying our child," he said.

Daria looked into his hazel eyes and remembered the first time he'd opened them, how they had captured her and held her in thrall ever since. Forever. "Aye," she said simply.

Her admission stunned her husband. Jamie's eyes searched her face, then fell to her abdomen.

"Spring, I should think," she said. "When the bog is drained." She covered his hand with hers.

He lifted shining eyes to her. "Mary, Queen of Scots, woman, why have you not *told* me?"

"I wanted to tell you on Scottish soil. I wanted to tell you at Dundavie."

He released a sigh of elation and buried his face against her, saying something in Gaelic. Daria didn't know what he said, but she could see his happiness.

So there it was, then. The last debutante of Hadley Green had a purpose to her life: she was leaving England for a bright future in a small glen in Scotland. Her broken wings had been miraculously repaired. She would bear this man a child — a son, if Bethia was to be believed — followed by three more. She would raise her brood in that rustic castle in the middle of a spectacular vista of hills and forest.

Daria didn't put much stock in second sight, but she would acknowledge that Bethia was right about one other thing: she would never leave Dundavie. She would make her nest there, she thought as Jamie covered her in kisses, whispering in Gaelic to her. She would feather it and tend it and keep it safe and warm for her brood, and she would love this man, who had been willing to surrender it all for her, until she drew her last breath. He was the love of her life, her purpose, her meaning.

Whoever would have believed that Daria Babcock would have found her heart's true desire in the wilds of Scotland? She laughed and turned her attention to her husband.